Mo

1st Place winner for best Mystery / Suspense in the 2014 Chatelaine Awards, recognizing emerging new talent and outstanding works in women's fiction and romance novels.
~ *Chanticleer Book Reviews*

"Donna Barker's dark humorous novel has a fresh, snarky voice that will leave readers laughing out loud and turning pages right until the end."
~ Eileen Cook, author of *With Malice*

"Best friends Tara and Betsy's journey toward psychic enlightenment is a hilarious, terrifying and heartwarming roller-coaster ride. The power of positive and negative energy becomes crystal clear on the pages of Ms. Barker's unique debut novel. The locations of Vancouver and Sacramento were painted with talented prose, but it is the landscape of the heart and soul that makes this story truly shine."
~ Jacqui Nelson, award-winning romance author

"Donna Barker has created an entertaining read full of heart, humor and meaningful messages."
~ T. Rae Mitchell, author of *Magic Brew*

"I loved this book! It's quirky. It's weird. It's hilarious. Barker creates a world a quarter-turn towards magic realism where super powers of the mind are a real possibility and could be responsible for a string of odd ball accidents, coincidences that are stacking up a bit too high for normal mishaps.

"There's romance, there's murder mystery, there's black humour, there's an irreverent spiritual journey and under it all, there's a subtle exploration of the difference between right and wrong and how each of us has to grow up a bit to bring that into focus. A smooth read from start to finish, great pacing, compelling characters, a plot that keeps unspooling and some juicy twists to keep you jumping."

~ Michele Fogal, author of *The West Coast Boys* series

Mother Teresa's
Advice for Jilted Lovers

Justin—
May your white light sparkle!

Donna Barker

Library and Archives Canada Cataloguing in Publication

Barker, Donna, 1966-, author
Mother Teresa's advice for jilted lovers / Donna Barker.

Issued in print and electronic formats.
ISBN 978-0-9730619-2-5 (paperback)
ISBN 978-0-9730619-3-2 (html)

I. Title.

PS8603.A73554M68 2016   C813'.6
C2015-907880-6
C2015-907881-4

To Dad.

*I'd have never published before you
had you not cheated to let me win.*

R.I.P.

Chapter One

Killing James wasn't my top-of-mind thought after we made love that morning.

In fact, after four months of sharing sheets, I was feeling good about my relationship with James. *Relationship.* Okay, so we hadn't actually said that we were a couple. But I knew it was coming.

James got out of bed to make coffee and connect with his head office. I stayed put to hold onto my post-sex buzz just a bit longer. I imagined the conversation I'd have later that day with Betsy.

"I think we're getting serious," I'd tell her.

She'd be skeptical and snarky.

"Better you than me," she'd say.

"He bought me a toothbrush when he replaced his own. Feels like a sign."

"Yeah, a big, orange caution flag."

I heard the coffeemaker sputter and James clinking mugs. I got up. His laptop sat on the table open to an exchange with his boss, Sandra. As I dropped to the couch, two words jumped out at me as though they'd been typed in large, bold, red letters—'blow job.' *He must mean something about not blowing a job he has to do for Sandra.*

I picked up the laptop and started to read. Nope. The only job that Sandra was worried about blowing was his. From only six one-liners, back-and-forth between them, it was obvious that James and Sandra were lovers. And by 'lovers' I mean it was obvious that James's penis played an integral role in his weekly job duties.

James called from the kitchen as I put his laptop down, "Hey, Tara, you want your coffee in bed or are you getting up?"

I couldn't speak through the bile in my throat. James walked around the corner and saw me sitting on the couch. He smiled—*he bloody smiled at me!*—and put one cup of coffee down on each side of his laptop.

"What's wrong? You look pale. Are you feeling sick?" he asked, touching my forehead like a concerned dad.

I pointed at his laptop, stood, walked to his bedroom, and closed the door. Hard. I wanted to leave but didn't have the energy to get dressed. I sat on the edge of his bed. I didn't scream. I couldn't cry. My only thought was whether I should puke in the toilet or on his bedroom floor. I decided to stay where I was.

Unfortunately, all I did was dry heave. *If only I'd had the coffee first, then I'd have something to bring up.*

James sat down beside me and put his hand on my back. I jerked away.

"I get that you're upset. And I'm sorry you saw the emails. But let's not make this into something that it's not," he said.

I glared at him and saw something in his eyes that made me want to believe him. I started to soften and then thought, *No! You've been cheating on me. That's not okay.* I turned away from him.

"Tara, look at me. Let me try to explain." He crouched on the floor directly in my sight line. I looked in the other direction.

"Fine. Do you want to be juvenile about this or do you want to talk about it?"

Apparently that was the right question to break through my stunned speechlessness. Oh, I gave it to him. I don't even remember what I said but I had a sore throat and ringing ears at the end my tirade. And the whole time, he stood there with a stupid little smile on his stupid little face.

"Are you done? Do you feel better?" James asked when it was clear that I was done and that I didn't feel better. "I really like you. I do. I've been thinking that we have something special—"

See Betsy, I was right. He was ready to go to the next level.

"—but this job is...well, it's my life, Tara. You and I, we've only been together, what, a few months? This thing with Sandra, it's just a thing, it's not love, but it's been three years. I can't simply stop, it's complicated. I want to be with this company for the rest of my career, and she kind of has me over a barrel, if you know what I mean."

He stopped talking and I wished my eyes could do to him what my heart was feeling. He seemed to understand that this approach was not doing the trick...ha! Doing the trick.

"Tara? It's not like you and I ever said we were exclusive, right? I mean I really love...the time we spend together. I do. I'm happy that it looks like we might be moving into a more…you know…serious kind of relationship. But, that's not where we are now. If anyone should be mad, it's Sandra," he said with a frigging smile, "since I've kind of been cheating on her with you. Look, I'm sorry. Aren't you going to say anything?" he asked.

I looked around James's bedroom. *I'm going to miss waking up to your view of Kits beach … And I love the colour of your walls. I wish I'd asked what it was…Too bad you're an asshole 'cause I was getting comfortable here.*

"I'm taking my new toothbrush." I packed up my things, dressed in silence and left without saying good-bye.

Chapter Two

Icalled Betsy while I waited for the bus and told her what had happened, keeping it short so I wouldn't get emotional.

Sitting adjacent to the beach, watching tired but seemingly happy people on their way to work, I wished for rain. My dark mood didn't want to be diluted by the bright, early morning August sun. Twenty minutes into the bus trip, rolling along East Hastings Street, even the down-and-outers looked like life was treating them well this morning.

Betsy was waiting at my apartment by the time I'd made it over to Commercial Drive.

"I'm not going to say I told you so," she said before even saying hello.

"Betsy! Jesus! Can you maybe let me mope? Cut me some emotional slack? I need you to side with me here. Five minutes?"

"I'm sorry," she said, dropping her backpack and grabbing me in a back-breaking hug, her short, spiky hair poking at my cheeks.

"I'm sorry. I really am. But you know I never liked him."

"You haven't liked a single one of my boyfriends since high school."

"And have I been wrong? If he's not a liar or a cheater he's some other kind of prick. They all are."

She did have a point. I had a history of making some pretty bad choices in men. Guys who believed that once I'd laid with them in the Biblical sense, that my body became their property to treat as they desired, which typically meant with as much care as a 1975 Gremlin; the beater they were going to drive until it died then leave at the side of the road, licence plates removed, registration number pried off, so someone else could clean up the mess.

But there had been a couple of nice guys, too. Men I could see a future with. Unfortunately, they were both dead.

"First thing," Betsy said as we entered my apartment, "start your laptop. Log in to email and Facebook. We have to get James out of your e-life as fast as possible."

"You think, maybe, first thing we could sit and have a cup of tea? You think you might allow me half-an-hour to be sad? To cry?"

As soon as I was safe inside my apartment the floodgates opened.

Betsy sighed, unzipped her bag and emptied it onto my kitchen table.

"Chamomile tea with valerian. Rescue Remedy—take five drops under your tongue right now. Wine, for later. And—" she did a passable Vanna White impression as she pulled a box of chocolate croissants from her emotional emergency kit.

"I love you," I said, crying harder.

"I know. And I love you, too. That's why I put up with your bad choices in men."

Betsy and I drank tea and ate all six croissants before she ordered me to hand over my computer. I launched Facebook and scrolled down the page to see what some of my 323 'friends' were posting before unfriending James.

Outrage. Pontification. Disgust.

For a flash of a second I wondered how they all knew so quickly about what James had done. Then I stopped to read a few of the media links. Some politician-wannabe had publicly stated his opinion that there are situations where rape is legitimate and that 'some girls rape so easy.'

I tried to read the quote to Betsy but choked on the last words. It was such a vile and ignorant thing to say; my whole body contracted and stomach acid pushed up into my throat. I grabbed my knees, hugging myself in the kitchen chair.

"Breathe, Tez. You're okay."

She wrapped her arm over my shoulder and took several slow, deep, loud breaths for me to follow. Of course, once I was breathing again, the sobs came. Betsy held me as I rocked myself. Although she had no patience at all for my adult love life crises, she would sit silently with me all day—and had several times—when old hurts surfaced.

But I didn't want to go there today.

"Shower," I said, slumping sideways into her.

"Good idea."

Standing, face into the hot water, I saw images of men I wished I could drown. Men who looked like the politician,

13

like the kind of man my mother had always hoped I'd marry. A well-fed man in a suit with a good education, a high-paying job, and the bastardized words of Christ on his lips. 'Girls who get themselves in trouble deserve the consequences,' he said to me. I screamed him out of my mind.

But he was quickly replaced with another and another and another image of a man. Men I knew, or knew of. I made a wish that all the men who cheated and lied their way to two-point-five children and a white picket fence *and* the rock-star life, would come home from work to find an empty fridge and a note from their wives saying 'I can do better than you.' I wished that all the assholes who'd intentionally hurt women in the bedroom, in bars, but especially in their parents' basement while their folks were out, would get theirs.

But, like every birthday candle I'd blown out since I was five years old, I expected nothing to come from my wishing. So, on that day, I decided that the smartest thing I could do was to simply be done with dating. To stop intentionally putting myself into situations where I was going to end up hurt.

Betsy was sitting on the closed toilet seat when I pulled open the shower curtain.

"That was some noise."

"I'm done with men."

"About time," she said, standing and passing me my towel.

"Yeah, well, we all learn at our own pace. You happen to be ahead of me on this curve."

"There's still fifty-percent of the population to build your life with."

I grimaced. "Not my thing."

"You never tried."

"You want me to throw up again?"

Betsy smiled. "Nothing to trigger your gag reflex—"

"Except the very *idea* of going down on a woman."

"You —"

"Betsy! I love you. But shut up. You can't bully me into being bisexual." I wasn't angry. In fact, I was amused that she hadn't given up on the idea that, like her, I could enjoy sex with women.

"So, you're going to give up men *and* give up sex? Not bloody likely."

I shrugged my shoulders. "Doesn't seem to have hurt Aunt Linda or Auntie Paula. I could ask them to be my mentors. I'm sure they'd be thrilled to share their spinsterly advice with their only niece."

"You'd take spinsterly advice over sisterly advice? Hmph."

Betsy. My sister from another mother. Better than a sister since we had no sibling rivalry and all the protective ferocity of being blood.

We'd met in grade three when she was taken in by her fourth foster family. I remember my mom talking about that 'poor girl' who was going to end up on the streets. Mom knew of her from the gossip the church ladies spread at their weekly luncheon meetings:

"Hazel said she heard that Betsy had thrown the urn of her foster mother's father's ashes on the floor in a fit. Well, of course she couldn't stay there anymore, could she? And Celia said that she heard that when another family was caring for her, she had this old ratty blanket that she carried everywhere. Well, they thought she was old enough

15

to not need such a thing so they threw it away. Betsy cried and fitted for days so they had no choice but to put her back in the government's care."

Mom had lots of stories that I'd eventually asked Betsy about. Some had bits of truth in them, but what made Betsy a hard-to-love child was her mouth. She had fight in her the day I met her sitting at the top of the jungle gym at recess and it's only gotten worse over the years.

I admired Betsy from day one, the way she'd talk back to teachers if she thought they were being unfair.

"You're an idiot," she was known to yell, arms outreached like she was throwing magic from her fingertips at the teacher who had given heck to the wrong kid in class for having passed a note, or snickered when Uranus was spoken of in science lesson.

It took me two weeks to get up the courage to finally talk to her. I was new at the school since my mom and I had to move after my dad left us. I didn't know that Betsy had also recently moved and didn't have any friends yet either. I thought she was so cool that she didn't want to hang out with the other girls.

One day I sat across the lunch table from Betsy and told her that I agreed with her, that Ms. Boddom was really mean to some kids and nice to others. I told her that I wished I could say what I was thinking the same way she was able to.

She scrunched up her nose and gave me a look. I was sure she was going to tell me to bug off. But she said, "All you have to do is say it. It's not that hard."

"Yeah it is. What if they yell at you?"

"Who cares? Sticks and stones can break your bones but words will never hurt you."

She grabbed my lunch bag and dumped out the contents.

"Don't you have a cookie or anything?" she asked.

I shook my head, "My mom won't let me eat anything with sugar at school."

"Want half my Hershey's?"

Betsy's been my best friend for over twenty years and, since the day we met, she's always been the alpha-female. Sometimes, rarely, I'll stand up to her when she's being bitchy, but mostly we stick to our roles: I'm passive, she's aggressive, together we're a nice, emotional yin/yang balance.

And, we'd been pretty yin and yang in our dating lives, too. We both had serious relationships but I was always hoping for mine to be the last one, the 'one true love' relationship, while she had no interest in being tied down. That's not to say she didn't date or get involved with people, but she was a runner. She'd had this guy Josh, and they were great together. She tattooed his name on her belly. They bought matching Kawasaki motorcycles. And they'd been living together for over a year. But Josh wrecked it all by proposing to her. Idiot! I'd warned him not to try to tie her down but he wouldn't listen. He was sure that the tattoo meant something.

"It's only ink," I told him.

"But it's permanent. It's not like she can erase it. And she put it on that spot on her belly that I love to…"

"Stop, Josh. You don't have to tell me."

I didn't have the heart to tell him that his wasn't the first name Betsy'd branded her body with. The vine that wrapped around her wrist? If you look closely you could see "Paul," in scroll-font, is all twisted inside it. Once you

17

know it's there it's quite obvious. And the "DAN" on her left shoulder with the Amnesty logo below it doesn't stand for 'Direct Action Network' like she says, but for that lovely British musician who I was so sure would whisk her away to London and a life of delight.

When Betsy gave up on men and started dating women I was the only person who wasn't surprised. But then, nobody else knew her like I did. What surprised me was that it took until she was twenty-four to admit to herself that she was bisexual. And even though she and I had had some fun make-out sessions—only at parties when we were drunk and wanted to make a scene—I never felt uncomfortable being naked in front of her or even sharing a bed with her. She's my sister.

"Do you have any deadlines today," I asked her.

"No. It's quiet. Dead, actually."

"Want to do something crazy?"

"Such as?"

"I don't know. Something fun. Something that'll replace my James-is-an-asshole memory for today."

"How about skydiving?" Betsy suggested.

"What?"

"Skydiving. Nothing to make you appreciate life, as shitty as it might feel right now, than risking it by throwing yourself out of a plane."

"I wish I could throw James out of a plane," I said.

"My treat."

"Skydiving?"

It was a crazy idea. Not something I ever thought I'd do. But then, it was a crazy day and there's nothing like pure terror to clear your mind.

Chapter Three

Betsy booked us for a jump at 3:00 which gave us time to walk the twenty blocks—in gorgeous sun, of course—along quiet treed-streets, with a view of the North Shore mountains, to the sporty co-op car I'd rented for the afternoon.

"Could life be better?" Betsy asked.

I wanted to say yes, and to scream at my bad luck with men, but I was having such a great day with my best friend I had to agree, "No. We are blessed."

Even the drive to the Fraser Valley was nice. Traffic was light and drivers were polite, letting us merge easily in and out of lanes through the many construction zones.

Less than four hours from suggesting the idea, Betsy and I were standing in a small plane hangar putting on bright purple, one-piece jumpsuits and soft leather helmets that would not hold in our brains if our heads were to hit the ground from bicycle height let alone eighteen thousand feet.

"Why?" Betsy asked Max, her buff Australian jump partner, pointing at her leather cap.

"To keep your hair from covering my face."

"Seriously? Do I have to wear this? My hair isn't flying anywhere, it's too short. And I paid to have pictures taken. Can we skip the helmet? Please?" she asked, doing her best imitation of a woman flirting.

"Maybe. Let's get this harness on you and see how well we fit together," he said with a wink.

"How many times have you jumped?" I asked my small French Canadian tandem partner, Alain, as he kneeled in front of me, adjusting a harness hoop around my left thigh.

"Hundred. Maybe thousand," he said without looking up.

"How many have you lost?"

Alain looked up, eyes questioning.

"Lost," Betsy chimed in, "as in, how many have you not strapped on properly and let fall to their untimely deaths?"

"Skydiving, she's safer than climbing the ladder," he said, rolling his eyes.

Max smiled and nodded, "We'll take care of you, girls. Now…Betsy is it? If you'll kneel on this bench, I'll be able to tell you if you need to wear that helmet."

Betsy kneeled and Max pressed himself tight against her back, clipping his harness to hers. He ran his fingers through her short hair from her neck up to the crown and tugged gently at the top, pulling her head back, chin up.

"Should be fine," he said, holding Betsy's head in that position several seconds longer than he needed to.

I had a wave of mixed feelings watching the two of them. Betsy was a guy magnet and played up her natural ability to excite men even though she wasn't going to follow-through anymore. She was living proof that men aren't as attracted to magazine-thin women as they are to women with breasts and solid legs. Betsy is a Botticelli beauty with a Sid Vicious haircut. I, on the other hand, at five foot ten, have a lithe body that would make me look like a man in drag if I put on a glamorous dress and false eye lashes. Men who were attracted to me liked me for my personality, not my figure. On the upside, in our twenty-year friendship, Betsy and I had never once had to deal with one of our boyfriends flirting with the other.

Once we were suited up, the guys told us to walk across a field and wait beside a small plane; they were going to check their chutes one last time and meet us there.

"Are you nervous?" I asked Betsy.

"Not in the least. The universe knows what it's doing. If I die...must be some other place I'm supposed to be."

"I wish I had your faith...hell, I wish I had any faith."

"You have faith in me."

"But I don't *worship* you," I pointed out.

"You should."

"Yeah, so you keep telling me."

Ten minutes later we were sitting in the cargo hold of a Turbine Pilatus Porter—the pilot appeared eager to connect with Betsy and babbled on about our plane until the engine got to speed so we could take off.

Betsy had been right. James was the last thing on my mind. While we climbed to fifteen thousand feet, Betsy and I pointed this way and that at landmarks and scenery. I was almost surprised when Alain tapped my shoulder and told me to lean back so he could clip us together.

"What if I've changed my mind?" I yelled over the engine noise.

He smiled, put his hand on my collarbone and pulled me hard against him until my back arched uncomfortably. I was happy to move toward the door, if only to change position. Less happy when Alain told me to drop my legs out and lean forward until I started to fall.

"How fast do we fall?"

"Two hundred kilometres per hour," he said, pushing his own weight against me.

Once I'd stopped screaming and had the courage to open my eyes, I was awestruck. The valley, with all its squares of different coloured crops, was even more beautiful without the framing of the airplane windows. I felt as inconsequential as I did all-powerful, gliding above the world with the air in my face. I was flying without wings. I was an angel. I was a Goddess.

Alain's arms disappeared from beside my face and we started to spin, or roll. Whichever direction we were rotating, I didn't like it one bit. I closed my eyes and held my breath. We levelled out again and he pulled the chute. The new resistance pulled me backward.

"Having fun?"

"Please don't spin again. No, no, no, no, no."

He laughed, "But dat is what you pay for, no? Feel like you will die but go home after?"

"Maybe."

The rest of the fall was amazing. Not scary. I didn't want it to end. I wanted our parachute to turn to wings so Alain and I could spend the rest of the day flying together.

But, there was no way to slow gravity so after eight or nine minutes, we were splatter distance from the ground. Alain told me to put my legs straight out in front of me, like I was sitting on the grass.

I did as he instructed. His feet hit the ground running, while mine pointed out our direction. Once he'd slowed to a quick walk, he told me to drop my legs. We walked a few steps together before dropping to our butts.

"Good job," he said, holding his hand in front of my face for a high-five before pulling me hard against him to unbuckle my harness.

I looked skyward and saw Betsy, still high enough to not be recognizable. Her photographer floated a dozen feet in front of her and Max. A threesome in the sky. That was the Betsy I knew and loved. I wished I was up there with her. The ground felt so limiting after the freedom of the fall.

Alain and I watched as Max and Betsy prepared to land.

"Shouldn't Betsy have her feet out front by now?" I asked.

"Oui. It will be ugly."

Ugly is one way to describe Betsy's landing. Hilarious is another. Since Max had at least six inches on her, his feet hit ground first and his legs moved fast. Betsy's landed a couple steps along, moving much more slowly.

The image made me think of a gazelle. Not a graceful one, though. A baby gazelle that's just learned to take his first steps when a lioness appears from the shadows. The baby's instinct tells it to run, but its feet don't yet understand how to work together. Front legs tangle with back legs and the lioness and her babies have a nice dinner.

Betsy's front half-gazelle did just that with Max's back-half and they twisted and fell in a mess on the ground.

"What. The fuck. Was that?" Betsy screamed. "First time landing?"

Max silently pulled her shoulders back until she was laying right on top of him. As soon as her harness was unclipped, Betsy was on her feet.

"Seriously, though. Land much?"

"I told you to put your legs out in front of you," Max said, obviously trying not to smile.

"Well, excuse me for wanting to land on my own two feet."

*   *   *

Back in Vancouver, we went out for dinner and a glass of wine.

"How you doing?" Betsy asked.

"Good. I'm good. Leave it to you to take me from crying over a break-up to celebrating still being alive, all within a few hours."

"It's what I do. Make you feel better when you're sad."

"Yeah. Too often. And what do I give you?" My shoulders collapsed forward as my neck muscles decided my head was suddenly too heavy to hold up.

Betsy put her hand under my chin and looked directly into my eyes. I blinked to clear the uninvited tears and bring her into focus.

"You let me be me without judgment. You're the only one. And…" she paused and wiped a tear from my cheek. "And, that, my friend, is why I put up with all your sensitive heart and stomach crap."

"A day without crying or puking is like a day that you're not fully alive," I said with a small laugh.

She shook her head. "You need a new mantra."

"I do."

"How about, 'a day without Betsy is like a day you're

24

not fully alive?'"

I laughed out loud. "I like it."

We sat quietly, drinking our wine, making friendly faces and random body movements to each other for a few minutes.

"It's amazing how a different perspective can make you see things you hadn't before," I said.

"Meaning?"

"Well, obviously seeing the world while you're falling toward it, but also seeing the world with a different expectation, I guess."

She raised her glass, we clinked and drank.

"I realize that I only ever see what I want to see with lovers. It was especially true with James," I admitted.

Betsy rolled her eyes, as if to say, "Duh."

"I should have known he was working on something other than spreadsheets with Sandra. Now that I think about it, he made lots of direct hints about it that I didn't catch at the time."

"Such as?"

"There was the day he came to my place after work and wanted to take a shower before dinner. I asked why he was feeling dirty and he'd said, 'I'm covered in sex and candy.' Of course, I thought he was joking so I laughed. And then he kissed me. And then we had sex in the shower—before—he'd washed—Sandra—off of him!"

"He was a pig."

"You know, I met Sandra last week. First time. Coincidence. James and I were having dinner at a restaurant on Fourth Avenue and she saw us in the window and came in to say hello. She was lovely…"

"Lovely? Really?"

"Yeah. Bubbly and fun." I replayed our conversation in my mind. "And, a total bitch because she told me that James was a keeper and I agreed with her. I thought she meant for me, not for her."

My eyes filled with tears but I pushed the hurt feelings back down my throat with a big swig of wine.

"No more assholes," Betsy said refilling my glass.

"No more assholes."

Chapter Four

When I saw Sandra's name in my email inbox I almost deleted the message without reading it, expecting it to be some sort of apology. But I noticed that the 'To' line had 206 names in it. What a bimbo, not knowing how to use blind cc, I thought. I figured she'd sent it to everyone in James's email address book, which is why I opened it. It's not a normal thing for a boss to do. That and the fact that the subject line read, 'Sad news.'

It's with deep regret that I'm writing you all to inform you that our dear friend and good colleague, James Tucker, passed away two days ago, succumbing to injuries he sustained from a two-storey fall while cleaning the drain pipes and gutters on his house.

For all who knew James you'll remember him as a team player, always eager to do whatever it took to get the job done, even if it meant staying late, working on projects both on and off-the-side of his desk.

The message went on and on but I didn't read it. I closed my laptop and cried. I cried so hard I threw up. All over my living room carpet. *A day without puking is a day without being alive.* God knows why, but that thought made me laugh. I laughed so hard I threw up again. *People die like this. I can't die laughing at James's death. Betsy would be furious.*

It took a few more minutes but I pulled myself together enough to call Betsy.

"He's dead," I said, realizing that I was still sort of cry-laughing.

"Who's dead? Sounds like it's someone we're glad is gone," she said.

"No. James. He fell. And he died."

"Oh, no! I'm so sorry," Betsy kept talking but I couldn't hear anything she said since I started to cough, trying to hold back the laughing.

"Death is not funny!" I yelled. It helped. I caught my breath.

"Tara," Betsy said, serious all of a sudden.

"What?" I asked between deep breaths.

"This is the third time one of your boyfriends has died. That's more than weird, don't you think?"

Images of the last two men I thought I'd had a chance with popped into my head and I started to laugh again.

"Tez, you really should see someone about this nervous laughter thing, you know. It's kind of disconcerting. Like, serial killer creepy."

I pictured myself floating over the city, pointing a bony finger down on mere mortals, which made me laugh harder. I had to hang up since my stomach ached so much from the laughing and coughing and vomiting.

Thirty minutes later, Betsy was standing at my front door with her backpack of remedies to calm me down.

It took several eye droppers of the remedy, a pot of chamomile tea with fresh ginger, three ounces of scotch, and two hours before I was able to hold a conversation, but Betsy's natural cure worked like a charm.

"I guess the universe thought it was his time." Betsy shrugged like her statement was a fact as inarguable as the colour of my living room wall.

"Seriously, Betsy?" I said shaking my head. "You seriously think the universe killed James?" I didn't have patience for her metaphysical blah-dee-blah.

"What we're seeing is old systems failing and falling apart. New systems are ready to take their place based on equality and respect. Enlightenment," she told me.

"Give me a break. If we're in this universal movement toward enlightenment, how do you explain that the last three times I was either in love or moving in that direction, my man has died? If that's what enlightenment is, I think I like the old way better," I said.

"I think you have to believe that the universe knows better what's best for you. Obviously, you weren't in the right relationship with James. That's why he died. And the universe knew that as long as he was still around, you'd be holding on to some hope that you might get back together with him," Betsy said.

"Bullshit."

"What do you mean, bullshit?"

"I mean, you know as well I do, that I was never going to go back to James. So, bullshit."

"Well, then maybe the universe was eliminating a bad person from the world to make room for a good one,"

Betsy said.

"I don't buy it. Bob wasn't a bad person. Scott wasn't a bad person. So why did the universe kill them? Sure, James was a shit, but shouldn't the universe be taking out people like rapists and murderers and child molesters first? I mean, what are the universe's priorities?"

"I'm not 'the Universe,'" Betsy said waving her hands in the air, "so I can't say for sure. But I do know that neither Scott nor Bob was right for you, either."

And I knew that continuing this argument would lead nowhere good.

"I need to clear my head. I'm taking a shower," I said.

"Don't worry about me. I'll just…" Betsy grabbed a magazine from the pile on the floor beside the couch. "I'll read about gas fracking."

I ignored her. Standing in a hot shower when I'm upset is almost a reflex, like laughing when I'm nervous. As I stood, water hitting me squarely in the face, I replayed scenes from my relationships with Scott and Bob.

Scott had been an architect. I was deeply in love. He was old-fashioned and proposed before we started living together. I was thrilled. A week after I'd moved in he told me that he'd kept a secret from me.

"It's not a big deal," he'd said.

"So why'd you keep it a secret?" I asked.

"Because I know you don't like it and I lied about it on our first date."

"Oh sweet Jesus, you're not Catholic are you? You don't want me to convert now that we're living in sin?" I closed my eyes and held my breath. I wasn't joking.

"Dear, God, no."

"Oh, thank heavens. Then what?"

"Every now and then, like when I watch hockey with the guys, I like to…" he couldn't say it.

"What? You like to dress in women's clothing?" I remember I'd tried to lighten the mood by making him laugh. But he didn't laugh. I started to get that bad sinking feeling.

Scott looked at the floor for several seconds then looked up at me and spoke auctioneer-fast, "I smoke a few cigarettes, okay? I'm sorry."

I deciphered what he said, "That's all? Honey, that's fine. Rare occasion?" He nodded. "When I'm not home?" He nodded. "I can live with that," I'd promised him.

I breathed a huge sigh of relief. The way Scott had looked I'd half-expected he was going to tell me that he was the son of a mafia kingpin and had just been told he had to join the family business.

It was Betsy who'd gotten upset, telling me that if he'd lied about such a small thing I couldn't trust him with big problems. I'd shrugged off her concern and life carried on all sweet and lovely with Scott.

I turned my back on the water and breathed in deeply through my nose, as I'd done so many times to try to find the smell of cigarettes on Scott's breath. I never did. I was happy enough to know that if he was smoking at home, he did it while I was away and aired out the apartment when he was done.

My mind flashed forward a month or so and I had to sit down on the shower floor. It was the third Monday in November, I'll never forget. I'd come home from having dinner with Betsy to find a fire engine and ambulance parked outside our building. My first thought was, "I hope nobody's hurt," followed very quickly by, "but if they are and the apartment becomes free, I wonder if they'll rent it to Betsy." I remember imagining how perfect life would be with Betsy living down the hall and I wasn't paying attention to the commotion in the foyer. Then our neighbour from 3C grabbed me in a bear hug and started to cry.

Single words created images, both in that moment and as I sat sobbing in my shower. Toaster...cigarette... explosion...

A knock on the door brought me back to the present.

"Tez? I'm coming in." Betsy turned off the water and held open my towel. I stepped toward her and she wrapped me up like a child, hugging me. "It's okay. I'm here. I love you."

"Then why aren't you dead, too?"

Betsy was smart enough not to answer.

"Were you thinking about Bob?" Betsy asked, rubbing my back.

I shook my head and pulled away from her embrace, the irritation that I'd taken a shower to try to dissipate, back stronger than before. I spoke as I got dressed.

"Bob. If your whole universe-justice idea is true then Bob's death makes the least sense of all. He was nothing if not a good man. There was absolutely no reason for the universe to want to replace him. He was..."

"He was old, Tara."

"He was only forty-five!"

"Well, he was too old for you."

I scoffed.

"Don't you remember how you used to worry about what it would be like in fifteen years if you stayed with him? He'd be sixty and you'd be forty-five. He'd die first and leave you alone when you were too old to find someone new. We talked about that."

"You talked about that," I argued. "It's always you doing the talking. You don't even notice that I'm not adding to the conversation. You assume that if I'm not arguing, I'm agreeing with you."

"Hold off. I'm the one who does all the talking? The day we went hiking in Squamish? It was all you talking, telling me about every goddamn kind of rock we saw and how Bob had taught you this and Bob would love that. Did you notice that I didn't care? I wanted to be hiking with my best friend, not listening to how wonderful Bob and his freaking rock collection was."

"Well, lucky for you his rock collection landed on his head and killed him, then, isn't it?"

"Lucky for you," Betsy muttered under her breath.

"Lucky for me?" I screamed. "How do you think you'd feel if you'd been the one to put those rocks on the bookshelf? How would you feel knowing that you're very likely the reason the shelf pulled free from its anchors and fell on his head? Huh? Think you might have a bit of guilt about that or would your little universe say, *Hey, Betsy, don't you worry about that. I'm the one who killed your lover.*"

Betsy was silent for several seconds and her energy became incredibly calm. "It's not *my* universe; it's our universe. You shouldn't feel guilt, Tez. You might have caused Bob's death, but that doesn't make it your fault. There is no fault. There just is. And Bob was meant to leave. You simply facilitated what was already predetermined. You were—"

"Shut up. Please. Stop. I don't want to hear it. Okay?

Enough. I need you to leave, Betsy."

"But, I—"

"Just…leave me, okay. Thanks for coming."

Chapter Five

It had been a week since I'd asked Betsy to leave. I was finally coming out of my funk and ready to join the living again. Betsy and I had made up by phone, both of us apologizing for our part in the argument. We'd spoken about how different we were in our relationships, how she would push a man away when he got too close while I would do the opposite—grab hold and never want to let go. She told me I was like cat hair on a black suit. I'd agreed so I guess she took that as a sign to give me dating advice.

"Keep the relationship in your head and your pants. The way men do. It's cleaner that way," Betsy advised me.

"Not that I actually need to know, since I've given up on men—"

"I'll believe *that* when I see it," Betsy interrupted.

"Whatever. But how do you do that? Keep it in your head and your pants? What does that even mean?"

"Glad you asked. It's called 'attentive disengagement.'"

"Betsy, that doesn't help," I admitted, rolling my eyes at myself for giving Betsy a platform to tell me more.

"It means, basically, that you act like you're interested in a relationship and you take advantage of the benefits—like great sex and a regular dinner companion—but you keep emotionally distant from the guy. Or woman. Whatever."

"You mean like hooking up? Random, sleazy sex with strangers, one-nighters? Not for me," I said.

"It doesn't have to be sex with strangers. God, Tara, you're so black and white sometimes. You can have a relationship—hell, you could have five, if you wanted. Just don't let your heart engage. Like I said, head and pants. And voila, no more hurt feelings."

*   *   *

Bumping into Glen on the SkyTrain gave me the perfect opportunity to practice this new approach to relationships.

"Tara Holland?" a deep voice called from across the platform.

I turned to see a face that was familiar, but not. By the way my breathing changed, I knew I'd looked into his eyes before but I couldn't figure out when or where or why. He saw my confusion.

"It's Glen…from high school?" He smiled

I inhaled quickly and was filled with all the joy that could fit in my lungs.

"Glen!" I jumped forward, not giving him any chance to escape my full contact hug, which surprised me as much as it did him since I'd never done anything full-body with Glen before.

"Wow. Not quite the reaction I was expecting."

"Sorry," I said, embarrassed, quickly stepping arms-length distance from him.

"No, no, it's fine. Actually, come here," he said stepping towards me, "I don't think we finished that."

Glen took me in his arms and hugged me hard.

"How are you? You look great. Exactly the same as when we graduated."

"Ha! And you still don't wear your contacts, do you?"

"No seriously, you have a Dorian Gray thing going on." He looked me up and down and I flushed.

"Stop. I look tired and old. But you look amazing. Different. *Really* different. But great."

He'd filled out in all the right places. His shaved head and full beard made me think of Jeff Bridges in Iron Man, but twenty years younger. Very sexy. He looked relaxed and comfortable with himself. Not the same as the scrawny, gawky teenager I'd snuck kisses with in the shadows behind the portable classrooms at the far end of the school. Different even than the young man I'd run into ten years earlier, dancing at a university pub event.

"Have you got time for coffee?" he asked.

"Uh," I had to think. The shock of seeing him made it so I couldn't remember where I'd been going. Betsy. Right. I was supposed to meet *her* for coffee. She'd understand if I bailed to meet with Glen. She'd be thrilled I'd reconnected. Ah, who was I trying to kid? She'd be furious. "I have to text a friend and let her know I'll be a little late." I wouldn't tell her all the details, only that I ran into an old friend. What she didn't know wouldn't hurt her.

We walked two blocks to Bean Around The World, where I could get a gluten-free baked treat with my coffee.

"You allergic to wheat?" Glen asked.

"Intolerant. It gives me gas. I get bloated. I've had people ask if I'm pregnant after a big spaghetti dinner. It's that bad."

Oh dear God am I really telling him about my gas problems? I cringed. No wonder I was such a dolt with relationships.

"Still the same old Tara." Glen said sounding pleased. "Has anyone found a subject that's off-limits for you to talk about yet?"

"Oh my gosh, you remember that?"

The years of hanging out with Betsy had made their mark on me. Although I never had the guts to talk back to adults like she did, I'd made it my mission to push the limits of acceptable conversation by nonchalantly talking about politics, body functions, religion, even sex, which I knew nothing about, to see how other kids would react. Some would run away from the conversation while others would run with my inappropriate intercourse and take it to new depths. Glen was always a 'run with 'er kinda guy.'

"Until the day I die I will never forget the afternoon we spent sitting in the football bleachers talking about genital mutilation. I remember being both appalled and turned on at the same time," he said with a shudder.

"Well, since I couldn't have sex with you that was my way of letting you know I was thinking about it. A lot."

"So? Has anyone found a subject you're uncomfortable discussing yet?" he asked again.

How about the fact that my last three lovers are dead? I smiled and took his hand in mine to give it a kiss. "It's so good to see you. I thought I blew it that last time we ran into each other. I had this crazy idea that we'd be able to pick up where we'd left off when we graduated. I was actually quite hurt that you didn't call."

"I am so sorry. I wanted to. I really did. You told me you lived in a shared house near the pub, and I got a pen from the bar and you wrote your number on the palm of my hand. Remember?"

"Of course I remember. And I remember telling Betsy that…" I couldn't finish my sentence. I blushed. "Never mind."

"What do you mean 'never mind?' What did you tell her?"

"It doesn't matter," I said smiling.

"A subject Tara Holland won't talk about? Come on. You owe me. I've never thought of foreskin the same way because of you…"

"I told Betsy…I told her…that I was going to lose my virginity with you. Sorry."

He laughed. "Sorry? Why in the world are you sorry?"

"Well, obviously you weren't still interested. I must have looked like an idiot that night."

"Tara. I *was* interested."

"Then why didn't you call?"

"When I got home I'd sweated off your number and couldn't read it. I even wandered around your neighbourhood—a couple of times, actually—hoping in vain to see you walking down the street. How cheesy, Hugh-Grant-movie-lame is that? I called your mom and asked for your number."

"You did? She never told me that."

"Well, I was never high on her list of favourites."

"True enough…you called my mom? You did still like me." I felt warm inside. "If only I'd had a cell phone back then…"

"Oh well, it's probably for the best," he said.

In one single instant my body switched from the sweet tingle of the memory of the crush I'd had on Glen to a feeling of having cockroaches doing *La Danza de la Meurta* in my gut, as my mind remade Hugh Grant's movie into Three Funerals and a Wedding…followed by fourth funeral—Glen's.

Definitely for the best because you'd probably be dead given my luck with men.

I stepped away, creating space between us. "Definitely for the best," I agreed.

"What's up? Did I say something wrong?" His eyebrows crunched up in concern.

"Let's talk when we're sitting down," I said, squeezing my stomach muscles as tight as I could to suffocate all the bugs in my belly. We held eye contact for several seconds.

"I still haven't met anyone else with grey eyes, you know. Most beautiful eyes ever."

"Are you flirting?" he asked.

"No. Not at all. At least, no more than I did back in grade eleven," I said, trying to sound lighter than I felt.

We ordered our coffees and muffins and took them to the low lounge chairs in the corner of the café. Glen sat first. Rather than sitting across the table from him, I swung the chair beside his around, so it was facing him.

"Do you mind if I get comfortable?"

Glen shook his head. I pulled my legs up to sit lotus-style then reconsidered, not wanting to dirty the chair.

"Mind if I take off my boots?"

Glen laughed. A sound that filled the room, deep and throaty. People turned to look at us and I smiled at them.

My date, lucky me.

Sitting cross-legged, knees touching Glen's, our conversation quickly got intimate.

"I can't tell you how much I'd hoped I'd lose my virginity with you."

"As I recall, I gave you several opportunities to move from locker necking to the next level—bathroom groping, I think it was—but you wouldn't go there with me," he said smiling.

"I know. You're right. It would have meant having to marry me, of course. I wasn't the kind of girl to grope without a ring. And, well, even though I imagined us having sex, I couldn't picture being married. Not at seventeen. Not to a guy who didn't even have an after-school job."

"You were pretty church-y back in the old days. Still?"

"No. It was my mom's thing. I guess I believed and all, but it was mostly fear that if I didn't do all the stuff the church said I had to do—"

"Or did do the stuff they said you couldn't do," Glen added with a wink.

I nodded, "Absolutely. If I didn't follow the rules, I'd go to Hell. And they didn't make Hell seem like a place I wanted to spend eternity."

"And...now that you're an adult, Hell looks like a better alternative?" he asked.

"Without going into details..." I stalled.

"Is that two subjects in one cup of coffee that you don't want to talk about? Tara Holland, you've changed."

"No. Just trying to find the right words, is all. I guess it's fair to say that I got myself into a situation that guaranteed I'd not be going to Heaven...so I thought, hang it. If I'm going to Hell anyway I might as well have fun getting there."

Glen put his hand on my knee and squeezed it. I felt a shiver run up my leg and right into my Hanes Her Way. The famous 'pants feelings' Betsy spoke about. *This is where I have to make the feeling stop*, I told myself. *Don't let the feeling move out of there*, I commanded my now clenched vagina, as Glen took my chin and looked me in the eyes. Bam! Shiver right into my heart.

"Glen," I whispered.

"Yes?" he leaned forward.

"I can't."

"Can't what?" he said.

I can't go down this road with you. I like you. I always have. I don't want you to die. I shook my head.

"Have dinner tomorrow?" he asked.

I stared at him. *I love your eyes.*

"Tara?" Glen said, crossing his arms in front of his chest, "Do you believe in fate?"

"Hm. I don't know. Like when someone is hit by a bus—" *Or a shelf falls on their head* "—it was something that was meant to be?"

"Well, I was thinking more along the lines of the fact that we met again after so many years and it seems pretty clear that there's still an attraction," he said, touching my leg again, sending another shiver from my knee through my pants, into my heart and this time, into the expanding blood vessels in my forehead.

I sighed. I had such good intentions to practice my emotional detachment and I was failing already. But this was Glen. Sweet Glen who never pushed me to do anything I wasn't comfortable doing. Lovely Glen who didn't simply tolerate me, he encouraged me to be myself.

I couldn't keep feelings for Glen in my pants and my head 'cause he'd been in my heart for almost half my life.

"It's only dinner," he said.

"I know, but..."

"We'll go somewhere wheat-free. I'm as interested in giving you gas as you are in having it. I promise you that."

I laughed. And relaxed. I really wanted to see him again. I desperately wanted to believe that James's, Scott's and Bob's deaths had all been coincidences and that I'd had nothing to do with them. I *needed* to believe that.

"The Naam?" I asked, "At six?"

"Just so you know, that hippy vegetarian food gives *me* gas. But if you're good with that, I'm game."

"Cool," I said.

"But, I'd like to pick you up, if that's okay, rather than meet there."

I pulled a pen from my bag and reached toward him. I pulled his arm toward me, pushed up his sleeve and wrote in large letters along his inner arm both my phone number and address.

"Try not to sweat on the way home," I told him.

"I'll take a cab to avoid any physical exertion at all. Except this." Glen took my arm in his hand and pulled me toward him. I expected him to write on me but he kept pulling until I fell forward into his chest. He smelled of apple pie. I breathed him in. Off-balance with my legs still crossed in front of me, I put my free hand on his leg and pushed myself back into a sort-of-sitting position. Glen took my chin in his free hand and tilted my head up slightly, leaning his own down.

"Can I kiss you? Or should we stand over there and try to hide behind the door to the bathrooms?"

My smile and pursed lips answered. *I promise you won't die. Oh, God, I hope you don't die.* My eyes filled with tears so as soon as our kiss ended I looked away and excused myself to the bathroom. My phone had vibrated several times during our coffee date so I took the moment to check it. It had been Betsy. She'd texted. And she was pissed off.

Chapter Six

"You ditched me, your oldest, bestest friend, for coffee with some loser you kissed a few times in high school?" Betsy rolled her eyes.

"I honestly didn't think you'd mind. I actually thought you'd be happy that I was getting out," I argued.

"You were already out, remember? To meet me? Christ, Tez."

Betsy slammed her mug of coffee down so hard it splashed over the rim, making a puddle that reached out to the milk and cream containers. I grabbed a wad of napkins to wipe it up as she carelessly — or intentionally, I wasn't sure — poured milk on my hand.

"Why are you so mad? It's not like you've never gone for coffee on your own before."

"I was looking forward to seeing you," she snapped.

"Well, you're seeing me now. Only an hour later. Why are you so upset?"

Betsy looked at her Doc Martens. She stomped her

feet a few times. I pictured her as a small child, throwing fits so intense her foster families couldn't cope.

"You don't want to know," she said to her feet.

I exhaled and moaned. I wasn't going to give in. *If I don't want to know then I'm not going to ask, am I?*

We sat down at the same table Glen and I had been seated at, but I sat across from Betsy, not beside her.

"Do you want to know?" she asked after a minute of silence.

"Not really," I said, defiant, knowing she'd tell me within another minute.

"Tez, do you believe in fate?"

I laughed, "Glen asked the same question, sitting in that same chair. Do you mean fate like running into a man I was in love with as a teen at a time when finding an old friend has extra-special meaning?"

"No, I mean fate as in, you fall in love and a toaster explodes in his face; you fall in love and a shelf falls on his head; you fall in love and a ladder slips."

"No, Betsy, I don't. I can't believe I had anything to do with any of those events. I can't. I didn't. I won't," I said standing up, ready to fight.

Normally I was pretty patient with Betsy's woo-woo, the-universe-is-talking-to-me crap. Hell, sometimes I even found it interesting. But this was going too far. Who tells their best friend that they're to blame for some type of universal hit man?

"Believe it, baby," Betsy said. "I love you and I hate to see you hurting. I'm telling you this to protect you. You have a power. And if you don't accept that fact, you'll have four men on your conscience. "

"That sounds like a threat. What is your fucking

46

problem?" I said, too loud. The manager of the coffee shop walked toward me with purpose.

"I'm sorry," I said before the manager spoke. "I'm sorry," I said to the rest of the patrons who were all looking at us.

"If you don't mind," he said, "I'll put your coffee in *To Go* cups and you can finish elsewhere."

Betsy and I parted ways with little more than a head shrug of acknowledgement. I decided not to tell her anything about dates with Glen, whether there was only one or there were a hundred. Glen would be my secret, just like he had been from my mother half-a-lifetime ago.

*   *   *

It wasn't hard juggling my dates with Glen with time I spent with Betsy since her evenings were usually jam-packed with meditation, Tarot readings, some esoteric book club...she had things going on almost every night of the week with a group of friends I didn't share. Glen and I became constant dinner-to-dawn companions and he stayed in touch through the day with text messages: short notes to let me know he was thinking of me, a link to a news story he thought I'd be interested in, a flirtatious invitation to try something new after dinner. I always let him know when I'd be with Betsy since I couldn't reply to his notes and didn't want him to think I was ignoring him.

He, of course, remembered Betsy from high school—people didn't forget Betsy. At first I told him that she was going through a man-hating phase, which wasn't really a lie, except that this 'phase' had lasted about seven years. After a couple of weeks I admitted that I'd promised Betsy I wouldn't date and said that since I didn't want to deal with her telling me it was a bad idea, that I was keeping our relationship a secret. After three weeks I finally told him about Scott, Bob and James. He didn't seem at all worried.

After less than a month, I was head-over heels. Again.

"I think I fall in love too easily," I told him while we lay in bed, him rubbing my naked back.

"Who is it this time?" he asked. "Daniel Craig? He's too old for you. Plus, he travels all the time for work…"

"And too cliché," I replied. "I'm more of a Will Ferrell kinda gal."

"I don't know if you fall in love *too* easily. I mean, this back rubbing…it's hard work. And it's taken, what…four or five weeks to have any effect on you."

I rolled over and kissed him.

"I love you," I said.

"I love you."

"I'm scared. Terrified, actually."

"Because if we have kids they'll be hairy like me?"

My heart skipped a beat. I looked into his eyes and saw him as he would look in ten years. I buried my face in his chest and breathed him in. "You always smell good."

"Don't deflect. Why are you scared?"

Silence.

"Tara look at me. I'm not going to hurt you. I can promise you that. We talk. Have you ever been with a man who talks as much as I do?"

I laughed and shook my head.

"I tell you everything. I promise, no half-truths. You know me better than anyone. When I'm with you, I feel," he paused and took my face in his hands, "gay."

I laughed out loud. "Gay? Not what I was expecting."

"Yeah. Gay. You know, all emo and talking about feelings and shit all the time. Stuff real men don't actually have a vocabulary for," he tried to look serious.

"Bob was pretty good with gay, too," I said. "I guess I like gay."

Glen stared into my eyes. I willed him to read my mind, but he kept smiling, dammit. "I know this is going to sound crazy—that *I'm* going to sound crazy—but there's this very slight chance that…" How was I going to word this?

"You'll eat too much Fettuccini Alfredo one night and you'll explode, killing me in my sleep?"

I considered that idea and said, "Well, yes actually. Exactly. Or something as equally outrageous and unexpected."

"This is about your other lovers?"

I nodded, tears putting Glen into soft focus. He took my face in his hands and rubbed his thumbs gently over my eyes, pushing the tears out the sides them wiping them away.

"But there's one thing I didn't tell you."

He didn't speak, but the tilt of his head and smile in his eyes invited me to continue.

"I think, well, Betsy believes, that I'm…in some way… responsible for them all dying."

"Because?" he asked, rolling his hand.

I shrugged. "Because…I don't know why. Something about the universe and powers."

"Well, I hate to be a skeptic, but, I'm not buying it."

"But the last three men—"

"Tara, you're not going to kill me. I don't believe you have that power 'cause if you did, last week a dozen Telus

49

operators would have dropped dead when your phone service glitched."

"You're *really* not worried?" I asked.

"Not in the least. The way I see it, you've had some bad luck. That doesn't mean that you are bad luck."

"I'm going to tell Betsy about us. You good with that?"

"Of course. I'd love to see her again. We'll be the Three Musketeers."

"Larry, Curly and Moe," I said.

"Jesus, Mary and Joseph."

"Nah, I don't know about that one. If I were Mary, you'd be Joseph and that would make Betsy Jesus. I don't think I could stand the preaching. She has a bit of a God complex as it is," I said, shaking my head.

"Then how about Fred and Ginger? And Betsy can be Betsy, and she can join us for dinner and a dance every once in awhile," Glen said, moving his hand to my breast, gently squeezing my nipple, getting the response he always got: my full attention.

"Dinner only," I sighed, "I want to keep all our dances between us." I kissed Glen on the mouth, rolling up and on top of him at the same time. "Can I lay on you for awhile? Listen to your heart?"

"Would you like me to rub your back a little while longer?"

"Mm."

'A little while' turned into an hour. Glen was a master of recognizing when I needed emotional space and when I needed physical attention. Even though we were both hungry to experience our new connection the first time we slept together, Glen didn't push when I said I wasn't ready. He waited two weeks before I finally felt I could let him in emotionally. Not coincidentally, that was the same night I let him in physically. Since that night we'd made love every time we were together; we never had sex. I could feel the difference. He said he could, too.

We dozed, woke up, ran our hands over each other, gently, sensually but not sexually. We dozed more, woke up, talked about work, politics, and old English teachers. Although I'd only known Glen for a couple of years as a pimply teen and hadn't seen him in almost sixteen, aside from one drunken conversation ten years earlier, I felt like we'd known each other forever. And, I was starting to imagine forever with him. Forever was looking pretty damn good.

Chapter Seven

A few weeks passed before we talked about letting Betsy in on our secret again. I wasn't in a rush to turn my time with Glen into time with Betsy and Glen. I liked the way things had been going.

"So," Glen circled his finger lightly around my tail bone as we were relaxing before sleep one night, "Have you talked to Betsy yet?"

"You mean, about us?"

"Yes," he whispered in my ear, making me shiver.

"Not yet. It's just, well you two didn't like each other back in high school and in a way it's easier for me not to have to listen to the…you know… smack-talk. I love you both."

We lay in silence for several minutes. Glen continued to run his fingertips lightly over my lower back. I was almost asleep when he finally spoke.

"Obviously, I can't control what Betsy says about me, but I can promise you that I will never say a bad word about your best friend."

I rolled over to face Glen. I wanted to look into his eyes, "*You're* my best friend. Betsy's my sister. She's my bat-shit crazy sister and I love how she challenges me to think in ways that don't come naturally to me, and we've always been there for each other, and I would do anything for her...but you—"

I stopped to find the right words. A million thoughts went through my head but I couldn't express them. Emotion filled my eyes and Glen wiped my cheek with his gentle touch.

"The problem is," I decided to take another approach, "that Betsy is convinced that I need to take time to be on my own, to get to know myself before I throw myself at another man—her words."

"Too bad, 'cause I already caught you," Glen said, kissing me on the mouth. I accepted the affection then pulled away and rolled my back to him; I needed to separate myself to say the next part.

"She thinks that the universe is making sure I take some time and make the space to be happy with myself. With who I am. Who I grew up to be—"

Glen didn't let me finish my thought. He rolled me back toward him and asked, "Who did you grow up to be, Tara?"

A sinner. An atheist. A girl who gets herself into trouble and deserves the consequences. A killer, maybe even. The negative mind chatter overwhelmed me and I shook my head, "I don't know."

"Tara, what did you do today as we were walking home from the market?"

"Uh, I tripped on the curb," adding 'clumsy' to my

internal list of flaws.

"Not that, you goof," Glen said with a smile so sweet I forgot what I'd been thinking. "You gave that man outside the liquor store our roasted chicken."

"I'm sorry, but he looked so hungry—"

"My point is not that you gave away our dinner, it's that you're the most compassionate woman I've ever met. And one of the happiest. I don't know what Betsy sees in you that makes her think otherwise. But I have a good idea of the ghosts you're holding on to. And I have one thing to say about that…"

Glen paused to kiss the tears from my salty cheeks. "Fact: God is recognized as the all-powerful force in the universe—"

"But, I—"

"But, you don't believe in God. Fact?"

"Fact," I nodded.

"Therefore, you can't believe there is an all-powerful force in the universe."

"But, I—"

"But, you believe that you were in some way involved in your previous lovers' deaths, right?"

"Well, Bets—"

"Let me finish," Glen said smiling, "So, since only God can have God-like powers, then…either your powers don't exist or…you're God and, since you don't believe in God, you should cease to exist right…about…now!" He snapped his fingers.

"So…you think I'm batshit crazy, too?"

"Most definitely. But in a good way."

I laughed. "I think your logic is flawed."

"Really?" Glen asked, distracting me with a series of

gentle kisses on my eyelids, cheeks, then lips, "Can you prove it to me?"

"Probably," I whispered, "but I'd much rather prove that Betsy is wrong by having a fifty year relationship with you."

Chapter Eight

Sucking up my courage, I invited Betsy for dinner to tell her about Glen and me. It was the first night in over six weeks that Glen and I would spend apart. I missed him before the rice pilaf was even cooked.

Betsy arrived with a bottle of Riesling and a store bought apple pie. I smelled it and smiled, thinking of Glen and how he'd smelled the day we'd met. We chatted about work—and a lack of it—during dinner. I wanted to have the serious eating done before I moved on to the serious talking. I also needed time to finish my share of the bottle of wine for the relaxation buzz to hit me.

"Dessert in the living room?"

As I poured us each a double scotch and put a quarter of the pie on each plate, Betsy pulled a cushion from the couch and put it on the floor at the end of my old, oak coffee table. She sat cross-legged, straight-backed in a yoga pose. She pushed the magazines into a neat pile to make room for the plates and glasses.

"Thanks," I said, slouching into my Value Village couch and wrapping my favourite crazy quilt around my shoulders. My apartment wasn't cold but I wanted the security of my grandma's blanket.

"So, Glen and I," I said, raising my eyebrows, hoping Betsy would fill in the rest.

"Who the hell is Glen?"

"Glen. From grade eleven," I said, happy as a court jester.

"The guy you ran into a couple months ago?"

I opened my mouth wide, to relieve the face cramp I was getting from my uncontrollable grin.

"What about him?" Betsy asked, rolling her eyes.

I shrugged my shoulders and a deep sigh spontaneously erupted from my open mouth.

"Meaning, please," Betsy was clearly not feeling my bliss.

"We've been seeing each other. I think it's getting serious."

"Obviously. Way to keep it in your pants, Tez. And of all the men in the world you decide to date, you choose an old high school boyfriend? You're insane."

A better reaction than I'd expected. I was counting on a more general tirade about the danger of my getting involved with any man. I was pleasantly surprised.

"Batshit crazy!" I said.

"How serious is this?"

I nodded and clapped like a wind-up tin monkey. "Serious enough that I can picture Glen as the last man I ever share a toothbrush with."

Betsy wrinkled her nose. "Well, congratulations, I guess. And now, can we talk about something other than who you're swapping spit with?"

I was happy to change the subject. I picked up where we'd left off in the kitchen. "So, what are you going to do about work if you don't land a new client soon?" I asked.

Betsy dropped her head and sighed.

"Would you go back to being an employee?" I asked.

"Never. I'd rather drain all my savings than have to do office politics again. You know?"

"Yeah. I'd never go back either. And anyway, it's stupid to think that people like us can turn on inspiration at 9:00 AM and then put it on hold at 5:00 if the words or design are flowing," I said.

We clinked glasses and sipped our scotch.

"You know…I have one client right now who has a terrible website. I'm writing new copy that they were planning to drop in to their existing crappy design. Maybe I could convince them to move some of their budget over to hire you? I'll try," I said.

"That would be awesome. I'd appreciate it."

"Happy to ask. You know I'd do anything for you."

We sat in silence for a minute or two before Betsy took the conversation back to Glen. "So, how long have you been seeing him?"

"Basically since that day we met again. Six, seven weeks?"

"Seriously? You've been dating him for *seven weeks* and this is the first you're telling me?" I couldn't tell if she was more angry or hurt.

"You *told* me you didn't want to know anything about my love life. Remember?"

"Well…that's because I didn't think you had a love life. I was trying to make you feel okay about not having

58

any man news to update me on."

"Oh, for God's sake, Betsy," I said, laughing and finishing my scotch. "More?" I asked, holding up my glass.

She shook her head, no. "So what does high school lover do?"

"He's a watercourse design consultant."

"Excuse me?"

"He advises people who want water features in their yards of what they could do and then he designs it." I looked around my sparsely decorated living room and imagined how different it would look and feel with Glen's eye for design.

"Like pools?" Betsy asked.

"Not usually. More like he goes to a super expensive property in West Van or Dunbar and he figures out how to add a waterfall or a pond to their yard. He's done jobs all up and down the West Coast. He had this one client in California that wanted a small water park for their kids in their yard. So, he designed it, did the budget, mostly hired other people to do the hard work. Cool, eh?"

"So has he got money?"

I shrugged, "Enough, I guess. He never seems stressed about it."

"Wouldn't that be nice," Betsy said, looking sad.

"Hey, maybe Glen would hire you to redesign his company website? Want me to ask?"

"I don't know. It would be weird. He wouldn't be able to say no to you. That would feel like charity. I don't do charity," Betsy said, mood changing from somber to snarly.

"Never mind. Just trying to help."

"I know. Sorry. Why don't you give me his URL. Don't tell him you gave it to me, though. I'll take a look at his site and if I think I can improve it, I'll give him a call. Lots of web designers make cold calls. I should probably do more," Betsy said.

I was thrilled. "You're going to love him, Betsy. I know you will."

"Doubtful. I suspect we'll both love you and that will be as much as we have in common."

"We should all get together on the weekend if he's free—he usually has site visits on weekends but maybe Saturday night? You won't recognize him. I didn't. And he's so sweet, Betsy," I said, grabbing her hands and shaking her arms.

"Maybe," Betsy said, pulling away. "We'll see. You know, I should get going."

"But it's only 9:00. Stay. It's been ages since we've had a girls' night. I miss you."

"I saw you three days ago," she said with a scowl.

"For like two minutes."

"I have yoga at 7:00 tomorrow morning. I need to get home and to bed early."

As soon as I closed the door behind Betsy I called Glen to see if he wanted to come over. He didn't hesitate, twenty minutes later he was wrapped up with me in Nana's crazy quilt.

"You know the saying, 'much ado about nothing?'" I asked him.

"All those weeks of stress about telling Betsy... I'd say I told you so, but instead all I'll say is, I'm glad."

"You can say I told you so. You were right. Happy to admit it. So, now we can move in together without worrying about the wrath of Betsy O'Khan-er."

"Nice one."

"Thank you."

Since it was my joke that drew the response from Glen, he left me unsure about what he thought of my subtle proposition of living together, but I decided to leave it for now. I was happy enough not having to curl up alone in cold sheets.

"Want to go to bed?" I asked, feeling exhausted from the combination of alcohol and stress.

"It's still early. I'll be awake at 4:00 AM if we go to sleep now," he said.

"Who said I wanted to sleep?"

"I can see it in your eyes. You've got that glazed look. As soon as you get warm you'll be out."

"Well, will you lay with me until then?"

"I'd love to. But don't be upset if you wake up and I'm not there, okay? I've got to get some work done, a few client emails. I'll come back when it's real bedtime."

Glen was right again and I was asleep in minutes. I woke briefly when he lifted my arm and rolled out from my spooning body-hold. He kissed me on the forehead, told me he loved me and left me to fall asleep again.

I was surprised and a little upset when I woke up to my alarm the next morning and his side of the bed was empty and cold. I lay quietly, wondering if he'd gotten up early to make coffee but I didn't hear any noise in the kitchen. I opened the bedroom door and called, 'Good morning, gorgeous,' as I pulled on my robe. His shoes weren't at the door and there was a note on the kitchen table.

Dear Tara,

You were right; my logic was flawed. I had an epiphany

61

last night and had to leave. I'm so sorry.

Glen

P.S. The film we were trying to remember last night was 'The Prestige.'

There was no, 'I love you.' There was no 'XOX.' The first time reading it, I smiled, expecting a joke ending, which is what I thought the P.S was since we hadn't talked about films in a few days and hadn't been trying to remember the name of any film ever.

The second time I read it my heart was pounding in my ears. The third time I could only see a blur on the paper; it wasn't so much reading as it was staring and willing the words to be different once I wiped my eyes, which of course, they weren't.

Was he breaking up with me? If his logic was flawed that meant he did think I might kill him. But that didn't make sense. None of it made sense.

I called his cell. It was turned off and went straight to voice mail. I did my best to keep my voice from sounding panicked, in case I was over-reacting or misreading his note somehow.

"Hi Glen, I missed you this morning. Got your note. Not sure I understand it. Can you call me? As soon as you get the message? Please?" By the time I said *please*, he would have known I was crying. I took an unstable breath. "I love you. Call me."

Betsy was already awake and on her way to yoga when I called her. She got off the bus and arrived within half-an-hour with coffee, muffins and her Rescue Remedy kit. I could neither drink nor eat until after noon, and even then, the tension in my stomach fought every sip and swallow. I tried to call him at least five times and sent him three text messages but he didn't answer any of them, even after his phone had been turned on. Betsy finally took my phone away from me, telling me I was torturing myself.

After a lunch of chicken noodle soup she asked me to tell her everything about my conversation with Glen the night before. I edited a little, but did mention my joke about moving in together and that he didn't seem to hear me.

"He heard you," she argued.

"I don't think he did or he would have said something."

"He heard you. Guaranteed. That's why he ran."

Betsy told me that I was lucky to have her since she, more than anyone else I knew (which in truth was very few people and even fewer I'd confide in), understood the psyche of people who were afraid of commitment. She explained how feelings of love would turn to feelings of being slowly drowned when the pressure to commit became too intense.

"Tez," Betsy said, with tears in her own eyes, empathy, I figured for my pain, "You have to let him go. The faster you breathe him out of your system, the quicker you'll heal and move on."

"I don't want to let him go. I don't want to breathe him out of my system. I want to know what the fuck happened. It doesn't make any sense at all." I threw a cushion and hit my Georgia O'Keefe print. It slid down the wall behind my bookcase.

"Fuck!" I screamed.

"Let it out. You know the stages. Denial to anger.

Gotta move through them," Betsy said. I wanted to hit her. "You're better—"

I didn't let her finish. "If you tell me I'm better off without him I swear to God I'll kill you." My tone of voice told the truth though: I didn't have the energy to swat a fly.

Betsy's eyes widened for an instant and then she smiled and zipped her lips, throwing away the invisible key. I don't know what she hoped to accomplish with her bit of theatre—a laugh? Rage? Either might have been possible in another situation. I felt exhausted, like giving up.

"Do you mind if I go to bed? You can stay if you want, or leave. I'll be fine. I feel like I need to sleep all of a sudden."

"Sure you're okay?"

I nodded.

By 2:00 PM I was asleep and ready to never wake up again. My dreams were vivid and so real I knew that they were meant as a direct call-to-action.

Chapter Nine

The next morning, I swaddled myself in my comfort clothes: sweat pants, a hoodie over a tank top, no bra, and my oldest Doc Martens. I didn't care how I looked. Nobody would be looking at my clothes anyway. If they saw me at all, they'd be staring at my puffy eyes and blotchy cheeks.

It was almost ten when I arrived at my destination. A big building. A cold building. Imposing. A God-awful place. A space I hadn't visited since I was twenty-one. A church. I had no idea if there would be anyone there to meet me, anyone for me to talk to. It almost didn't matter. I knew I needed to push open the heavy oak doors and sit on a straight-back pew. I wasn't going to kneel. I had no intention of inviting God back into my heart but I needed to stand face-to-face with Him to ask my burning question, "What the fuck?"

I sat for several minutes, oddly calm. What was so calming? The energy of the room? I doubted that since my recollection of the sermons was that I always left feeling like a sinner. In reality, I rarely sat with the congregation. As a small child, I'd only sit for a few minutes before being whisked away to Sunday School in the church basement with all the other 'Under Tens.' As an older child, teen and young woman I'd stood at the front of the church in a too-large maroon robe, singing with the blue-haired ladies, a handful of balding men, and two other young people like myself.

The air was always cold in the church. I'd never thought about it before but as I sat now, coat pulled tight around me, I wondered if it was strategic, 'discomfort and cold keep you paying attention,' or if it was efficient, 'do you know how much it costs to heat the twenty-two feet of the heavens over our heads?' I decided that would be my ice-breaker question to the pastor, if he ever appeared. Better than what my original opener was going to be.

The sun must have come around a building because suddenly several images of Jesus in varying degrees of discomfort lit up to my right. What had been dark panes of coloured glass started to glow and spread their parables over the pews and bibles. I turned sideways and pulled one leg up so I was sitting partially cross-legged. I'd never sat like this, disrespectful I'm sure, in church before and wondered if it was an actual sin. I didn't care. It was the most comfortable position to watch the movement of light and shadow and colour. I slid toward the heat of the sun and tilted my head up to receive its warmth. For a minute I felt like I belonged here.

The sound of a door drew my attention. It was an older woman, entering from the same door I'd used to walk single file to my Bible lessons so many years ago. Our eyes met. She smiled but didn't speak. I imagined people often came to pray quietly and rarely looking for chit-chat.

"Hello," I said, standing and walking toward her. "Is the pastor in today? Is he available for a conversation?"

I wasn't actually sure why I was asking to speak to the pastor when it was God I had an issue with.

"Are you a member of the congregation?" she asked.

"No. I mean, maybe. I used to be. And I haven't joined any other church." I was hedging my bets, as it were, not wanting to be expelled for not being a card-carrying member.

"Did you have an appointment with Father Sparrow?"

"Father Sparrow is still the pastor?" I asked, flabbergasted. He must be a hundred-and-fifty years old. I thought he was a hundred when I was a teen.

She scowled and lowered her head, mumbling something that sounded like "young people...no respect... elders...the cane," then raised her head and showed me all her false teeth, "This is his forty-fifth year with us."

"He married my parents," I said to Father Sparrow's gate-keeper, who wasn't moving me any closer to knowing if I could see him or not.

"Oh, he doesn't do weddings anymore. He's too tired for all that nonsense now. And anyway," she seemed to speak to herself again, "young people don't take their vows before God seriously anymore."

"So, is Father Sparrow in? Is he available?" *Why do you want to see him? What will you say?*

"Yes, dear. He's in. He's having his tea. If you wait, I'll find out when he can see you." She turned and walked back through the door that led to the Vestry and the hall. From behind, she looked like every church lady I'd ever seen in this congregation in her shapeless cotton dress, clinging tight around her bottom, sitting just below her knees on panty-hose-clad legs, atop plain, black, square heeled shoes.

As I watched I wondered if ladies from all churches and of all religions developed this same body or, if the body-type drew these women to this church. I decided at that moment that no matter how convincing Father Sparrow might be, if I was going to consider becoming a Christian again, I'd shop around for a congregation that was a little more top-heavy, and a little less grounded.

Father Sparrow's teacup must have been as big as a beer stein; the sun had moved away from the stained glass and to the brick corner before he came out to meet with me.

"How can I help you, my child?"

He put his hand on my arm and my stomach tensed. Suddenly, I couldn't breathe. I didn't want to talk to him. I should have left. I didn't want to see him. Him of all people.

"You look exactly the same as you did last time I was here," I blinked away the tears that were trying to collect. Father Sparrow hadn't changed in ten years. But I guess by seventy you've already got all your wrinkles. And although he wasn't in robes, he still looked daunting in his black suit and collar.

"You look familiar, but I can't recall your name."

"Tara Holland."

No recognition.

"Lynn and Tony Holland's daughter," I offered.

He looked thoughtful for a minute, rubbing his chin with his finger. "You had a spot of trouble a few years ago, didn't you?"

A spot of trouble? You don't remember all the years I sang in your choir? All you remember me for is my spot of trouble? My emotions were changing quickly.

"Yeah," I said tentatively, "I guess you could call it that."

"And how old is your young one now?"

I stared at him, teeth clenched, holding my breath for fear that if I exhaled, a decade worth of anger and hatred would explode from me and drown Father Sparrow in the blood of the innocent.

"You got pregnant out of wedlock, did you not? I believe I offered to find a home for the child but you said you were going to care for it yourself."

Close but not quite. I said I'd take care of it.

At any other time, from any other person, that comment would have resulted in an uncontrollable wave of grief. But from Father Sparrow, it fuelled my rage. My fists clenched and I took a steadying breath. I suddenly remembered the last conversation I'd had with him. I'd been sitting in his office, my mother standing on his side of the heavy oak desk. They'd ganged up on me, telling me I'd sinned. Telling me I must have asked to be raped.

"Girls only get pregnant when they're enjoying it."

The fact that I wasn't even conscious during the date rape didn't matter. The fact that I'd been drugged with Rohypnol was of no consequence to them; or if it was of consequence, it was to tell me that I shouldn't have been using drugs. The fact that I lost my virginity to a man whose last name I didn't even know had felt like the worst thing that could have happened to me. Until I found out I was pregnant. And even that moment paled in comparison

69

to how it felt to be blamed for my situation by the two people I thought I could trust to help me find a way out of my 'spot of trouble.'

"Sex out of wedlock means you'll burn in Hell," my mother had said.

'Fine,' I finally had the courage to say, 'if being raped condemns me to Hell already, then why not have an abortion? At least I'll be happy in this life if my afterlife is already fucked.' My mother collapsed to the floor and Father Sparrow called 9-1-1 as I left the room. At her funeral two years later, Father Sparrow said in his eulogy that my mother had died of a broken heart.

Why had I thought coming back here would be a good idea? Somehow, even though it all ended so badly, I had loved the peace of the church when I'd been younger. The hymns had filled my heart. I hadn't hated God back then, even though I didn't always understand or agree with His expectations.

"Tara?" Father Sparrow asked.

I looked into his watery, grey eyes. They didn't scare me now. He was nothing more than a man, an old and tired and weak man.

"Why did you come to see me?" he asked.

I shrugged my shoulders, shook my head and turned without saying a word. There was no way to explain that it never occurred to me he'd still be there. That I'd assumed, like the monsters under my bed, he was something from my childhood that I'd outgrown. There was nothing to say. Lots to scream, though, like, "How could you have given such bad counsel to a young woman in need of serious spiritual support?" Or, "How could you have sided with my mother when I needed one person to understand my situation?" It took all my willpower not to yell through the church, "How dare you condemn me to a life of guilt and an afterlife in Hell? What the fuck, Father?"

As I opened the heavy oak doors I heard Father Sparrow's shaky voice call, "God be with you, child."

I turned and pushed the door open enough to throw my voice in, "God left me years ago, Father."

On the upside, I hadn't thought about Glen in the last half-hour. On the downside, I was reliving the most awful moments of my early twenties. Feelings and pain I'd successfully buried. Of course, I didn't have an abortion. I couldn't, despite my tough talk. But the fetus spontaneously aborted at five months, after I'd started to show. After I'd accepted I was going to be a single mom. After I'd started to think of names and how I'd be the kind of mother I wished mine had been, accepting and nonjudgmental.

"Goddammit!" I yelled to the stellar jays in the maple tree. I interpreted their back-talk as "We hear ya sister."

Chapter Ten

I tried to reach Betsy. She wasn't answering. Not wanting to sit home alone with my voices, I blinked my way to the downtown library. The library had been my church for the last decade. A quiet place filled with people searching for answers. I knew that I could sit undisturbed, invisible if I wanted, hidden by stacks and rows of musings of people more learned, more balanced, more enlightened than me. My normal destination was the area that was home to books about finance, the economy, and political science. But today my feet took me in a new, unexplored direction. I sat down on the floor, mid-row, and looked left, right, and up. Had I been in a better frame-of-mind I would have laughed but in my current state I was more inclined to pull the shelf of books down on top of myself in a life-ending avalanche. I'd sat myself down in front of books categorized as 'spiritual.'

"Fine," I said, too loud for my environment. I closed my eyes and pulled a random book from the shelf, something

I often did when I didn't know where to start the research for a new project. Thinking about my own life as a new project did offer me a brief moment of levity. My hand settled on a spine. It was large and hard-covered. Without opening my eyes I decided that this random selection was not what I wanted. I wanted something lighter so I ran my hand right along the shelf until it felt a small book. I put my hand on top of the book, tilted the spine forward and pulled it off the shelf before I opened my eyes.

"*The Four Agreements*," I read aloud. Nice cover art. I flipped it open. One-hundred-thirty-two pages. Less than a two-hour read. Perfect. I'd be able to finish it before my growling stomach insisted I had to find lunch. I picked myself up off the floor and walked to a wall lined with upholstered, straight-back chairs. I'd always wondered if the chairs were meant to be comfortable or uncomfortable. They had an inviting look, but ten minutes into them, my bum was always numb so I pulled one chair out from the wall and sat on the floor behind it. The librarians were used to seeing me in "my spot" as they called it, and left me alone.

Since I was young, reading was one of the only ways I could settle the chatter in my mind. I often joked when trying to hold a conversation while looking at a menu that although I can walk and drink, I can't read and think. And right now, the last thing I wanted to do was think. The author, Don Miguel Ruiz, kept my attention for over an hour, the time it took to read his short treatise on self-love, integrity and finding peace. I checked the book out so I could reread it and take notes. My life as a research project.

Betsy called me mid-afternoon. I was back at home.

"Hey, Tez. How's it going? You called?"

The sound of her voice seemed to invite the emotions I'd successfully repressed all day to rain forth. As usual, she was on transit within minutes and at my house within half-an-hour with her healing bag. I could not have asked for a better friend.

"I know the hurt is still fresh, but you know that men are bastards. I don't understand why this surprises you," she said as she handed me a full eye-dropper of Rescue Remedy. "Double dose. You may as well keep the whole damn thing. You use it more than I do."

"Thanks," I said, squeezing the liquid under my tongue. "I thought Glen was different. I really did. It felt different. It felt…"

"Permanent?"

"I guess."

"The only permanent relationship I expect to have is with my best friend. All others I look at as distractions from the person who is most important in my life," Betsy said, wrapping her arm around my shoulder.

"Thanks," I sobbed, overcome by both the sweetness of Betsy's words and the grief and guilt of wishing I was hearing them from Glen instead.

"Come on. You weren't even together two months. It's a blip in time. You'll be over him in two weeks. Tops." Betsy saw the book on the table, "You read this?"

I nodded.

"I read this a few years ago. I thought it was pretty well all touchy-feely crap. But there was one thing I remember agreeing with," she said.

"What?" I said, irritated that Betsy wasn't going to let me wallow in my grief for even a day.

"The part about letting go of the past. Something about living in the present, looking to the future, but not focusing on what's happened before. Giving up the whole victim thing."

"Personally, I like the way he describes how love is the real creator."

"Yeah. Look at all that love's created in your life," Betsy said, rolling her eyes.

I moved quickly from grief to guilt to *grr*, "Agreement Two. Don't take anything personally. Do you remember that one? I think you're saying that because *you* don't believe in love, not because love has actually hurt *me*."

"Right. That's some pretty fine denial you got going on there, Tez. Maybe love hasn't killed you, but how do you explain the deaths of three men you loved and the sudden disappearing act of your most recent lover?"

"I don't. I can't. Coincidence," I said feeling a wave of nausea. "Why do you keep bringing that up? I really would like to forget that."

"You can't forget it—"

"You just said you thought the only good part of this book," I said waving it in her face, "was about letting go of the past. So let me let it go, all right?"

"I see it differently. I think you have a special power so you should look at it as your present. And your future."

I scoffed.

"Fair enough. What if we can prove that you have the power to affect the future well-being of other people?"

"Yeah, right. How?"

"Seems obvious. You think of someone who's hurt you and imagine how you'd hurt them back. I don't know. How did you do it with the others?"

"I. Don't. Know. I didn't do anything. I didn't think anything. At least, nothing specific."

"So, what's the harm in testing this? Who's hurt you recently? Aside from numb nuts who just walked out."

I was furious that she was bad-mouthing Glen but I held my tongue and said, "Stupid Father Sparrow."

"Your old pastor? What in the world has he done?"

"I saw him today. He pissed me off—"

"You saw him? Where did you see him? And why did you stop to talk to him?"

"I went to the church. I—"

"You what?" Betsy froze with her hands in front of her, as if to stop a large flying object.

"I didn't know he'd be there. I mean, still be alive."

"But why did you go to the church?" Betsy asked in sincere disbelief. "No judgment. Just curious 'cause last time you were there…"

"It's not like I planned it. I was walking by like I have a thousand times and I felt…compelled. I don't know. I can't explain. Anyway, I want him to feel abandoned while he drowns in his own grief. That's what I want him to feel. And fear. I want him to experience the hell that he promised was my future. I want him to feel the pain of being so alone in the world that even happiness feels like poison in his blood. I want him to feel everything I felt."

I was surprised at my own words. Betsy looked surprised, too.

"Really? You want him to suffer like that? Because if you have a power…"

"If I have a power then that must mean that God exists. And if God exists then Father Sparrow should be *grateful* that I've helped him finally meet his Maker." I was a woman possessed.

"Okay," Betsy said slowly. "Picture Father Sparrow in your mind. Now picture all that rage you're feeling and send it to him. Send that energy right to him."

I wanted to stop sending my rage at him. I wanted to embrace the words I'd read in *The Four Agreements*. I desperately tried to refocus my energy to that of love, but I couldn't do it. Seeing him this morning had opened old wounds that now bled hate. I pummeled a pillow and screamed profanities to the heavens.

"Don't kill the man," Betsy said.

By the time I'd released all my rage, I was exhausted. Betsy made me mint tea. She lay down with me in bed and promised she'd spend the night, in case I woke up and needed company, which I did.

I asked her if she'd spend a few days with me, work from my office rather than her own. She agreed. We didn't speak of Father Sparrow or of Glen or the men who were no longer with us. We spoke only about work and bucket list dreams. We played a lot of cribbage. I drank too much scotch. After five days, I told Betsy she could go home. She'd started to get on my nerves, leaving the milk out, finishing cereal and crackers but not telling me. Walking in on me in the bathroom and telling me to ignore her. Flashbacks to the days we'd been roommates, a time we both referred to as our 'dark days.' Living with Betsy in university taught me the lesson that even though you love someone it's possible to hate living with them. Living with Betsy convinced me that I'd never get married without 'living in sin' first.

That afternoon, taking my book back to the library, I passed the church. The stellar jays were still chattering in the maple overhead. I said a much more pleasant hello to them this time as I walked by. And strangely, I had no negative feelings about Father Sparrow. The church was a big old building, nothing more. The same old building I'd walked by a thousand times. Nothing more. Nothing less. I was pleased. I wondered if perhaps I'd finally—finally— processed all that pain. I laughed to myself thinking that I should have raged against Sparrow years earlier and saved myself all the counselling money.

After dropping off *The Four Agreements* I stopped for coffee and grabbed a day-old newspaper from the magazine stack to keep me company. The A section was filled with bad news about national issues which I scanned more than read. International news was more interesting, filled with stories and opinion pieces about how the United States and Great Britain were playing politics in several other countries' internal affairs. It took most of my cup to read these stories. With little more than a sip left, I flipped through the local news section to see a quarter page photo of Father Sparrow. Below it, his obituary. Words jumped out at me, 'heart failure,' 'pre-existing condition,' 'eighty-seven years old.' I managed to get to the bathroom before I vomited.

Chapter Eleven

Betsy moved back in with me during the days, treating my house as her office and social hub, going back to her apartment only to sleep.

"Aren't you afraid that I'll kill you if you piss me off?" I asked early on from the darkness of my mid-afternoon bedroom.

"Pah!" she said. "You don't scare me. Whatever power you have, I'm pretty sure I could match it!"

"You think your tarot cards and witchy potions could undo what I seem to be doing?" I asked.

"I don't know if I could protect people you set your sights on, but I feel pretty confident that if we put our powers head-to-head, I'd beat you in a psychic second."

This provided a welcome laugh. And I believed her.

At the same time I gave up believing in God back in my twenties, Betsy started down her own spiritual path. She'd shared broad strokes about it, but since we generally ended up arguing whenever she pushed me to adopt her beliefs, we did our best to avoid evangelizing our very different ideas about faith. As such, she'd built a whole community of friends through her spiritual life whom I'd never met.

But now that I appeared to have a connection to a spirit — a Spirit — that acted on my behalf, I had to rethink my staunch atheism. I was okay with that. Atheism hadn't added to my quality of life. It's not like I had to give up an important part of my identity or social network. I'd never made it a practice to gather with non-believers once a week to chant, "*Hallelujah! Praise the Big Coincidence!*"

Of course, realizing that I had some power to will things to change in the world, I heard a whole lot of "I told you so" for the next month while Betsy educated me in the finer points of connecting with my own spirit guide by bringing me into her other life. Sure, many of her friends were as flakey as homemade cherry pie, but they were also warm and welcoming and, the best part—over ninety percent of them were women. And since I'd decided to give up the whole men thing for real this time—both to give my own broken heart time to repair and to keep from accidentally killing anyone else—it was nice to build a new community that wasn't over-run by a bunch of know-it-alls in suits. Really nice.

Every day Betsy invited one or more of her gang over to meet me, sometimes for afternoon tea, sometimes for dinner. I could tell they were checking me out, probably trying to figure out if I was one of them. And to be fair, I was doing the same, trying to see if or how I might fit into this subculture. Some of the ladies brought me books that they insisted I read. Others gave me gifts, talismans, cards, incense, scarves…my office started to look like an eastern bazaar. And I started to feel a little bit Bohemian, injecting new vocabulary into normal conversation, wearing a little less black, or at least, adding colourful highlights to my otherwise goth look. I bought and read all of Don Miguel Ruiz's books as well as his son's contribution, *The Fifth Agreement*.

One thing that struck me among Betsy's friends was that, like her, none of them appeared at all perturbed by the fact that it seemed I'd been responsible for four deaths. I, on the other hand, was suffering greatly from this realization. I spent hours each day trying to live by the Fourth Agreement, "Do your best." I tried not to focus on the past, not to feel the guilt, not to make assumptions (like that I did actually cause those deaths), and not to make myself a victim in my own crimes. I worked hard to feel, project, and grow love in all my communications. By the end of a month, I thought I was doing pretty well.

I'd missed Glen a great deal at first, but knowing that I had such a terrible power and had already, quite accidentally taken the life of lovely Bob, whose only crime was being fifteen years older than me, I was able to all but forget about the man who'd taken my heart twice. And, the fact that he never tried to contact me assured me that he was no longer interested anyway. Betsy and her cronies said it was for the best. So I believed them. I had to.

It was Betsy who first suggested that I use my power to earn an income. Since James's death I'd barely worked. In my tenuous emotional state I wasn't able to focus on business writing, on reading about the stock market or on anything requiring more concentration than watching my favourite 80s shows on the ReRun Channel.

The idea was prompted by the conversations that

flowed the night Dorothy was over for dinner. It was her fourth Saturday with us. Dorothy's special skill was dream interpretation based on the Jungian model. I loved Saturday nights with Dorothy in part because she had a dark and dry sense of humour, but also because she was one of Betsy's only friends who didn't drown the room in patchouli-scented floral scarves and non-stop chatter. Dorothy was quiet, a listener, an observer. And, she wore almost as much black as I. When Dorothy was over, I felt that I was part of the flow of the conversation, and not simply swimming to keep up.

"Any interesting dreams this week, Tara?" she asked, putting down her glass of wine and making a real effort to be present.

"I did," I said, thrilled to share with her. "It was disjointed but it felt…well, like truth, if that makes sense."

"Of course. What happened?"

"I was in a house. Kind of like a mall though. It was filled with women. Only women. Some seemed happy but most seemed very sad. They hid their faces from me, like they didn't want me to really see them, who they were. After I'd walked through the whole house-mall place, one woman approached and asked if I was the one who could help her. I said no. She said she was sure I was. Then all the other women started to push towards me, asking me to help them.

"I finally agreed even though I had no idea what I'd agreed to do. So they all lined up and one-by-one they floated up to meet me near the ceiling. I don't know when I started floating but there I was, watching myself meet these women in a beautiful domed skylight, a hundred feet from the ground.

"I didn't talk. They didn't talk. We simply sat together and when they were ready, they floated back down and another woman floated up. Weird, eh?"

"Did they seem happier when they left you," Dorothy asked.

"Oh, yeah. They were laughing and some were singing."

"Okay. So, where do you want to start? What aspect of your dream do you want to be?"

"I think I want to start as the house that turns into a mall."

"Okay, house that turns into a mall, what aspect of Tara are you?" Dorothy asked.

A funny thing always happened when Dorothy started to ask questions of my dreams. I immediately relaxed, breathed deeper, felt peaceful. The sensation never happened when I described the dream but as soon as she said, "Okay, object of Tara's dream..." I was transported. I inhaled, exhaled and the image of the cathedral-like skylight dome filled my mind's eye.

"The house-mall is where—" I started but Dorothy interrupted.

"I am the house-mall," she said.

"Right. Sorry." I never got it right to start. It felt weird to say I *am that thing in my dream*. I started over with my eyes closed, trying to see the images again. "I am...the answer. I am...where happiness lives. I. Shine light. In darkness. I. Bring hope. Peace. Love."

I paused long enough for Dorothy to step in.

"Anything else, house that turns into a mall?"

I thought for several seconds, "No, that feels like everything."

We carried on, analyzing different elements of my

dream, the women I met, their changing emotions, the potted plants on the ground that I remembered as I embodied different elements from the dream. When I felt I'd exhausted everything, Dorothy said, "Well, there's something to think about," which is what she said at the end of every dream interpretation session.

"It's a puzzle," I said, not having any idea what in the world that dream might have been pointing to. Dorothy left with a promise to come back the following week. Before she'd even made it to the sidewalk Betsy blurted, "I know what your dream means."

I was skeptical but opened the door by raising my eyebrows.

"It's telling you that you have a gift to help women be happy."

Maybe it was the wine, perhaps it was the hours and days and weeks that Betsy had been spending in my space, but my response was not something either of us expected.

"You're insane. Nothing I've done would make anyone happy. Being somehow responsible for James's and Scott's and Bob's deaths doesn't make me happy. Having to spend twelve fucking hours a day with you since I'm too afraid to be alone doesn't make me happy. You're driving me up the fucking wall with your constant nattering about spirit this and energy that and the universe whatever-the-fuck else. Give it a break, Betsy. Give *me* a break. I'm done with it. I don't need a babysitter anymore okay? Thanks for the support, now can you let me get on with my life? Leave me alone. And stop fucking talking about this power you think I have. Okay?"

I excused myself to my room by throwing my arms in the air and walking away. I left Betsy to let herself out.

I didn't worry about the ramifications of my irrational explosion. Betsy and I were old hats at getting over emotional outbursts. Sister-like.

Before I fell into a semi-drunk sleep, I had a waking dream, in that moment of still being awake but on the edge of falling asleep. It felt like what I imagined being in a trance or being hypnotized would feel like.

I'd had a waking dream once before, with Bob after he died, an experience that left me disoriented for days, unsure of whether or not the conversation had actually taken place. In the end, I had to resolve that I'd simply never know.

This conversation was with a woman I didn't recognize physically but who made me feel that my grandmother was in the room with me energetically.

"Your friend is right," she said, hovering near the ceiling in the right corner of my bedroom.

"But it doesn't make sense," I argued.

"That's because you're clinging to your belief that life is all one big coincidence. That there's nothing more permanent than the life you experience on Earth, that death of the body means an end to the life that called that body home for a blip in time."

I closed and opened my eyes. She was still there. Rather than feeling awed by the presence of this spirit, I felt imposed upon.

"You're right. That's my belief. So, float along and let me be a happy atheist."

She laughed. "Even if you don't believe in gravity it will still keep you pinned to the Earth. Even if you don't believe that microbes can devour a human body but leave the spirit intact, they will eventually do their job with you.

Whether or not you believe you have a role to play helping others, you will fulfill that calling. It's the nature of your gift."

"Gift? How is having the power to kill people with my thoughts a gift? If that's my gift then you can have it back. Please, take it back."

"I didn't say your gift was to kill. Trust your instinct. And don't let others mislead you. Your spirit is strong but there are others around you that are stronger."

I pulled the duvet over my head and when I came out for fresh air, she was gone. That's what I'd wanted, but now that she'd left, I wanted her back.

"Wait. Come back," I said to the corner of my empty room. But she didn't. I fell asleep listening to the voices inside my head argue about God, the universe and my role in it.

As I expected, Betsy was back the next day, previous night all but forgotten. She arrived with two fancy coffees and biscotti for us both. As my apology, I told her about my vision. She was guarded; she didn't show her typical enthusiasm or give me her standard eye-rolling, I-told-you-so-look. We were in unknown territory here and were both treading carefully.

"I'm not saying you have something here. I'm not saying you don't. But tell me what harm there'd be if we tested the theory?" Betsy asked.

"Tested? How?" I asked, mind immediately dark, stomach tense.

"If you could use this power to help other women get themselves out of dead-end relationships and break free from good-for-nothing men, wouldn't that be a good thing?"

"No way. Not if it means I'm responsible for one more death."

Betsy rolled her eyes.

"Betsy, I don't even know how I did it the first times. How in God's name can I figure out how to do this without becoming known as Aileen Wuornos or the Belle Gunnus of the twenty-first century?"

"Okay, hear me out. Don't react until you've really thought about my idea," she said, handing me her own biscotti, an obvious peace gesture meant also to fill my mouth. "So, this is only a rough idea. Something I've been thinking about for a few days...okay, maybe a few weeks. We'd need to work out the details and, of course, you need to add your flare to it, but I think this could be helpful and make people happy and make us lots of money—"

"Jesus, Betsy! Get on with it. What's the idea?" I said, waving the biscotti in the air, in a hurry up motion.

"We set up a service to help women who are in bad relationships."

"Like counselling?"

"No, more concrete. Using your gift—"

I deflated loudly, interrupting Betsy's flow and changing her excitement to irritation in one sigh.

"It's a fucking gift, Tara. Accept it. You have the power to change lives—"

"*Take* lives," I whispered, my chest contracting.

"Take one, change another. It's all good," Betsy said.

"No! It's not all good, Betsy. It's bad. Very bad. Disgustingly bad. If I have this power, and I'm still not convinced that I do, because, well, that's not who I am, then I will never, ever use it. Ever."

"Did you know that in the States, in Canada, in the

UK and God knows where else, there's domestic violence in one out of every four households? Tez, the audience for this would be huge. It's a marketer's dream."

I scoffed.

"We could," Betsy paused and gave me her best stare down gaze, "Tez, *you* could help to reduce that statistic."

I shook my head. "No."

"I'm not saying we should kill guys who forget to buy flowers on Valentine's Day. But there are men out there who deserve—"

"No," I said again.

"But these assholes are hurting women. Innocent wives. Girlfriends. Daughters. Don't you see that you'd be doing good?" Betsy said. She seemed to be getting frustrated with me but this was one time I wouldn't let myself be bullied.

"Killing another person is never doing good. That's why we have laws against it, Betsy. What you're suggesting is some kind of fucked-up psychic vigilantism. I'm not going there. If this is so important to you, you figure out how to do it, 'cause I'm not going to," I said. It felt good to stand up to her for a change.

"Who said anything about killing them? Do you want to help women-in-need?" she asked.

"Of course I do. That's not the point."

"And do you think that life for a lot of women would be better if they didn't have abusive and controlling men in their lives?"

"You're not hearing me, Betsy."

"Do you agree?"

"Of course they'd be better off. But that doesn't mean the guy should die. Why is this so hard for you to understand?" I said.

"You have to agree that the government is doing a shite job taking care of the most vulnerable people in society—the women and kids who have no choice but to live with assholes who hurt them."

The truth was that I'd never thought about how well or unwell the government was doing its job on this front. But Betsy, having been taken from her father when she was three after her mom died, had lived as a child of the government foster system and had no love for it or most of the families who played a role in raising her. There was no way I could disagree with her assertion. I gave in.

"Yeah, I agree."

"Then turning your power into a full-time job would be like providing a social service that government isn't able to," she said.

We sat in silence for several minutes. I replayed her words over and over in my mind. I was shocked that she was suggesting we kill people because, in her opinion, I had the power.

"Betsy," I said, coming from a place of love, "Do you think that we could, I could, help people without hurting anyone? From what you know about all that spiritual stuff and energy and all that, do you think I could learn to make this gift work so that nobody ever died again? Because, if I could learn to control whatever the fuck it is that I have, then I'd be willing to try whatever it is that you're suggesting. But I have to know that nobody is going get hurt. Heart yes, but nothing more."

"Yeah, yeah, yeah," Betsy waved, "No problem. The first thing we have to do is help you figure out how to communicate with your spiritual powers. You know, tarot cards, chants, meditation…your spiritual niche. You have any ideas what that might be?"

I wanted to show Betsy that I had a positive attitude about her idea, and I really did like the idea of being helpful to women-in-need, but aside from Dorothy and her dream analysis work, none of Betsy's other friends or their powers spoke to me. I didn't know how to say this without sounding negative.

"As much as I like all your flakey friends—*Rats. Bad choice of words*—I'm not sure I'm like them. You know, they're really committed to what they believe in. I haven't found anything that makes me feel…authentic? I love Dorothy's work, but I'm not sure she's actually got a power other than being a good listener and question-asker, you know?"

"Fair enough. It took me awhile to figure out that cards were my thing. But I think you'll be able to figure this out faster because…" Betsy stopped talking and reached into her purse, pulling out two all access passes to the annual *Psychic Faire* in Portland.

"…we'll make it a road trip. I'll pay for everything. All you have to do is promise to attend every event and talk, and visit every table and booth. It'll take all three days but by the end you'll have the best spiritual education possible."

"Every booth? Every talk?" my inner skeptic started to rebel.

"Yes. Especially the ones you feel most uncomfortable getting to know," she emphasized, "since those are probably the areas you need the most help getting in touch with."

Three days later we were eating at Taco Bell and sleeping in a shared queen size bed. She said she'd pay for

90

everything, but she never promised we'd travel in luxury.

At the conference I felt like a fraud. And I knew everyone else there could see I was a fake and phony. Not because I believed they all had mind-reading powers, although many claimed this ability of course, but because I was dressed…normal. That's the only word I can think of.

The flowiness of the Psychic Faire conference attendees' attire was incomparable. It made me think of a whirling dervish made of thousands of bolts of fabric, unfurled, flying about the contained room, wild, excited, moving as if driven by a hurricane wind.

And there was me, feeling conspicuous as I slunk from booth to booth, head low in my Doc Marten boots, tight-fitting jeans and black t-shirt.

Everything about this room challenged every belief system I'd held in my thirty years of life. The Christianity I was raised on and the atheism I'd adopted a decade ago. I could picture my mother, looking down from the heavens at me with all these 'witches,' she would have called them. She didn't let me believe in magic even when I was small. If something was unexplainable it was 'the power of the Lord.' Unless it was a bad unexplainable, in which case it was 'the Devil's work.'

Standing still in the middle of an aisle, I pretended I was eight years old again and that all these women (and the handful of men) were actually able to make wishes come true, like the tooth fairy I was never allowed to believe in. And that they had magic powers. I wanted to have magic powers, too. I did. I wrapped my hand around the crystal in my jacket pocket and silently asked, "Can you hear me?"

A chorus of voices rose from across the room. All they

said was, "Yes! Yes! Yes!"

I pulled the crystal from my pocket and stared at it, asking another silent question. "Bob? Are you here?"

In the week before Bob's carpentry skills undid him, he opened a large box filled with crystals that he'd picked up over the decades and told me to take any one I wanted. I'd spent at least two hours sorting and playing with those crystals, looking for the perfect one. Bob thought it was hilarious that I was putting so much effort into this but I had a feeling that there would be one that would be better than all the rest. None of them 'spoke to me' so I placed all the crystals back in their box and as I was putting it away in his filing cabinet, I felt a pull to another box in the drawer. It too, was labelled 'Crystals.' I asked Bob if I could look through those. I swear one of those crystals actually jumped out of the box and into my hand as soon as I took off the lid. My whole body vibrated as I held my egg-sized amethyst.

Although I'd kept this keepsake from Bob, I'd all but forgotten about it. It was Betsy who suggested I bring it with me. At the Psychic Faire Betsy paid a woman two hundred dollars to teach me how to cleanse the energies in my amethyst, then charge it and program it so that it would help me in my psychic development.

I spent five or even six hundred dollars of my own money on CDs and books, all meant to help me develop my connection to the universe. I thought it would be hard to choose from the thousands of items on offer, but, much like my experience finding the right amethyst, the CDs and books seemed to choose me. Sometimes it was an image on the cover, sometimes I actually enjoyed the chanting, in one case, I kid you not, a CD fell from the table and into my open shopping bag. Of course, I had to buy it. It was called *Deva Premal Sings the Moola Mantra* and I had to laugh since the only word on the case that I understood was "sings."

Chapter Twelve

Together, Betsy and I are pretty smart. We've both managed to run our own businesses with relative success for over a decade and people generally consider us to be intelligent. We didn't expect to have much trouble writing a business plan for our new endeavour with my expertise as a technical writer and Betsy's marketing and web development savvy.

It took weeks to come up with the perfect business name, though. I researched names of other successful advice services and found that every single possible word combination that included variations of the words 'spirit,' 'relationship,' and 'psychic' had been used. I was quietly relieved since I was still getting used to the idea of making my mark in the world as a psychic advisor and wasn't keen to be the President and CEO of a company called Killer Psychic Services.

"How about Immaculate Immolation? It's got great alliteration," Betsy said nodding with enthusiasm.

"I don't even know what that means," I admitted.

"Immaculate, like immaculate conception? Hand of God? And immolation means to burst into flames."

"Betsy. That's awful."

"I thought it would be a nice nod to Toast Master Scott—"

"No. Okay. Jesus."

"No. You're right. It's too esoteric," Betsy said. "Good call."

I rolled my eyes.

"We need a name that suggests what service you provide, but doesn't actually say it outright. You know? It has to be broad enough that Mary-Jane Suburb can see herself using your powers."

"Mary-Jane Suburb?"

"You know, the women who drive minivans and play Celine Dion in the car when they pick their kids up from soccer practice."

"Celine Dion? Nobody listens to Celine Dion anymore," I argued.

"Are you kidding me? Nobody *admits* to listening to her but she's made a zillion dollars from people who secretly play her music on their iPods or when they're alone in their cars. They sing her praises in code so only other Dionites will recognize them. That's who you'll be like in a few years."

"Really?" I said, not understanding at all.

I Googled 'Celine Dion' to see if she was as popular as Betsy was suggesting. I scrolled down the page, reading headlines and the two-line descriptions until I came to one called, 'Famous Mothers.' I'd forgotten that Celine was famous for being a test-tube mom. It was a strange list that included many former president's moms, Carol Brady from the Brady Bunch, Jodie Foster, Rosa Parks and Mother Teresa, the 'caring mother to thousands.'

I didn't know much about Mother Teresa other than that she lived in abject poverty by choice for most of her life so, as I tend to do when I should be focused on working, I followed the links to learn more.

I'd always assumed that Mother Teresa had been a devout Catholic, being an almost-saint and all. Turns out she spent most of her life questioning not only her faith, but the actual existence of God. I thought, *Now there's someone I can relate to.*

"I wonder what kind of spiritual advice Mother Teresa was giving all those people who were dying of leprosy and AIDS," I said to Betsy. "Must have been hard to say, "God is with you. Trust in the Lord," when apparently God was distracted watching butterflies while entire countries of people were dying horrible deaths."

Betsy was irritated, "Why are you reading about Mother Teresa? You're supposed to be working on web copy."

"I am. This is…brainstorming. You know, take the idea in as many crazy directions as possible to find something new?"

"Whatever. And as I understand it, Mother Teresa is a pretty questionable nominee for sainthood."

"Why? This says she won the Nobel Peace Prize," I added.

"She held some wacky philosophy that basically told people that the most beautiful gift for a person is that he can participate in the sufferings of Christ, or something like that."

"Well, I guess if you're surrounded by suffering day-in and out, you find ways to justify it. You know, if I had been Mother Teresa, I'd have focused on fixing the root of the problem. They'd have called me Mother Hood; I'd have dressed in green robes and worn a feather hat and empowered the poor people to take what they needed from the rich to be comfortable and healthy."

Betsy laughed. "And if I'd been Mother Teresa I'd only have empowered the women who needed to stand up for their rights at home. I'd have told them to collect their babies, pack food and water then poison the well and get the hell out of Dodge."

"You'd be a Mother Teresa who gave advice to jilted lovers," I said laughing. And that's when we had it. Our business name. Mother Teresa's Advice for Jilted Lovers.

Betsy said that my spirit moved me to find our business name and a psychic persona of Mother Teresa, which offered me a great deal of latitude to speak from my experience and my heart. It didn't seem to matter that we weren't planning to work only with jilted lovers. Betsy said the marketing would handle any possible confusion.

I wrote copy but we had a hard time agreeing on it. The biggest challenge was that Betsy wanted to play up my apparent ability to give men what they had coming to them, a kind of 'you break her heart and my spirits will tear your heart from your chest and leave it for the hounds of Hell.' Her words, not mine.

I, of course, wanted to project the service I hoped I'd be able to offer: a loving, more conciliatory healing. Never death. I was one hundred percent certain that, if I had special powers, my spirits weren't as murderous as Betsy believed.

Although I had joked about pushing James out of a plane, and then he fell from that ladder, I never thought he should *die*. And even though Scott had lied to me, I never, ever wished him to burn—in Hell or otherwise. And then there was Bob who I'd never had a bad thought against. And Father Sparrow, I told myself, was an old man with an existing heart condition. Yes, I'd raged against him and yes, I had directed as much hate as one body could contain at the man, but I couldn't believe that a man who stood beside God could be undone by an atheist who wasn't even very committed to that belief.

Point being that our very different perspectives on the kind of results that my 'advice' was going to bring made it next to impossible to come to agreement on the marketing copy.

The other challenge, which I couldn't admit to Betsy, was that if I didn't believe I'd been responsible for the deaths that Betsy was certain I'd caused, then why and how could I possibly believe that I had any powers in the first place?

I was confused and concerned but Betsy's confidence and enthusiasm were like a riptide, dragging me further and deeper into unknown waters.

"Tara, this is insane. We have to come up with something, anything to get started. Two weeks is way too long to still be trying to figure out marketing copy," Betsy complained.

"Well, if you'd let me do what I'm good at, the copywriting, this would have been done twelve days ago."

"But you're not getting it. You know that wishy-washy copy won't work and that's what you're coming up with."

She was right. But I'd never written anything in this

area before. I could write technical documents until the bio-engineered cows came home. But I had no context for writing about a service that wasn't grounded in anything real.

"If you took this long doing client-work you'd be fired," Betsy challenged.

"Well, if I had clients like you, I'd quit."

We laughed. Despite the challenge of not being able to figure out how to sell our business idea to women-in-need, we were having a blast working together. Something had changed in me after Father Sparrow died. Life felt lighter. I felt happier. I still thought of Glen every single day. I missed him but Betsy was keeping me from ever feeling lonely or alone.

"I'm useless writing this woo-woo stuff so I have an idea. Tell me," I said to Betsy, "what normal business or industry does our business look like? What could I use to help me see our business the way you see it but in words and visuals that I understand? You know?"

Betsy thought, and finally suggested, "I think we should look at other business models that profit based on the misfortune of others, since that's what we're doing. Can you agree to that premise?"

"Sure. I guess. If women weren't in crappy relationships they wouldn't need Mother Teresa's services, so yeah. That works."

"That's not quite what I mean. Yes, we need women in crisis, but that's the easy sell. The hard one is how to sell your service, which might do harm to that woman's man, without having people focus on the negative outcome for the man. We need them to focus on the positive outcome for the woman."

I sighed. Betsy was hell-bent on causing suffering but I'd decided not to waste any more energy arguing with her. If I had a power then I was going to wield it my way.

"So how does the oil industry get us to focus on the positive and ignore the negative?" I asked.

"That's dead easy. They use the *'Look over there! A shiny castle'* approach."

"The what?"

"Oil industry. What do they do? They dig huge pits, cut down forests, pollute lakes and rivers and oceans and make products that are toxic and cause cancer. But, to keep us from saying, 'Hey, wait a cotton-pickin' minute,' they point in the opposite direction saying, 'Look at how much we invest in renewable energy. Look at how happy our well-paid employees are. Look at how well the economy is doing because of us. Besides you love your car, don't you? Shiny castles.'"

"So I need to figure out what shiny castles we can point to."

After hours of B.S.ing—Betsy's professional acronym for brain-storming—we decided, or were *guided* to understand, that the service we were going to sell was kind of like a new drug being pitched to the public: the positive impact on the user is what is sold, but—and there's always a big 'but' in small print—use of this drug could lead to dry mouth; watery eyes; swollen hands; itchy feet; diarrhea or constipation; leg cramps; black vomit; vaginal infection; spontaneous, bloody erections; heart attack; stroke; suicidal ideation; irritable, hostile or aggressive behaviour; death; breast enlargement; runny nose; dizziness; and/or hiccups.

Something that became quite clear to me was that big

pharma put their shiny castle at the front and tail ends of their long lists of possible side effects, hiding the ones they didn't want people to see in the middle, where most of us scan over, noticing that the symptoms escalate in seriousness, starting quite minor, expecting to find the worst at the end.

"Well, Pa, it says here that if you take this drug you could have dry mouth or watery eyes or swollen hands—God, this is a long list—or dizziness or hiccups. Or maybe a couple of them problems."

"Well, Ma, that don't sound too bad. Pass me four of them pills."

"Pa! Pa! Wake up! Your Tiny Tim is squirtin' blood all over my Sunday chair! Pa, wake up!"

"He's dead, Ma. I think them pills killed him."

"Couldn't be the pills, Junior. Was prob'ly the moonshine. Go get the shovel."

Unlike big pharma marketing, we couldn't provide potential clients with a list of possible side effects, or, in our business model, solutions to the problems we'd be helping them address in their relationships since, as far as we could tell, every situation would create a unique 'side effect.'

"We need to write some sample stories," Betsy said, "Think of the typical situations a woman will want to use your services for and give her an example of the kind of solution she may get from you. We'll put a little asterisk at the end with the note, 'Results may vary,' like all the diet ads do."

While I worked on the words, Betsy created what she called 'tear sheets' that looked exactly like they'd been pulled out of many of the popular women's magazines.

They even had pictures of the women who the case studies were supposed to have been written about.

"Who is that picture of?" I asked, feeling a little unwell about the questionable ethics of what we were doing.

"Some random woman. I bought the right to use her image from an image bank."

"Seems wrong."

Betsy looked at me as though I'd told her I voted for Charlie Sheen for president. "Are you really that naïve? Tara, this is advertising. This is the way it's done."

I wrote ad copy to appeal to three different kinds of women and the problems they might want to fix. And I still struggled with the ethical dilemma of what we were doing. On the one hand, I didn't actually believe that I had any service worth paying for, so I felt guilty about the real possibility that we'd be scamming women who were desperate for help. On the other hand, if I did have the powers that Betsy was certain I had, then I felt guilt that unless I learned how to control that power…I didn't want to think about it.

No matter how I looked at this, I was writing ad copy to sell a service that I was morally opposed to. But every time I tried to explain how I felt, Betsy managed to convince me that what we were doing was part of a higher calling, something I might not understand and might even feel icky about, but which I had no choice but to accept. And, since I'd spent my first twenty years practicing a religion I didn't believe in, I actually felt sort of at home with the moral ambiguity of our new business.

HEADLINE: Do you have extra weight you'd like to lose?

BODY COPY: I'm not talking about a few extra pounds around your waistline, ladies. Your body is perfect and deserves to be loved exactly the way it is. And if you're carrying around the weight of a whole other person who tells you otherwise, then it's time to get rid of *that* fat!

Are you ready to burn off those extra pounds? Let the compassionate weight loss experts at Mother Teresa's Advice for Jilted Lovers turn that dead weight to ashes for you. Call now for a free consultation with one of our Guides.

HEADLINE: Does your beautiful home have one room that's a fixer-upper?

BODY COPY: Most of us have them: that corner of a room that we can't seem to keep free from bad odours, annoying noises, beer cans and chip crumbs. Some of us are lucky enough to get a few hours each day to clean this corner before the offensive entity takes over again.

If you never get a break from smell and the sounds and the mess, the compassionate cleaners at Mother Teresa's Advice for Jilted Lovers can disinfect your home of unwanted life forms for you. Call now for a free consultation with one of our Guides.

HEADLINE: Has his midlife crisis turned your world upside down?

BODY COPY: Maybe he left you for another woman. Perhaps he spent all your retirement money on a Ferrari—and then left you for another woman. You'd committed your life to him and now he's gone and you feel like you're drowning in a sea of uncertainty.

If you're ready to get your feet back on solid ground, the compassionate counsellors at Mother Teresa's Advice for Jilted Lovers will help you bury your past. Call now for a free consultation with one of our Guides.

Betsy turned my words into art and we placed the ads in a dozen magazines. It cost all our retirement savings — which was a few thousand dollars from me and close to forty thousand from Betsy — but she was so certain in the need for the service and had such confidence in our business model that she emptied her accounts without a hint of concern.

I wasn't as confident since my amethyst had gone silent on me half-way through writing the web copy. I didn't tell Betsy since she would have forced me to re-calibrate the crystal and I didn't think it was a problem with crystal calibration; I thought it was a problem with Betsy's motivation.

Chapter Thirteen

Having committed to being a Jilted Lover Advisor as my new, full-time gig, I revamped my office. I was sure that ten years of filling the space with the dull and pedantic energy of a technical writer had certainly sucked out any potential for supporting the opening of my third eye. I started by painting the walls and ceiling a very light blue, the colour I see in my mind when I imagine light entering through the top of my head.

I lugged my filing cabinet, desk, and office chair down to the building's common storage room, just in case my new beanbag chairs (or the business) weren't a good fit for me. I replaced the imposing, oak bookcase and my technical, jargony hard-cover textbooks with a small glass-top table that held a stone Buddha statue and three pillar candles. Cinnamon-scented. I kept my old Persian-style rug even though the reds and browns clashed horribly with the sky blue walls and the jade green chairs.

My amethyst sat on its own small side table to the right of my beanbag so I could either hold it or simply sit in its energy, as needed. I put a matching side table on my left to have a place for my cup of tea. And, since Betsy thought my favourite, 32-ounce beer-stein-cum-tea-mug wasn't a very spiritual-looking vessel, she bought me a beautiful, if not outrageously tiny, teacup and saucer.

With everything in its place I hoped, would have prayed had I believed in God, that my amethyst would come back to life and start talking to me again. I mean, I worked hard to give it a home worthy of its power. In my frustration with its silence, I picked it up and without thinking said, "Come on Bob, talk to me" and from that moment imagined that any advice coming from the crystal were words straight from poor, old Bob.

Betsy overheard me and thought I was talking to her, so she came to my door, "What's up? Hey, looks good in here. But you need music," she noted as she gave my meditation room the once-over.

"I've always worked in silence," I said. "I can't think with any kind of noise"

"But you're not thinking anymore, Tara. You're supposed to be doing the opposite of thinking. What do you think all those CDs you bought are for? Making your bookshelf look good? You need background music to welcome your spirits into the space with you. And you need incense."

"I'm not even sure where I put that bag…good idea. I'll find it and start listening. But no to the incense. I have scented candles," I argued.

"Not the same."

"Excuse me, Little Miss Know-it-all, but I've done

my research. Cinnamon is used in about a hundred spells that I think relate to the work I'm trying to do here. It helps increase clairvoyance and…lots of things," I said, frustrated that I couldn't remember even one more.

"I'm not arguing that cinnamon is a bad choice. In fact, I think it's perfect since it's well-known to promote psychic ability and high spirituality…but as a pure wood in incense. Not as a chemical scent all mixed up with a petroleum-based wax," Betsy said rolling her eyes.

"Oh," I said, knowing full-well I'd been out-smarted. "Do you happen to have some?"

Room ready, I committed to spend at least seven hours every day developing my psychic abilities. For three weeks I sat earnestly meditating. And by meditating I mean I spent hours every day fighting off leg cramps while sitting lotus-style in my beanbag, trying to empty my mind of thoughts. The first several days went like this:

Put on a CD of background sounds, like ocean waves. Work to clear my mind of all chatter. Sit for ten seconds hearing only the ocean, being one with the room, maybe even the universe. Then, my stomach would grumble and I'd think, *I sure could go for some waffles right now. Oh, but I think we're out of maple syrup. Dammit, Betsy, I wish you'd replace what you finish. Maple syrup is expensive. How much…twenty dollars for half-a-litre…that's forty dollars a litre. How much does gas cost, like a buck fifty a litre? I think I need to fill the car before I go grocery shopping. Shit, supposed to empty my mind.*

I don't think I managed more than a couple of minutes of empty thought in that first week. I'm told that's why meditation is called a practice, since it takes a lot of it to get it right. Since I had bought so many CDs at some point during my second week *Deva Premal Sings the Moola Mantra* was sitting at the top of the pile, next in line for a listen. The blurb on the back called it a devotional Sanskrit mantra and yoga music to use in Oneness Blessings for healing, yoga and relaxation. I loved it immediately. Deva Premal, it turned out, is a person, a woman. And her voice did what rustling leaves, cooing doves and whale sounds couldn't—it transported me to another place.

The first chant, the title track, was simply called "Invocation: Part One." I thought this singer could use some of Betsy's and my marketing skills to help her give her songs more inspirational titles. Once the breathy flute-like sound stopped, the singing started. Wow. I had no idea what she was saying, having opted to take French rather than Sanskrit in high school, but it spoke to me. And, for almost ten minutes I didn't hear my gurgling stomach, or think about the heating bill or Visa bill or rent that was due in three days. I just…was.

Turns out this particular chant combines three very powerful Sanskrit words, making it one of the most important meditation chants there is, which I learned is what Moola Mantra means. The words, Sat, Chit and Ananda mean wisdom, consciousness and bliss. The way Deva Premal sings, though, it sounds like she's saying them all as one word, "satchitananda."

This chant stuck in my mind like an ear-worm. Better by a long shot than the Blondie hit I'd had in there the night before, but an ear-worm is an ear-worm and must be extracted. After lunch I paused Premal and postponed my afternoon meditation practice to find out what this chant meant. If I can trust the good people in the online answers world, "Sat Chit Ananda is the most perfect expression of our primordial self which is energetically inseparable from the power of love that creates the universe and to reside in this state is the experience of pure bliss and the essence of life itself."

I wasn't sure I understood the full meaning so I asked Betsy.

"It is exactly what it says," she said. "What *I* don't understand is why you're focused on a mantra about love. What we're doing is kind of the opposite of love, you know? Ending bad relationships, not starting new ones."

"I see it differently," I said. "If I can use my power to flow more love, peace and joy out into the world, then I'd be doing a great job. Well worth two thousand dollars."

"That's not what women will be signing up for," she argued.

"I think it is."

"And I think you're wrong. They'll want revenge, Tez. To make those men go away, like James and Scott and Bob."

"I wish you'd stop mentioning them. Especially Bob," I said, losing all the benefits of having spent the morning trying to develop a direct link to the Creator of the Universe.

"Whatever floats your boat. As long as the clients are happy."

Back in my room, I reconnected with the Moola Mantra, this time holding Bob in my hands. I won't go so far as to say I had a conversation with Bob, but I did feel his presence. He was definitely chanting with Deva and me. Of course, I still had no idea whether this sense of higher connection was what I needed to experience to take on Mother Teresa's work since I didn't have any real challenge to test the universe, or my spirit guide, or Bob, or *whoever it was* that was going to be receiving my connection and sending the energy back to the client-in-need.

Sure you do. I felt the words come through the amethyst.

I stared at it, expecting it to do something, which was ridiculous, of course. I picked it up, held it cupped in both hands.

What challenge can I test my new connection on? I asked Amethyst Bob, expecting an answer.

Yourself. You're a jilted lover. And just because you aren't talking about him doesn't mean you aren't thinking about him. A lot.

I put the amethyst on the table, freaked out that it, he, Bob appeared to be reading my mind.

I still know what you're thinking, it communicated.

I broke into a nervous sweat. Of course I had talked to Bob before and thought I'd felt his energy, but he'd never talked back. And he'd certainly never initiated a conversation. It felt like he was sitting beside me. His voice sounded like it was coming from across the room, not from inside my head.

Okay, I thought, picking up the crystal again. *So what that I think about Glen every day. The fact is, he got scared and he left so my services aren't needed. Problem already solved.*

Bob agreed. *You're right that he got scared. But you never figured out what he meant in his note about the movie. Watch the movie.*

And then he, or it, the voice, the energy, was gone. I could feel it. I lay back in my beanbag chair and fell sound asleep.

Chapter Fourteen

"Knock, knock," Betsy said at my door, opening it before I could answer. "You busy?"

I was startled and tried to sit up before she noticed I'd been asleep.

"You're *sleeping*?" she said.

"Meditating. I'm in the zone, you know?"

"Hm. Well, I was thinking while you were 'meditating'" she said making air quotes, "that while we're waiting for this business to take off, and since money is kind of tight—"

"That's an understatement," I said, feeling my chest tense at the mention of money.

"I was thinking that maybe we could try to live together again. You know, share one rent, one internet bill, one hydro…instead of paying two?" Betsy said.

My hand dropped straight down to my lower abdomen which had suddenly developed a terrible cramp at the same moment bile rose in my throat. I had a series of flashbacks to a decade earlier when we'd shared an apartment. It had been an unequivocal disaster. Betsy must have seen the pain on my face which most certainly screamed, "I'd rather be destitute and homeless than live through that again."

Betsy spoke quickly, "It'll be so different this time. Neither of us have a man in our life. And we can make a pact that as long as we're living together, neither of us can have a man – or a woman."

Our challenge with men wasn't that there was ever jealousy between Betsy and I. The problem with having men share our space came from the inevitable, in our experience, triangles that were created, where one person always felt left out. Usually the man. And when that happened, the men—at least the two we were seeing when we'd lived together—got jealous. That had lead to all kinds of bad behaviour, broken windows, and police reports. And then there was the men's response, which was no better.

"I'm not saying I'm not open to considering the idea, but…" I sighed. I'd been dreaming about Glen, living with him. I didn't want to make a pact of celibacy with Betsy. What I really wanted was to understand why Glen had left the way he had, and then remove the spell that spooked him. Looking up at Betsy my eye caught my amethyst.

"I think this would be a great time to call on my spirits for advice. Are you okay with that?" I asked.

"Should I light the incense for you?" Betsy asked.

I started by switching my CD for a new one, a compilation of heart sutra mantras. I figured it was more important to connect with my own heart on this question than with the universe. I sat with my legs crossed, back arched slightly to open my chest and heart, fingertips lightly touching each other in an open-prayer hand pose as my room filled with the spicy scent of cinnamon. I'd put my amethyst on the floor in front of me and stared at it in soft focus. I breathed slowly, consciously and deeply, filling first my belly, my root chakra, then allowing the oxygen and energy to fill me to the top of my head, my crown chakra.

I focused my mind on one question: What should I do?

Nothing. Not a word. For an hour I sat and tried to focus on hearing the message but I couldn't turn off the replays of my previous experience having lived with Betsy. It was like watching a poorly edited historical documentary, blurry images jumping from one conversation to another without any logical segue, certain scenes repeating over and over and over.

"Be quiet," I said out loud to my inner voices. Maybe this was my message.

The door creaked open a few inches and Betsy poked her head in.

"Oh, that doesn't sound good. Are you arguing with Mother?" she asked.

Betsy and I had taken to calling my spirit guide 'Mother' when we spoke of her since Betsy rebelled when I first mentioned Bob might be my guide. So even though in my head I knew I was talking to Bob, since calling him 'my spirit guide' was both cumbersome and something I was still not entirely comfortable saying in public, I accepted Betsy's suggestion: Mother.

And since Betsy had taken to playing up my connection to the universe in even the most banal situations, like grocery shopping, "Tez, should I buy organic apples imported from California or local, non-organic apples? Ask your spirit guide," 'Mother' felt like a safe alternative. So now if anyone overheard us, it was more along the lines of, "Hey Tez, ask Mother if these leather gloves or the man-made pleather ones are more ethical," to which I could answer, "Mother says go with gloves made from New Zealand wool."

"So what did she say?" Betsy asked.

"Mother's quiet today," I mumbled. *And so is Bob*, I thought giving the amethyst a disappointed stare. "Let's ask the Tarot cards."

"Okay. Which one of us should read? You or me?"

"Both of us. We each have to draw one card," I said feeling light and relaxed for the first time since I'd lit the incense.

Betsy had years of experience reading Oracle cards and I'd always been amazed at how often her readings would resonate with either what I'd been thinking about a certain issue or hit me with one of those, "ah, that's so obvious! Why didn't I think of that?" feelings. I'd only started practicing with my Motherpeace deck in the last three months so I wasn't nearly as conversant and comfortable with my interpretations. But I had developed a strong intuitive sense that seemed to guide me pretty well.

I nodded to Betsy to sit on her beanbag. She dragged it right in front of me, keeping Bob between us. I shuffled the deck until it felt right then handed the cards to Betsy to do the same. We didn't have to speak; we knew what to do. Once Betsy felt the cards had the right energy she handed them back to me and I held them until I was ready to place the deck on the table where the crystal usually sat. Since the cards were round, when I fanned them out I moved them in a circular motion that left the cards looking like a snail's shell on the round table.

Betsy and I held hands and took three deep breaths together. We pulled our cards at the same time. She handed me hers and pushed the deck along the same path I'd used to fan them, to bring them back into a single pile. She placed the pile on the edge of the table and I placed our two cards face down beside it.

"Ready?"

She nodded. I flipped the two cards over and we both looked at them for a minute or so. I was hoping she'd speak first. Apparently she was waiting for me to start.

"I wonder which one of us pulled the Hanged One card," I said.

"Doesn't matter," Betsy said, "the cards knew that two would be pulled so either one of us could have pulled the card. Same result, same meaning. So, do you want to read first or should I?"

Thank you, Mother, for getting her talking first.

"Go ahead. Please," I said.

Betsy took a deep breath and closed her eyes. She kept them closed as she spoke, "Okay, what I feel is… compassion…surrender…I don't know…cleansing, I think. We'll struggle but once we both give up our ego… this will be good. Very good."

She opened her eyes and smiled at me. I nodded and smiled back, still not sure what I saw in the cards, hoping Betsy would continue. She didn't let me down.

"And the Shaman of Swords is all about power and control. And communication, speaking your truth. What do you get, Tez?"

I closed my eyes and saw an animated Visa bill, its

115

balance increasing by the second. I saw my bank account statement with a dangerously low balance. I saw myself eat Ramen noodles, wearing fingerless gloves sitting inside my unheated kitchen. I tried to draw Glen into the picture but he wouldn't join me. I opened my eyes and looked right into Betsy's. She was smiling.

"Moving in together. My truth says that it's probably a good idea," I said. *And my gut says it's a very bad idea so I'll ignore my gut.*

Betsy got out of her lease without any trouble since the landlord had wanted to renovate and raise the rent. We spent days packing and moving bits of both of our belongings to create a home that was equally ours. What we didn't need—my ratty, old couch, Betsy's dining room table and chairs, kitchen ware, my spare bedroom furniture— we put in storage since I wasn't quite as confident in the "foreverness" of this arrangement as Betsy was. Between moving my extra furniture out and moving Betsy's in, we painted almost every room. My landlady was happy to pay for the paint since I was a quiet tenant who always paid my rent on time and she didn't want to lose me.

I had to admit that Betsy not only had nicer furniture than me, she had a much better sense of how to give a crappy rental apartment a warm, homey feel. It was simple things like choosing the right paint colours: canary yellow for the kitchen, jade green for the living room, a bright but neutral colour called Florida Sand for the windowless hallway that connected the bathroom, two bedrooms and my meditation room.

We pulled down the heavy, beige curtains that probably hadn't been washed in ten years and replaced them with multi-coloured, patterned Indian saris that allowed some light in even when they were pulled closed.

We donated my mis-matched table and floor-lamps to the women's shelter and used a set from Betsy's place, with chrome bases and pale, fabric shades. Even her light bulbs were warmer than the ones I'd be using.

My Georgia O'Keefe Poppies print was rehung on a wall better suited to its size and I swear I felt the pride those poppies felt being so well-displayed.

I painted the bathroom light blue and Betsy decided to splurge and buy all white bathroom towels and facecloths, bath mat and shower curtain. It cost her a hundred dollars but made the bathroom look like a million bucks.

"I feel like I'm walking into a spa," I said.

"Not a bad transformation from the Motel 8 shit-hole it used to feel like."

"It wasn't that bad," I laughed.

"Oh, yeah. It was," Betsy said.

When my landlady came over to see how great the place looked, she joked that she was going to have to double the rent now. And if she had, I would have paid it. I loved the space that Betsy and I had created together.

While Betsy and I drank a celebratory bottle of the cheapest shiraz we could find, the phone rang. It was after ten o'clock and I didn't recognize the number so we let it go to voice mail. I checked the message as soon as the phone started to flash.

"Hello. My name is Hazel and I'm looking for advice from Mother Teresa's guides. I'm not really sure how this works. Please call me back."

Chapter Fifteen

Our first client. Were we happy? I know Betsy was by the way she danced around the living room, whooping and hollering and thanking the universe. I hushed her, saying I didn't want to upset our neighbours. But really, I needed her to be quiet so I could understand what I was feeling. Light-headed? Check. Tingling extremities? Check. Feeling of wanting to vomit? Oh, yeah.

"It's weird, Betsy. I've been working so hard to develop my powers and I thought I wanted a chance to see if it's working. But now that we have our first client...I don't feel so good."

Betsy sat down beside me and rubbed my back.

"That's normal Tez. It's called performance anxiety. Stage fright. Let it flow through you. You'll be great. You should call Hazel now." She handed me the phone.

I placed it back on the table, shaking my head, 'no.'

"Tara," Betsy said with her stern, I-am-you-mother-listen-to-me voice.

"It's after ten. I'm not going to call now."

"She's clearly awake. She just called us."

"Betsy," I replied in my rude-teenager voice, "I'm not calling her now. She can wait until tomorrow. We're not a twenty-four hour take-out pizza joint. And anyway, I need time to sit with this, okay?"

Betsy grunted and left the room. I slumped into the couch wishing I'd never agreed to this idea. *I'm not a psychic. I have no idea what to do. Ohhh...and I don't want anyone to die because of me...Mother-Bob, where are you? Help me.* Several minutes passed. I experienced wave after wave of dizziness. I tried to focus on deep breathing but found myself unconsciously holding my breath with every inhalation. The effect wasn't pleasant, calming or quiet since each time I exhaled I made a dramatic 'ahhh' sound. Once I became aware of what I'd been doing, I opened my eyes and took a normal breath.

Betsy was standing against the wall watching me.

"Wow. That was intense, Tez. What did she tell you?"

"That I should never commune with a spirit guide when I'm intoxicated." I had no idea where that idea came from; it was one of my classic, say something snarky without thinking lines.

I was about to apologize when Betsy said, "She's right. It's disrespectful to seek advice when you're drunk, let alone give it. We should do this in the morning."

"Please don't wake me up early. Let me sleep if I need to, okay? Maybe Mother will give me something in my dreams," I said, hoping that would keep Little Miss Enthusiastic from clinking a cup of coffee on my bedside table at six AM.

I fell asleep hoping for a sign that what we were doing,

what I was doing, was right and good.

Morning came too soon for me. I like my coffee and toast at 11:00. Betsy had already finished her second cup of tea before 7:00 and done an hour of yoga. In my half-sleep I had heard her pacing outside my door for over an hour. I dragged myself out of my room at 7:45. To Betsy's credit, she asked how I'd slept and if I wanted breakfast before casually placing the phone and an orange coloured, pleather notebook on the kitchen table in front of me.

"What's this?"

"I bought it ages ago. I wanted it to be a surprise when you got your first client."

"What is it?"

"It's a diary. D'uh."

I gave her a look.

"Good lord, Tara you can be thick sometimes. Look," she opened the book to the first page. She'd written the date, Hazel's name, phone number, and the word 'Problem' on the first lines and half-way down the page, 'Solution.' "We'll keep track of all your advice in this book."

I took the book from Betsy. It was funky. The cover was padded and embossed with a simple floral pattern. It felt like leather but was made of something faux. I liked how it felt in my hands. Solid. Real. The opposite of what we were going to be diarizing.

"I think we should add two more pieces of information," I said. "How much money we charged, maybe in the top corner, so it's easy to track?"

"That's a great idea," Betsy agreed, taking the book from me and putting a dollar sign to the right of centre at the very top of the first page.

"And maybe one more header called, 'Result' so we can

start to understand how my thoughts on certain problems actually manifest in the world."

"That is such a great idea!"

"Thanks, Betsy. This is a lovely gift," I said, standing and giving her a hug. *I'm going to stall for as long as I can before I have to use this thing.* "I'm going to meditate and then call Hazel. Okay?"

"Okay. But don't take too long. You need to strike while the iron is hot, as they say."

My meditation consisted of playing Bejewelled on my phone for almost an hour. Whenever I had trouble relaxing to fall asleep, that distraction seemed to help settle my mind, so I thought it would be a legitimate way to clear my head before having to talk to Hazel. Once I'd 'died' for the second time I lit my incense, held Bob for a minute, then called Betsy into the room.

"You want to sit with me while I do this? Please?"

I dialed.

"Hullo?" said the old woman's voice.

"Oh hello. Is this Hazel?"

"What? I can't hear you, Dear. My show is on. Call back when it's over." Then she hung up.

Betsy and I looked at each other and laughed so hard we snorted. That was exactly what I needed to break the tension I'd been holding since her call the night before.

"Do you think I should call back at 9:30 or 10:00? What if her show is a movie and isn't done until 11:00?"

"Call at 10:00. The worst she'll do is hang up on you again."

I waited until 10:15, to give Hazel time to make a cup of tea or go to the bathroom after her show.

"Hullo?" Hazel answered.

"Hello. Is this Hazel?" I asked.

"Yes. Who is this?"

"Hazel you called me last night looking for advice. I'm...Mother Teresa." As I said the words I got that feeling you get when you tell a lie and you know the other person knows you're lying. "Hazel, do you mind if I record our conversation? It will help me and my Guides in case we need to listen to your problem again, to hear details we might miss while we're talking now?"

"Oh that's fine, Dear. But you're not going to put it up on the websites are you? I don't want my neighbours to know about this. They wouldn't want to visit anymore if they knew."

I nodded at Betsy and she turned on the recording device which also made it possible for her to listen to both sides of my conversation with Hazel though headphones.

"No, just for our use. Thank you, Hazel. Now, before you tell me your problem, can you tell me how you heard about this advice service?" I asked. Betsy had told me it was critical that we knew which magazines had given us the best results for future marketing efforts.

"Oh. It was at the doctor's office, Dear."

"Your doctor told you about us?"

"Oh, no, Dear. He doesn't know about this. I haven't told anyone. I was seeing Dr. Jacobs about my gout."

"So, it was in a magazine you saw at the doctor's office? Do you remember which one?"

"I'm sorry, Dear. I'm not interested in your survey." And, Hazel hung up.

"This lady is loopy," I said. "Her poor husband must have his hands full with her."

"Kind of makes you wonder which one of them needs

the advice," Betsy said making a face.

I called again.

"Hullo?"

"Hello, Hazel? This is Mother Teresa. We were just speaking about some advice that you were hoping to get. We seem to have been cut off."

"It's him. He never lets me talk on the phone. I think he's cutting the wires. I can hear him in the other room. He doesn't know I hear him creeping around. And when I go in he's sitting in his chair pretending to be asleep," Hazel paused for a second and then yelled, "Go and take a bath you smelly old man and stop eavesdropping on my calls." She spoke quietly again, "Your advertisement said you can help me get rid of bad smells in my house. Well, he smells something awful. Can you help me, Dear?"

"Sorry to have to ask, but is this your husband you're talking about, Hazel?"

"Of course it is. I wouldn't have other men sleeping in my house, now would I?"

"Of course not," I said. "What's your husband's name?"

"It's Eddie. Edward. Mr. Edward Rollit."

" And you'd like him...taken care of?"

"Well, yes, Dear, that's why I called you. For goodness sake. Can you come over today? I'm really quite tired of this."

"That's not how I work, Hazel. I'm not going to actually come to your house. I'll talk to my Guide and she'll take care of the problem in the way she thinks is best." I looked to Betsy and shrugged my shoulders. For all the practice runs we'd done, none of our imagined scenarios were quite like this; in fact, they weren't at all like this.

"And we have to talk about payment, too," I said.

"Wait a minute, Dear, let me get my purse," Hazel said.

"No, Hazel, you don't need to get your purse. I can't take credit cards—"

"Well, I wasn't going to give you my charge card number. I was going to give you cash. I was at the bank yesterday."

"I don't take cash either. You don't happen to have PayPal, do you?" I asked, knowing the answer. I swear I saw Bob vibrate with laughter.

"I don't know what a pay pal is. You come over and make this bad smell go away like it says in your magazine advertisement and I'll pay you in real money. Okay, Dear?"

"Ask her where she lives," Betsy whispered.

"Hazel, where do you live?

"I'm in Maple Ridge. Do you have a pen handy? I'll give you my address. Can you come this afternoon?"

An hour later, Betsy and I were on Highway One.

"We'll have to charge extra for gas," I said.

"She didn't even agree to a price. What if she tries to give us twenty dollars?"

I sighed, "This isn't quite the way I'd envisioned it would work. And I'm not thrilled about having to meet Mr. Edward Rollit. That's going to make it…"

"Too personal?"

"Yeah."

"Have you considered that maybe Mother set it up this way? Maybe you have to meet the men before you can, you know…?" Betsy said.

"That is *not* part of our business plan. If we were going to work that way it wouldn't have made any sense to run ads in magazines in Toronto and Montreal. And frankly,

I'm not up for that level of intimacy with clients."

"Actually, Tez, you were extremely intimate with three of the four men you already helped move along, so saying 'Hello' and shaking hands with the client's husband shouldn't be too much of a strain by comparison."

We found our way to Hazel's without any trouble. The grass was knee-high all around her small bungalow. I knocked on the door and heard her yelling to her husband, "Eddie, the cleaners are here to take care of you."

Betsy and I exchanged looks and the door opened. Hot air pushed its way into the cool outside like a prisoner emerging from an underground tunnel, struggling, gasping. Or was it Betsy and I who struggled and gasped?

"Hazel?" I said, trying not to breathe in again.

"Come in, Dears. Eddie's in the back room in his chair. He won't get up for you. Stubborn old mule," she said.

"Hazel, it smells terrible in here," Betsy said.

"Like death, Dear. That's why I called. No matter how much I clean I can't get rid of that smell. And Eddie's not lifted a finger to help."

*   *   *

Betsy talked to the ambulance attendants and the police since my nerves wouldn't let me put even four words together. We stood at the curb while Eddie's decaying body was put on a stretcher and taken away. Hazel was still arguing with one of the police officers that he was fine and only needed a bath and some extra sleep since his operation. Betsy drove home while I lay in the back seat dry heaving, not able to get the putrid smell out of my nostrils.

The first thing I did when we got home was light

two sticks of cinnamon incense and take a double dose of Betsy's natural calming tonic. We sat silently in my meditation room, listening to a soundtrack of ocean waves. Betsy said it would help purify us from the vision of D'Eddie, the nickname she'd given poor Mr. Rollit. I filled in the first page of the diary:

$ - 30 (for gas)

Problem: husband, D'Eddie, was smelling up the house

Solution: call the morgue

Result: probably nightmares for the rest of my life

*   *   *

"Mother seems to have a sick sense of humour," I said.

"Really? I don't see it that way. You helped a woman do exactly what we talked about: you helped her move on from a dead-end relationship."

"Oh, Betsy, that's terrible."

"That didn't come out right. But I'm serious. We helped Hazel where nobody else had or could since she wouldn't have told anyone she knows about that smell. She was too embarrassed. We did do a good thing, Tez. Thank you, Mother," Betsy said, looking skyward.

"Fine. But this was the opposite of helping pay the rent."

"*Au contraire, mon cherie,*" Betsy said, pulling a small pile of hundred dollar bills from her pocket.

"Betsy, you didn't steal that?"

"Not at all. While you were calling the police, I told Hazel we needed to be paid up front. She asked if a thousand dollars would be enough. I said it would be okay."

126

I grabbed the orange diary and added '+ $1,000 = $970!'

"Can you take one of those bills down to the off-sale and splurge on a fifteen dollar bottle of wine?" I asked. "I need a drink."

Chapter Sixteen

Almost three weeks passed before we received our second call, which, much like Hazel's, was a woman who'd misunderstood the between-the-lines message of our 'cleaners' ad. I was actually quite surprised. I assumed everyone watched mob movies and the meaning would be crystal clear.

Betsy followed up with the magazines; they'd all run the ads. To say we were disappointed would be an understatement. Betsy managed to scrounge up a little work from two old clients and I made a few dollars writing new content for one of my old client's websites. Although money was tight, we were managing to pay the rent and eat.

Of course, as soon as we'd both given up expecting our ads to generate any income, the phone rang. At 4:00 AM. We hadn't thought through the fact that people might not keep their calls to regular, west coast business hours. I answered as a reflex to stop the noise and immediately regretted having done so.

"Hello?"

"Is this Mother Teresa's Advice for Jilted Lovers?" an excited voice said.

"Uh, yeah," I yawned.

"Did I wake you up?"

"Yeah."

"Huh. Well you should have a twenty-four hour answering service. When people need you, they might need you right now, you know?"

"Um, can I get your number and call you right back in about five minutes? I need to wash my face to wake up a little. Is that okay?"

"Sure. But don't take too long. I only have the house to myself for a couple of hours this morning before the ladies arrive for tea and bridge."

She gave me her number but not her name. I recognized the area code as being from Newfoundland. *Not so bloody-awful-early on the east coast.* I was going to wake up Betsy but she was already in my meditation room by the time I got there.

"Ready?" she asked. "Don't forget to get her email address right away."

I dialed.

"Hello," said the voice.

"Hi. I didn't get your name," I said.

"Not telling you my name," she said.

"Okay, that's fine. But I need your email address so I can send you the invoice for services."

"Huh," she said.

"Do you have an email address? And a PayPal account?"

129

"Huh," she said again.

"You're losing her," Betsy whispered. "Ask her how you can help. She doesn't trust you yet."

"How about we wait for the technical stuff. What can Mother Teresa's Guides help you with? It seems urgent," I said.

"Urgent? I should've called you weeks ago when I saw the first ad. I don't know why I listened to that busybody Belinda. She doesn't think you can help me."

"Just to be clear, tell me what your business is," she paused, "because my girlfriends and I can't agree."

"Well, what service do you think my business provides?" I asked.

"For lack of a better word, I think you are a witch. And I need your services. And I need them fast."

"I'm not a witch, actually. I seem to have a special ability to will certain events to happen. But, I can't promise anything quickly. I don't have any control over timing."

Betsy whispered, "Is she in danger?"

"Are you in a situation where you should be calling 9-1-1, maybe, instead of me? Is someone threatening you?"

"Jesus, Mary and Joseph, no. It's not me. It's my little girl. She's gone and gotten herself all mixed up with a Mainland boy. Says they're getting married. Says she's leaving for Toronto. I can't have her go. I need her here at home with me. Lots of nice boys for her in Mount Pearl. Don't want her all mixed up with a Mainlander city boy. So I want it to end before it gets too serious," she said, barely taking a breath.

"Has this boy done anything to hurt your daughter? Has he cheated on her or treated her badly in any way?" I asked.

"Tarnations, no. Justin's a lovely lad. Got money, too. Treats her good. But he says he's going to take her away. Give her a better life in the big city. And I say no, she can't go. But they're going to do it anyway."

"How old is—"

"She's thirty-two."

"Oh. Um, well, I hate to turn away business," I said shrugging my shoulders to Betsy, "but, I don't know if I can help you. For one, I think if the man is good for your daughter, my spirit won't be inclined to do anything to harm him. And also, your daughter is certainly old enough to leave home."

"You Mainlanders don't get it. Belinda told me I was wasting my long distance minutes calling. I hate it when that old bitty is right. You got to prove her wrong. There must be something you can do. I don't want the boy hurt. Just...wash him out of my Paula's hair, like your ad says. I have the money. One thousand dollars now and one thousand dollars after the problem is fixed," she stopped talking and started to cry.

"I don't think I can take your money, Ma'am. I don't think there's anything I can do to help you. Now, if your daughter called—"

"Stop calling her my daughter. Her name is Paula. And she's not going to call. She's happier than a seagull on gutting day. Says she loves this boy. Don't want her to leave. Can't let her leave. I'll be all alone..." the woman's voice trailed off.

"Like I said, I don't think I can help—"

"I do not accept that answer. I am sending one thousand dollars to your PayPal account and then you'll *have* to do something. We'll have a contract if I pay you."

We sat in silence for thirty seconds. I felt defeated. I felt grief for the poor young woman, my age, who'd found love but had to overcome the hurdle of her overbearing mother to keep it. But more than anything, I felt like a fraud. I closed my eyes and saw Cate Blanchet as a psychic in *The Gift*, then, horrors, Carrie from de Palma's film flashed through my mind in the dark and silence. My inner voices stepped in to fill the void.

Those women clearly knew that they had a gift. You could see it on their faces.

Those were movies you idiot. Real psychics are much more subtle.

Based on what proof?

How about all the women we met at the Faire?

I'm sure half of them were fakes.

Which leaves the other half...

Betsy interrupted my inner dialogue with a tap on my arm and a glare, "Ask her what a perfect solution would be."

"Ma'am, can you see a way for this to work out so that both you and Paula can be happy?"

"Hmph. I do not. Unless that boy gives up his big city job and moves my Paula to St. John's. That wouldn't be perfect since it's a fifteen-minute drive from Mount Pearl and I don't have a car. But I guess it would be better than Toronto," she said.

"And, if Paula, were to marry this young man and move to Toronto. Would it really be that bad?"

"As long as I live I will not allow that to happen," she said. I believed her.

"Well, I'm not sure how I can help, but I promise I'll try," I said to her grunts. "One more question. Does

Paula already have a wedding date planned or are you just concerned that this will happen at some point in the future?"

"She's getting married in six weeks. That's why this is so urgent. You have to stop that wedding."

Chapter Seventeen

"I can't see a solution. And I don't even want to help this lady," I said to Betsy once we'd hung up.

"Why not?" she asked. "I think this is a great challenge for you and Mother."

"Are you kidding? Why in the world would I want to be part of ruining a relationship that's working...despite the obvious negative energy that lady is investing in it."

"Maybe it's not such a great relationship and the mother sees that," Betsy suggested.

"Which mother, Paula's or my spirit Mother?"

Betsy shrugged. "You're the one with the gift. You'll figure it out."

"I'm not so sure I will."

"Again with the fear of failure, Tez. Honest to God, get over it. Get over yourself. You've already done this three times. Four if you count Hazel. Five if you count old Father what's-his-name."

"Number one, Hazel's husband was dead long before

I came along—"

"Sure, but you saved her from any more suffering and now she's getting the help she needs. Isn't your highest goal to help women get out of bad relationships?" she asked.

"Yeah, but—"

"And wouldn't you agree that living with a corpse husband is kind of a bad relationship situation?"

"Yeah, but, what about Bob? I never wished anything bad to happen to him and…" I couldn't finish the sentence.

"Tara, you told me a hundred times that you wished he would stop getting older so you could catch up and be closer to the same age. Remember?"

I did remember. And in that moment had a terrible realization that I probably had willed Bob's death with my incessant wish. I got it, didn't I? He's not getting any older and one day I'll be forty-five.

"I have to lie down. I'm exhausted. Don't wake me up," I said through an open-mouthed yawn.

Hours later I awoke up with a start, my adrenalin pumping. I'd had a dream in which a faceless couple was standing at the altar in a cathedral made entirely of stained glass—walls, doors, even the ceiling. The pews were filled with people talking and laughing. It had the feeling of a celebration, like a wedding, but everyone was dressed in black, including the woman standing at the altar with a man who felt like her husband-to-be.

As I watched the odd celebration from my perch in a high corner, I saw a dark shadow start to cover the ceiling. A woman in a white wedding dress fell through the glass and landed on the young man at the front, killing him. She kept repeating, "Don't forget the rock, don't forget the rock." Then she died, too.

The woman at the altar flew straight up and at me, screaming, throwing an endless supply of rocks, breaking windows all around us. As her body flew into mine we both fell toward the ground. I awoke before the impact.

After I told Betsy about my dream she said, "I think Mother gave you a message in your dream. It sounds like a murder-suicide."

"Are you insane? Don't even think that. God, why would you put that image in my head, Betsy? That is so not cool."

"Well, what do you think it meant?" she asked, without any apparent appreciation for the damage she may have done to this couple.

"Nothing. I think it means I fell asleep with this awful situation on my mind and so I dreamt about it. And it got all twisted, the way dreams do. Jesus."

"Okay. All right. You don't have to get all snippy. It was only one interpretation."

"Sorry. But please don't tell me what you think until I've figured out how this all works. What if you just planted an idea that I end up focusing on and that's what comes to pass? That would be terrible," I said, feeling my chest fill with emotion. Anger. Fear. Grief. All rolled into one big, black ball of pain.

"Would it be that bad? I mean, you don't even know them," Betsy said with a shrug.

"Betsy, for the thousandth time, I *have* not, *am* not and *will* not kill anyone."

"Suit yourself," she said, leaving and closing my door behind her.

I sat for three days in my meditation room, burning

incense, rolling amethyst-Bob around in my hands for hours, talking to him and Mother. But it felt like talking to myself. I was no closer to understanding how my gift worked or what I should wish for this couple and Paula's mother. I made a conscious and focused effort to only think of positive outcomes. To picture white light and happiness. Each time a negative feeling overtook me or a dark colour filled my mind's eye, I quickly and forcefully pushed it aside.

For all the images that filled my mind while I tried to empty it, the only one that felt authentic was of hundred dollar bills, flying away from me toward the ocean. The meaning was obvious. I waited for Betsy to leave the house before I made the call. Although Paula's mother had not told us her name, her online payment was sent from Joanna Tope. I left a message since she didn't answer. Two days passed before I got a return call from Newfoundland. Betsy grabbed the phone before I could.

"Hang on a minute. I'll get her for you," Betsy handed me the receiver with an 'I don't know who it is' shrug.

Dammit. I don't want her to know I'm giving back the money.

"Hello?" I said, taking the phone into my meditation room, hoping Betsy wouldn't follow me. Of course, she did. And she turned on the recorder so she could hear the conversation first-hand.

"Hi, Teresa. My name is Paula Pitman—"

Oh, Sweet Jesus, no.

"—you left a message for Joanna a few days ago."

"I did," I said with great hesitation, wishing I could remember exactly what I'd said on the answering machine. *Please let me have been vague enough.*

Betsy gave me a look that I knew meant I had some explaining to do.

"I'm not sure of the service that Joanna hired you to take care of—"

There is a God!

"—but, I'm sorry to say, she's not going to be needing it now. She passed away three days ago."

"Oh, I am so sorry, Paula. Your mother…" I paused, not knowing what else to say.

"Oh, Joanna wasn't my mother, although she sometimes thought she should have that kind of control," Paula laughed.

"She wasn't? She told me you were her daughter, that you're getting married…"

"She always called me her 'little girl.' But I'm not her daughter. I'm a home-care nurse. I visited with her every day for an hour or so, made sure she was eating and taking her meds."

"Oh. That's great," I said with so much relief I all but forgot that Joanna was dead.

"How did she die?" Betsy whispered.

"I am sorry to hear about Joanna and for your loss. May I ask how she died? Was it natural causes?"

"No, it wasn't. Very sad, actually. It appears she was doing the dishes and broke a glass. She cut herself and bled to death. The doctor said that her blood thinners were to blame."

"I am so sorry," I said.

"So you called saying that you weren't sure if you'd be able to provide the service Joanna had paid you for…and, you offered to reimburse her money—"

Betsy threw me a glare that, had she had a connection

138

to a killer spirit, would most definitely have left me dead in my beanbag chair.

"Uh, yeah, um, uh, she, um, well, in the time between my leaving that message and now, I was actually able to complete the job she hired me to do, so, uh…"

"May I ask what that service was? A thousand dollars is a lot of money for someone like Joanna to spend. It's quite out of the ordinary," Paula said.

Betsy kicked me, fell backwards in her chair with Shakespearean flair, and said a bit too loud, "You are such a fucking idiot, Tez."

"I'm afraid I can't tell you, actually," I said, glaring at Betsy to please shut up. "It was a… secret service kind of thing," I added hoping that would satisfy Paula.

"Well, I think that given the situation, you can share her secret now," Paula's tone was less friendly suddenly.

"The thing is, Paula, she hired me to arrange a gift for you and your fiancé…Justin, is it?"

"Yeah, that's right. Huh."

Paula stopped talking. I had nothing to add. We sat in silence, Betsy looking at me with tarsier eyes from her prone position.

"Well," Paula said, "did she give you all the details you need? Date, location and all that?"

"Yeah, she gave me everything I needed to get the job done. I think she'd be… surprised at the outcome, but I am one hundred percent certain that she got exactly what she asked for."

"Well, okay,"

"And congratulations, Paula. From what Joanna told me, you're a very lucky woman."

'Thank you. Yes, I am. And, as impolitic as it is to

say, Joanna's passing actually makes my getting married a whole lot easier. She...wasn't particularly supportive. Which is why I'm surprised she arranged such a generous gift."

"From what she shared with me, it's obvious that she'd have given her life to ensure your happiness," I said, bringing Betsy off the floor to give me a half-hearted smile.

After I'd hung up, Betsy wanted to celebrate another Mother Teresa job-well-done. I wanted to cry.

"Mother Teresa had nothing to do with her death," I said. "I didn't do anything. I didn't do that."

"You don't even know what you can do or what you are doing. You're still too afraid to embrace this power."

"I might not understand it, but I'm not afraid of it," I argued.

"You know who you should be afraid of betraying? Me. I can't believe you called to cancel the service without talking to me first."

"Sorry," I snarked back, "I didn't realize that you were the keeper of my conscience."

"You could have ruined everything."

"Don't you think Joanna's life is kind of ruined? Our client is dead. That's not the way this is supposed to work. And I don't understand what happened because I sure as shit did not kill her."

Betsy stared at me for several seconds. "You have a fucking gift. Accept it, Tez."

Funny thing about gifts, I thought, is sometimes it's hard to return the ones we didn't ask for and don't want.

Chapter Eighteen

Betsy and I stayed out of each other's way for the next few days which suited me fine. I gave her use of the living room and I spent my days in my meditation room. And, I didn't meditate once. But I did do a lot of thinking. Mostly about Glen. I watched 'The Prestige,' the film he'd mentioned in his break-up note. The film he said we'd been trying to remember but had actually never spoken of.

It was about two magicians who became enemies when one accidentally allowed the other's wife to die during a trick. It was well-made and an interesting story but I couldn't understand why, as his last break-up words, Glen wanted to tell me to see it.

I watched it a second time and made notes since I had a feeling this film was the clue to why he left. I wrote words that seemed to describe the themes in the film: murder, love, wife, magic, betrayal, secrets, deceit, friend, rivalry, death, sleight-of-hand, trust, illusion, impostor, accident.

My gut, intuition, connection to the universe—

whatever you want to call it—told me that the story was somehow related to my own. But who was Glen suggesting I was among the three main characters? The dead wife? The grieving magician husband? Or the magician who killed his colleague's wife?

I assumed he meant for me to see that I *was* the person who was responsible, even if by accident, for the killing. It made sense in light of the rest of his note, that his logic had been flawed about my ability to use a power I didn't believe in.

I desperately wanted to call and tell him he was wrong. But the evidence from Mother Teresa's first real client, seemed to prove otherwise. And anyway, it had been three months since I'd seen him. Longer than I'd dated him for. Even though I still thought about him, if only for a minute every day, it was usually more in a 'I'm lucky to have had that experience,' kind of way rather than a longing for an impossible dream.

The third day after our fight I decided to make peace with Betsy. I mean, if I was one of the two magicians in the story that meant Betsy was the other and I certainly didn't want our relationship to follow the trajectory of the film's characters, hating each other and sabotaging each other's work.

"I'm sorry I tried to cancel a client without first talking to you," I offered.

She waved my apology aside the way she'd wave away a mosquito buzzing around her face.

"So I've been thinking," she started, "we made a mistake counting on the magazine ads to bring us business. It's been over two months since they ran, so all those mags—at least the ones that aren't in doctor's offices—

142

have been recycled. We can't count on too many more calls from them."

I cannot express the relief I felt that my days as Mother Teresa were over. The riptide was taking me back to shore. I tried to hide my happiness.

"Betsy, I'm so sorry you wasted your entire retirement savings on this. It seemed like such a good idea," I said, taking the glass of wine she was handing me.

"It's all good, Tez. We're not done yet. This can still work as long as you're ready to accept that even if you don't understand it, you make shit happen."

"I can't talk to them, Betsy. I get too emotionally wrapped up. I don't think I can do this. Our Mother Teresa days are over. I'm really sorry."

"And I don't think you have a choice. Fact is, even before you knew you were making things happen, you were."

Oh, no. Being dragged out again...

I dropped onto the couch beside her, sloshing my wine on my crazy quilt, which I was trying to wrap myself into.

"So we have to find a way for you to do what you do without getting personally engaged."

"But what if I have to be personally engaged to make this work? Like you said, so far I've personally known four and I've been connected by phone to the other two," I said, wondering why the hell I was arguing since I was not going to ever do that again.

"Maybe. But since you don't want to do it that way, why not test to see if you can still change things if you're a little more distant from the problem?"

I squeezed my eyes closed and wished I'd wake up in a different conversation. No such luck. Apparently I can unintentionally, psychically take people to the grave but I can't manage a small trick like changing the subject of a conversation. I decided I was going to have a chat with Mother once I was done listening to Betsy.

She laid out a plan in which she would become the face and voice of Mother Teresa's Advice for Jilted Lovers. She'd have the conversations with clients, collect all the relevant information and the money. Then she'd pass the important details on to me and I'd do whatever it was that I did to make things happen.

"But…" I was trying to think of an excuse, "we don't have any more money for advertising. How will we find clients to test out this approach?"

"Easy. Online. In fact, it's how we should have started from the get-go. I was an idiot."

"I don't get it. We have a website and it hasn't brought us one single client."

"Our website is where people go *after* they hear about us. The trick is to get them to hear about Mother Teresa's service. And how we do that is through other websites where people already go to get advice."

"But doesn't advertising cost money?"

"You don't get it. We don't advertise. We give Mother Teresa's advice online, in forums."

"For free?" I asked.

"Yeah. And at the end of the advice, we post a link to our website and see what grows from that. I'm pretty confident it won't take long to start getting at least one client a week."

"Kind of like Dear Abby or Anne Landers? Good advice? Not 'kill your husband' advice?" I said, wanting to be one hundred percent sure I understood what Betsy was suggesting.

"Yeah. I decided you were right. It's better to use the universe to create love. There's already enough suffering and death."

"Okay," I said, not sure if she was being serious. "What do you need me to do?"

"It would be great if you'd go online and post answers to questions the way I have...I'll show you."

Betsy grabbed her laptop from her room and entered a Q&A forum about relationships. "Here's a sweet one. I bet she's only a kid,

So like 3 months ago my best friend and me started to be friends with benefits. All we really did was make out a lot. We said it would be with no strings attached. But 3 weeks ago he asked me if I'd be his girlfriend. I said no cause I didn't want to ruin our friendship. And now he doesn't want to hang out with me anymore. I really miss him and I really wish I would have said yes. What should I do?

I was heart-broken by the story. I could feel this young lady's sadness and her young man's embarrassment at having asked her out and been rejected.

"What advice did you give?" I asked Betsy, a little scared of what I was going to hear.

"I wrote, *It sounds like you know exactly what you should do. You want him back in your life and so you should call and tell him exactly what you've told us: You said 'no' because you were scared it would ruin your friendship. I bet you dollars to donuts that he's not hanging out with you because he's embarrassed and hurt. In his mind you were already unofficially dating and he was trying to make it official. You*

145

saying no, even though your intentions were good, probably made him think you didn't like him as much as you do. My advice: Call and invite him over to talk. If he says no, write him a letter. Don't give up if your heart is telling you to keep trying."

I was speechless. How had the woman who railed against every one of my lovers come up with such a heartfelt response?

"Wow."

Betsy looked pleased by my reaction.

"Want to see another one?"

I nodded.

"These people are older. Long distance relationship question,

I just got home to Georgia after working in Australia for six months. Of course I met the man of my dreams there. We started as friends and then began to date. In all, we've been together five months and I love him. He loves me, too. But I had to come home when my work visa ended, a month ago. We've talked over Skype every day and are trying to stay involved in each other's lives but I'm worried about how long this can last. My friends say I'm crazy and should break it off but I'm crazy in love. Does anyone have advice for how to make a long distance relationship last?

"That's a tricky one. What did you say?" I was truly excited about what Betsy had been doing.

"Not tricky at all. I wrote, *Number one: never listen to friends who tell you to give up someone you love. They're wrong and that's just bad advice. Long distance relationships*

146

can and do work for people who are willing to make time to make them work. You can't be lazy about it. The most important things to remember to keep your relationship alive are to have regular communication—every day is best—and to trust the person you love. There are websites and communities of people who have successfully had long distance relationships for years. Connect with them for tips to keep your love strong."

"You wrote that?" I was in disbelief.

She shrugged her shoulders.

"Never listen to a friend who tells you to break up with someone you love? You wrote that?"

Betsy laughed. "Just because I can *give* the advice doesn't mean I'm going to follow it."

We spent two hours, heads together, drinking wine and answering questions about cheating boyfriends, drunken husbands, inappropriately behaved bosses, creepy uncles and dozens of other challenges that a user named 'TeresasAdvice4Lovers' would have credibility answering. Every response we gave was thoughtful and appropriate to the situation—call 9-1-1 if he hits you again, meet with your boss's boss if he hits *on* you again, etcetera—and included a link to our website every time.

"Oh, I edited our website a little, too," Betsy said, navigating away from the advice forums. "I replaced our phone number with an email address, so we'll have control over when people get in touch with us. No more middle of the night calls."

"Thank you. That means I can drink again, to excess if I want since I won't have to worry about providing drunken Mother Teresa's advice. How many answers do you think we'll need to do?"

"I figure if we can answer fifty questions a day—"

"Fifty? Holy cow, that's a lot."

"We did at least that many in what, two hours…while drinking a bottle-and-a-half of wine…it's easy. So if we do fifty a day, we should be able to generate at least one client every two or three days. And if we average, say, three clients a week, paying a thousand bucks up front, and the other thousand once the job is done…"

"Three times fifty-two is… Holy cow, that's a hundred and fifty grand. You really think this way will work?" My enthusiasm was unexpectedly dampened by the vague memory of a somewhat similar conversation three months earlier as we planned the magazine ads.

As if reading my mind Betsy said, "Those magazine ads were well worth the investment. People will have seen them, even if they didn't call or think the ad had anything to do with them at the time. But they give us credibility. And look—"

Betsy clicked to a new page in our own website that showed each of the ads and an 'As seen in *Happy Homemaker* magazine' or 'As seen in *Popular Dinners* magazine,' tag-line.

"But how does an ad give us credibility? We could say anything in an ad."

"Tell me, if you saw a company that you'd never heard of before and sounded possibly like a scam, would it give you more confidence seeing that the company had the resources to pay for all these magazine ads?"

I thought about it and had to say, "Yes."

"And so will Mary-Jane Suburbanite."

"Betsy, I need to understand one thing. Are you now, or have you—"

"—ever been a member of a terrorist organization?

Why, yes, I am a member of the cell known as the Mother Teresa's Advice for Jilted Lovers. We act on the radical belief that love, love will keep us together."

It was probably the wine, but her joke and then breaking into Captain and Tennille's famous song made me laugh so hard I fell over.

Once I recovered I asked her, "Are you finally onside with me? No more talk about killing? Mother Teresa is only providing two things—good advice on those websites and loving solutions to the people who send us money?"

"One hundred percent," she said.

"Why the sudden change?"

She leaned over and kissed my forehead. "Because I finally saw how much my approach was hurting you and I don't want to hurt you. I love you."

Before things got weird, *thank you, Mother*, Betsy's laptop pinged. It was a new message, addressed to motherteresa@adviceforjiltedlovers.com. By morning, Mother Teresa had received eight messages.

Chapter Nineteen

True to her word, Betsy took on the responsibility of making first contact with each of the potential new clients. It was an onerous task that got harder with every passing hour of the day since every hour brought at least one new woman seeking advice. To give the potential clients the feeling that they were being taken care of quickly, Betsy asked me to write an automatic reply email that promised to get back to them soon. She also wanted it to separate the gold from the pyrite by letting them know what the fee for Mother Teresa's service was since she'd removed that information from the website during her revamp. We debated whether or not to offer a money-back guarantee and came up with what we thought was a brilliant idea. I wrote:

Dear Blessed One,

Thank you so much for contacting me. I so look forward to helping you address your situation in a personal and intimate way.

As I hope you can appreciate, I am very busy helping women from all over the world with problems like yours. As such, I must ask your forgiveness that it may take me a day or two to get in touch with you personally. I work with clients on a first-come, first-served basis, which I believe is the most fair way to work. I hope you understand.

In the meantime, and to help me attune to your specific problem, if you would complete the short questionnaire on the attached link, I would be most appreciative. Please refrain from offering solutions to your problem. What I need to be of best service to you is a description of the challenge you face, in your words.

For more information on how the process works, please visit my website and link to www.adviceforjiltedlovers. com/method.

One thing you will not find on the website is the fee for my services since I like to be in conversation with friends-in-need, as we are now, before sharing that information. The fee to eliminate your problem is $2,000. I offer two payment options:

Either: $1,000 following our in-person conversation, before I start my work; and $1,000 once the job has been completed;

Or: $2,000 following our conversation, before I start my work. If you choose this option I will give you a full, money-back guarantee: if, after 30 days, your problem has *not been addressed to your satisfaction, I will refund your full payment.*

The choice is yours. I will provide exactly the same level of commitment to solving your problem no matter which payment option you choose.

With love and light and the promise of better days ahead, Mother Teresa

While I wrote the email, Betsy created a short survey to gather basic information about each client: Name, preferred contact method with phone number and/or email address, age, time-zone, number of years or months spent in the offending relationship, and cause of the relationship break-down.

She uploaded the questionnaire and I added the link to my email. After we'd sent the message to the fifteen women who'd contacted us in the last twenty-four hours, Betsy uploaded my email reply to Mother Teresa's email settings so that every person who contacted us would get it immediately. The rest was easy: wait for PayPal and the questionnaire software to send us messages that we had a new client.

From there, Betsy reviewed each response, contacted the person if she thought I needed more information, printed the sheet and passed it on to me, Mother Teresa, to handle.

To say I was stressing out would be an understatement. One minute I was manic, rearranging all the furniture and knick-knacks of my meditation room to try to make it more conducive to receiving guidance. The next I was falling asleep in my beanbag, chin hitting my chest and waking me up from what I thought had been meditation, but had turned into a nap somewhere along the way.

"Betsy, I don't know if I can do this," I said, walking and yawning from my room.

"Look, I'm working my butt off and all you have to do is sit and listen or talk or God knows what. All I'm asking is that you be receptive. Here," she said, handing me three sheets of paper, "your first clients. Two paid up front," she drew the words out for effect, "the whole two grand. The other paid half. Tez, we have five *thousand* dollars in our PayPal account."

I stood open-mouthed, not sure whether the mice in my gut were excitement at the amount of cash we suddenly had or nerves that I now had to perform some miracle acts that I still had no understanding of. What we had promised was to make a connection between the woman-in-need and the universal energy that would help her solve her problem. All she had to do was suspend disbelief, trust in the universe, and, pay us of course.

Betsy continued talking since I didn't say anything, "You want me to read them to you or do you want to take them and go over them yourself?"

"Read to me? Please."

"Okay. Client One. Isabelle from Oakland. She's forty-two and has been with this guy, Ian, since she was twenty-one. Half her life. Amazing, eh?" Betsy looked up from the page at me, laying face-down on the couch.

"Tara, what the hell are you doing?"

"Listening," I mumbled into the sofa.

"Why are you lying like that? Sit up," she scolded.

"I focus better like this. Keep talking."

"So twenty-one years. She says things were good until about two years ago. I quote, 'It used to be good but something changed when he joined an amateur baseball team. He goes out drinking, three or four nights a week with these guys now. The wives are only invited on Fridays, but I may as well not even be there since he spends the whole time slapping his buddies on the ass, yelling, "Yeah, baby!" He totally ignores me. And the other men are exactly the same, ass-slapping and ignoring their wives and girlfriends. The thing is, I DON'T EVEN LIKE HAVING MY ASS SLAPPED, but I hate that he's giving all this ass attention to his buddies! This is driving me crazy. Can you please make him stop, Mother Teresa?'" Betsy looked at me, probably to make sure I was awake, which I was.

"Anything else?" I asked.

"She paid the whole two grand up front and asks if you could please try to make things better before hockey playoffs start. I quote again, 'If I have to put up with having twenty, macho men all acting homoerotic in my living room again this year someone is going to leave with a hockey stick up his slap-happy ass.'"

"A little dramatic, don't you think?" I said.

Betsy shrugged, "Apparently this really bugs her."

"I'm stunned that she's willing to pay two thousand dollars to make that stop."

"Lucky us. You want the next one?"

"Hmm," I thought for a few seconds, trying to feel whether my spirit wanted all the situations at once or not. "Let me sit with that one for awhile, okay? I don't want to muddy the message by mixing things up. Sound okay to you?"

"But we could have twice this many cases by the end of

154

the day, you know. So, don't sit for too long. Okay?"

I agreed and walked back to my room. Rather than sit in my chair, I put the two beanbags side-by-side and lay across them. Once I'd wiggled myself into a comfortable position I picked up Bob. I'd taken to talking to him out loud since, when I spoke to him in my mind, I never knew which of my voices might be connecting to him: my creative and positive voice or the negative one that poo-poos everything. Speaking out loud felt like it gave me more control. It also quieted my pesky pessimist.

"Hi, Bob. I hope you're having a good day. So, I suspect you already know what's going on...Bob, I'm worried. You know that I never wanted you to die and that's what's got me so freaked out. I don't think an ass-slapping jock should join your team simply because his wife doesn't like how he expresses enthusiasm, but what if at some deeper level that actually is what I think should happen? What if I don't know what I think? What if my spirit guide, or whatever she is, does what she thinks is best regardless of what I think? Bob, I want *you* to be my guide. You were such a great teacher. Would you talk to my guide and ask her to trade me? Please?"

I stopped talking to leave space for Bob to answer. Sometimes, although rarely, he did. He'd give me a reassuring word or two that he was well and that he wasn't mad at me for his death. And I believed him. I believed him more than I was able to believe that I hadn't actually willed the shelf to fall on his head.

As amethyst-egg Bob rolled between my palms an image appeared, like a TV screen, in my mind. Isabelle was sitting on the couch with Ian and three of his friends, having a beer, enjoying a football game. Their team scored and the men jumped into the air and started high-fiving and ass-slapping. Isabelle joined in a second later, first whacking Ian's, then all his friends' butts. The men suddenly stopped. They looked at Isabelle, who looked sincere in her excitement. They looked at each other and sat down mumbling how weird that was.

Chapter Twenty

I threw myself down on the couch and Betsy joined me from her kitchen table office.

"I've done all I can with Isabelle for now. Can you send her an email, let her know that Mother Teresa has connected with her spirit guide and asks her to join her husband in the ass-slapping exuberance with a sincere heart."

Betsy raised her eyebrows but made a note on Isabelle's page in our client diary. "Good to go for Number Two?"

I nodded.

"Louise from Bokchito, Oklahoma. She didn't include how old she was. She wrote, 'I've been with this guy for two years and the relationship isn't going nowhere,'" Betsy stopped reading and rolled her eyes. "'The relationship isn't going *anywhere*. He moved in with me about six months ago and he don't give me no money for food or the bills or nothing. I pay for everything and he spends all his check getting drunk every night, yelling at my kids to shut up so he can watch his fighting shows that I pay for on the cable bill. I'm sick of it and he don't want to move out and I don't know how to make him. I can't afford to pay for another kid. Already have three. Mother Teresa, I'd be mighty pleased if you could help me get Luke to move along out of my house."

Betsy looked up from the paper and said, "Dead man walking."

I have to admit, my intuition told me it wasn't going to end well for this guy.

"You want to take it away, Tez? Able to handle this one right now?"

"Give me the next one. I have no idea if it'll mess it up, but I guess there's only one way to find out," I said, hoping my personal feelings for Luke the Leech wouldn't interfere with my professional role to simply send the love energy that Louise and Luke needed to get themselves out of this hillbilly hellhole of an existence.

"Okay. Last one for now. Pamela. She paid the whole shot up front. Poor Louise only paid half. I don't think we'll be seeing the other half even if you do solve the Luke problem."

"Maybe we should set-up a charitable arm if this really flies. You know, give deserving women like Louise a freebie. It's not like it costs us anything to help them," I said.

"It costs our time, Tez. That's worth at least a hundred bucks an hour each. Anyway, back to Pamela?"

I nodded, stuck on the thought that we should have a way to provide the service for free to some clients.

"She's 55, lives outside Seattle, Washington and has been married to Pete, her third husband, for four years. She wrote, 'Two years ago Pete and I were in a car crash.

We both suffered injuries. I broke my back and although I can walk again, I have constant numbness in my limbs. Pete smashed his head and since he came out of the coma he's developed a rare and most irritating condition called, Foreign Accent Syndrome. And he has a weird version of it. He doesn't have the same accent all the time. It changes depending on who he's talking to. The worst part is that he lost his job since his coworkers and bosses at the factory thought he was being racist whenever he spoke in their accents. He's not a bad guy, but I can't live like this anymore with him home all day long, moping around, talking like Alec Baldwin from *The Departed* with that awful fake Boston accent, Foghorn Leghorn sound-alike whenever the last person he's spoken to is from the south. Mother Teresa, can you please help?'"

"Is that for real or is he being an ass?" I asked, not able to hold back a smile.

"I looked it up. It's rare but it is a documented condition," Betsy said.

"I wonder if he does all accents badly or if he might have an ear for one or two of them."

"Do you think it matters, Mother Teresa?" Betsy asked with a hint of frustration.

"Well, if her real concern is that her husband has lost his job because of this, maybe he needs to find a job where that condition would be seen as a skill, rather than an insult to others. You know? If he did the accents well, maybe he could train actors? Or, he could read character voices for audio books? Jobs like that?"

"That's a good point. I'll find out for you."

"Thanks. And I'll go and see how the spirit moves me to help Louise. Can you give me her sheet, please?"

Betsy interrupted my meditation twice in the next ninety minutes with the excited call, "We got another one paid-up."

Since, for all I knew, my communications effort with Mother had achieved its goal as soon as Betsy told me about the situation, I figured I could stop laying in my beanbag, turn off the relaxing water-themed background sounds and open the window to air out the cinnamon scent. I wondered what was making me sleepiest of the three meditation tools, but wasn't interested in really knowing since I enjoyed the relaxation. As soon as I opened the door, Betsy thrust two more sheets into my hand.

"Read them," she ordered.

"Twenty-five-year old Jasmine Blayney. Lives in Rochester, Massachusetts. I thought Rochester was in New York."

Betsy waved me to continue.

"'Dear Mother Teresa, please help me. My husband and I got married seven months ago and he's changed. Or maybe it's that now that we've been living together for over a year his habits are driving my crazy. For example, whenever he's the one to drink the last serving of milk or juice or pop or whatever, he puts the empty container back in the fridge. Really. So I get up thinking there's milk for coffee and the carton is empty. WTF!

"When he takes off his socks, he leaves them in these little sock bombs which I have to unroll before I do the laundry. It's gross. When I asked him to unroll his own damn socks he spent the next five days sock-bombing me. I'd walk out of the bathroom. Boom! Sock-bomb in my belly. Turn off the light to go to sleep. Sock-bomb in the face. WTF!

"After dinner he likes to pick his teeth with a toothpick while we're still at the dinner table. He used to floss in the bathroom, but now it's a public display even when we have friends over. He thinks it's really funny to spin the toothpick around in his mouth doing tricks. I assure you, it's not.

"I could go on and on but that should give you a good idea of why I think I made a big mistake marrying Doug. I'd get a divorce but my dad would kill me since he spent a fortune on our wedding. PLEASE HELP ME!!!'

"And this young woman paid already?" I asked.

"A thousand dollars already in the account."

"Where do these people get that kind of money? And honestly, all she has to do is grow a pair and leave the guy. She should be easy to help. She needs to learn to love herself." I was thinking out loud and Betsy got impatient.

"Yeah, yeah. Love, love her do. Read the next one. She's paid the full two grand. Tez, we've made eight thousand dollars in one day. I'm going to post a hundred more bits of advice tonight. If you could do some, too, we might be able to hit ten grand before tomorrow morning."

A wave of nausea forced me into a fetal position.

"Betsy, what if this doesn't work? I mean, what if I can't actually make anything happen for these women?"

"Tez, I know you can do this. Hell, look at what you were able to do when you didn't even know you had any power. Now that you're focused on it...it'll work. And I'd think that sending love energy is a whole hell of a lot easier to do than creating situations where people, you know..."

"Not helpful," I said, still curled into a ball, trying to wash myself in the healing white light I was hoping I could send to all these clients.

"Well, on the very slight chance that it doesn't we have a back-up plan. We have to work hard and fast for the first month."

"Why?" I asked, hating how naïve I always felt around Betsy.

"Because, we've been clear on the website and in your email that they have to expect to wait thirty days for results."

"And?"

"Tara, nobody will complain about not having their problem resolved before a month goes by, since you've already told them it could take that long. If it turns out that what you have is actually a gag-gift from the universe, then we better make as much money as we can before people start posting bad reviews about your service. As fast as this has taken off, it will die if Mother Teresa is outed as a fraud," Betsy said.

"So then," I said, stretching myself out to get deeper breaths, "so then, we shouldn't actually be spending this money." I sighed, feeling a little better.

"Some of it. The people who paid two thousand dollars? No, we can't touch their money until we get word that you've done your job. But the ones who paid a thousand dollars, that's ours right now, whether Mother Teresa is a fraud or not."

"But that's totally unfair," I said rising up. "I *cannot*, with clear conscience, keep money from…what's her name…the girl who has awful grammar. That's probably her life savings."

Betsy got mad. "Oh, for fuck's sake, Tara. We had this conversation already. These people know what they signed up for when they paid a thousand bucks. *No guarantee.*

That's the deal."

"I've changed my mind. I want to send them back their money if I can't help them."

Betsy shook her head. "Not going to happen. I'm managing the money. You manage your fucking spirits and make it work. Okay?"

There was no point arguing. It wouldn't make me feel better and it wouldn't help me figure out if I was actually doing what Betsy was so sure I could do. Why wouldn't Bob or my spirit give me a sign that I was actually able to do this work? One sign. That's all I needed to feel better about this.

A loud 'thunk!' from my meditation room drew both of our attention.

"What the heck?" I said, standing and walking toward the room, Betsy following.

"How the hell…" Betsy said as I wondered the same thing. The curtain rod had fallen out of its cradles and was lying on the floor. Betsy started into my room to pick it up.

"Wait. Check that out," I said, pointing at my little round table. With the window curtainless, one ray of sunlight shone directly onto my amethyst. I never opened the curtain in this room since the window looked out into the neighbouring apartment's window. The buildings were so close, the sun never shone in anyway. Until today. And then, the angle changed and the ray of light was gone.

"Okay, that was weird," Betsy admitted.

I nodded and smiled, saying a silent thank you to Bob.

"Okay. Next one," I said, plunking myself into my beanbag chair with a brand new confidence. But Bob was a joker, throwing a nice new challenge into the next client's situation.

Chapter Twenty-One

B etsy handed me the client survey.

"Fifty-three-year old Alice Wrate and her husband Denzel of London, England... daughter-in-law is trouble...want her out of the picture...hmm," I stopped reading and said to Betsy, "This feels like mother-in-law meddling. I'm not sure about this one."

"What part aren't you sure about?"

"If this is an appropriate use of, you know, Mother Teresa's spirit power."

"Finish reading, Tez."

I did and Alice's P.S almost made me fall off my beanbag.

"She says, 'PS - Please do not confuse us with the Alice and Denzel Wrate of Windermere. We've spoken on the phone with them a handful of times since there have been occasions where mail goes awry. I understand they have a lovely daughter-in-law. I would hate for you to accidentally ruin the wrong marriage.' Oh, Sweet Mother, there's no way I can do this. How will I know which family to direct my thoughts to?" I shook my head to emphasize that this was a non-starter. "How much did they pay?"

"Full amount," Betsy said with a smile.

"Perfect. Send the money back now. I can't take this on. This is way too much pressure. And way too many places for it to go terribly wrong."

Betsy surprised me. She didn't jump down my throat, she said, "All right. But I'm not going to send it back today. Sleep on it, okay? I have faith that you'll be able to sort it out."

I threw her an 'are you kidding me' look.

She said, "Have faith, Tez. Have faith."

I looked at my amethyst and I swear I saw it vibrating; Bob was laughing at me again.

That afternoon I had a vision of Alice and her family while I was meditating. Or a dream while I was sleeping. Sometimes it was hard to tell the difference. Like in my first dream/vision, I was floating over the scene, but this time as an invisible observer.

*   *   *

Alice is asleep in bed with a man. Denzel, her husband. A loud crash wakes them both and she moans. He wraps his arms around her and a silent tear rolls down her cheek.

Denzel: "I'll talk to her again today, all right, Lovey?"

Alice: "Have you talked to Isaac?"

Denzel: "Yes, but he won't hear a thing I'm saying."

Alice: "We can't live like this anymore. I can't live this way."

Denzel: "We'll fix it by the end of the month. Can you hang on until then?"

Alice sighs and pulls Denzel's arms more tightly around

her, "I'll be counting the days, the hours."

Denzel: "Brave face. We don't want to lose Isaac, too."

*　　*　　*

Next I'm floating above a tiny kitchen. The table is in the middle of the room and there's little space to move around it with the two people who are already seated, eating eggs-in-a-hole and drinking coffee. He's a younger man who looks the spitting image of Denzel, but with a full afro where his father has his head all but shaved. Isaac. And his wife, Concepción, a beautiful Spaniard with long, jet-black hair and striking green eyes. They're in love, it's obvious by the energy in the room.

The energy changes. Alice and Denzel are standing at the door now.

Alice: "Good morning!"

Denzel: "Morning."

Concepción: "Morning, yes, but not good. There's no cream. *A madre que te parió!* Alice, you forgot to buy it when you went to the shop. After I told you we were running low."

Alice: "I'm sorry, dear. Seems you didn't look very well. It's in the fridge."

Concepción: "*Gilipollas.* I'm not blind, Alice. There is no cream in that fridge."

Isaac, turned his chair sideways and reached around to open the fridge door.

Denzel: "Put it in there myself. Isaac, it's on the left. Concepción, you might want to apologize to Alice for being snippy and maybe thank her?"

Isaac: "Thanks."

Concepción "What's this? That's not the normal

166

cream. How was I to know you'd bought a different kind? I was looking for the green carton, not a blue one. Someone might have told me. *Me cago en tus muertos.* Saved me drinking this black."

Alice: "Well, once one of you get a job and your own place, Concepción, you can buy whatever coloured milk you like."

Concepción: "In this economy. Not likely."

Isaac: "I am trying, Mum."

*   *   *

Another scene change. I'm floating over a small living room. Denzel is dozing in an old leather recliner. Alice is reading a book, under a blanket on a love seat, her slippered feet on the wooden coffee table. Isaac and Concepción join them, coming in from outside.

Alice: "What did you two get up to today? Any job leads?"

Isaac: "The chippy on Baker Street is hiring. I dropped off my application and have a meeting tomorrow."

Alice: "Wonderful!"

Concepción: "Wonderful? How would you like your husband to come home from work smelling of grease and fish every night, Alice? *Mierda!* I hope he doesn't get it. I'd rather live here for the rest of my life than have Isaac work in chip shop."

Denzel: "Concepción, where do you think Isaac should work?"

Concepción, looking up at me, not at the still-sleeping Denzel: "At the National Gallery."

And then, the vision was gone. I opened my eyes, found Alice's paperwork and wrote a note for Betsy: *Tell*

Alice to tell Isaac to apply for a job at the National Gallery.
I hoped they were hiring.

*   *   *

The next three days were a blur. Betsy woke me up by seven with a cup of coffee and two or three new client sheets. While I got in touch with my higher support team, Betsy replied to more advice-seekers. Betsy made lunch for us and after I'd eaten, handed me more new clients, never more than three at a time since I said I couldn't manage more than that in one sitting. Truth was, I didn't know if I could manage even a single case at a time since we hadn't gotten any feedback from any of the clients yet.

In the afternoon I'd sit with the new client situations, then have dinner. Since the opportunities and bank balance were rising faster than I was working, Betsy wanted me to take on clients in the evening, too, but I held my ground.

"Look," she said, "here are eight files you haven't looked at yet. By tomorrow morning there will probably be at least four more. If you don't work at night we'll never catch up."

"Look," I replied, using her identical hands-in-the-air motion and tone of voice, "if I don't take a couple of hours every day to sit with myself, not thinking about other people's problems and solving them, I'll burn-out within a week. I need to pace myself."

"So, you're going to meditate on nothing?" Betsy asked, nodding as if thinking that might be a good idea.

"Who said anything about meditating? I was thinking that tonight we should drink a bottle of good rum and watch *Mulholland Drive*. I could go for a pitcher of Cuba Libres and some good David Lynch right now."

Although Betsy argued against my idea, minutes after the opening credits had finished, Betsy was curled up on the couch beside me, helping empty the two-litre pitcher of rum, cola and lime. It was a good night. I successfully forgot about all the troubles of all the couples I was meeting in my mind's eye. On the upside, this work gave me a new appreciation for how easy I'd had it in my own relationships. A cake-walk compared to the people who were writing to Mother Teresa for help.

The best part about our evening off was that since Betsy drank half the rum, she didn't wake me up the next morning until 9:00. Unfortunately for my heart, she didn't use her typical gentle knock and clink of coffee on my bedside table as her alarm. No, this morning she used her, 'I'm being attacked by a dog-faced, nurse-zombie scream.'

"Betsy, what the hell?" I said, stumbling from my room toward the kitchen, feeling rather zombie-like myself.

"Since yesterday dinner we have twenty-thousand dollars more in the account. I haven't figured out how much is full payments and how much is half yet, but *ahhhh!*," she yelled again. "We're going to be millionaires!"

That woke me up. "How much have we made so far?" I asked, uncovering my ears. I started to laugh, looking at Betsy with her spiky, bleached hair and her five-dollar reading glasses, wearing a thread-bare Asexuals concert t-shirt and boxer shorts and tried to see her as a millionaire. Then I looked down at my own jammies—a tank top and two-sizes-too-big pink, waffled moose-print long johns—and knew that we were the most unlikely pair of old punk-rockers to be millionaires ever.

"Fifty. Seven. Thousand. Dollars. In five days. *Ahhhh!*"

Even though that wasn't even close to a million, I

jumped up and down in excitement and knocked Betsy's coffee onto the floor, breaking the mug she usually saved for me; the mug that said, 'Sometimes I wake up bitchy. Sometimes I let her sleep.'

After cleaning up the mess, we sat down and figured out how many more clients I had to focus on to catch up to the ones who'd paid. Things felt so complicated, I suggested we create a spreadsheet to track clients, payments, progress, successes and anything else we might need to remember. Betsy was happy with our notebook system and, she insisted, since she was the one taking care of the client and money management, I shouldn't waste any time trying to make sense of it all.

"You," she told me, "only have to read the sheets I give you and let your spirit take care of the rest."

Never one to not do what I want, I spent the entire morning inputting information from the client intake sheets into the tracking table I envisioned. And what it showed me, in no-nonsense black and white, was that as long as I kept thinking inside these boxes, I'd never catch up to the clients who were contacting Mother Teresa and we'd be repaying a pant-load of two thousand dollar fees. Before I left my room for lunch and to talk to Betsy about a new idea I had for managing contracts, I reviewed and focused on five client sheets, hoping that by having already done my daily quota by lunch, Betsy wouldn't get too upset that I'd spent so much energy on my spreadsheet.

"Hey," I said, with as much chipper as I could muster, "I managed five clients this morning." I was feeling proud.

Betsy looked unusually stressed. "That's great, Tez. Sure hope you can do another five after lunch and another five after dinner. We've had six more paid-up clients in the last three hours."

"Holy cow. I think you should stop posting to the advice websites for awhile. We've got all the work we need for now, don't you think?"

"I haven't had time to post any new links since Thursday. This is all word-of-mouth."

"But we don't even have proof of a real success yet," I said.

"Yeah, well, I guess someone up there," Betsy said, looking at the ceiling, "wants us to succeed."

"Bob," I said looking to the same spot Betsy had.

"Well, you think you could ask him to slow it down a bit, Tez? Otherwise I think we may burn-out and ruin our reputation before a month is up."

"Well, if we keep bringing in twenty grand a day, we'll be able to crash after a month."

"Six clients more since breakfast, so add another nine thousand dollars to today's take. Jesus. And odds are we'll have more before dinner. If this pace keeps up, we'll be making over a hundred thousand dollars a week, Tez. *A week!*"

"How many clients would that be?" I asked, blood rushing from my brain, making my arms feel like lead weights.

"Well, if they all paid two grand it would only be fifty."

"Only?" I said with obvious concern.

"Yeah, but only about a third are paying the full amount. So it would be closer to seventy-five."

"Seventy-five?"

"If the pace keeps at this rate. If it goes up…"

"If it goes up we won't be able to keep up," I said, always the naysayer.

"I know. You think your job is hard. Try doing mine."

"Speaking of…so, I know you told me not to focus on your job, but I had to make a plan for myself to keep track of which clients I'd already worked on—"

"That's why I left room on your sheets," Betsy interrupted. "To make notes."

"I know. And that was great when we had a couple clients a day. But I really need to see the big picture, so I made this," I said, handing her a print-out of my table.

She sniffed and snorted and harumphed, complained and grumbled and muttered while she looked at my outline. Then she said, "Can you email this to me? I think it'll help me stay organized too. But I'll want to add a couple more columns, like their contact info and stuff. That okay?"

"Of course."

"Can I ask, though, why'd you skip some of the contacts? You stopped doing them in order."

"Because, I figure until we know how long it actually takes to make something happen, I should focus on the clients who've paid the full amount, since, if they don't get results in thirty days, we have to pay them back. With the others—"

Betsy interrupted me. "Good idea. And you know what I just realized?"

"What?"

"All those people who've only paid a thousand dollars? Well, once they get results they should all give us another thousand. So, that means we haven't brought in," Betsy scribbled on the table, "fifty-six thousand dollars, but," she stopped and counted again, "twenty thousand more."

"Which means that we've made seventy-six thousand dollars? In under a week?"

"Yes and no," Betsy said. "We've *brought in* that much in a week, but we haven't *made* that much in a week since we started with those expensive ads months ago. And I know we haven't talked about it, but I was thinking that it would be fair if we repaid my retirement money before we start splitting this money."

"And my savings?" I asked, not wanting her to forget that although I hadn't invested as much as her, I had put money in.

She nodded.

"And, if this continues to go well, I want to take ten percent off-the-top of every client fee and put it in a separate account so we can do free work, too," I said.

"We won't have time to do free work," she countered.

"We'll make time," I said, grabbing my coffee and heading back to my room with a stack of new client sheets.

Chapter Twenty-Two

I'd read business case studies about the snowball effect in market research among hidden populations that are often difficult to access, like drug addicts and prostitutes. I had no idea that the same principle might apply to the group of people Mother Teresa's advice was targeted towards. But apparently, like snowballs in the wild, our marketing snowball was rolling along, gathering flakes very nicely without any help from Betsy or me.

On the one hand, this was great since Betsy had enough to do tracking the new clients. On the other, it meant that we had no control, zero, zilch, on managing the flow of work.

As we'd discussed, once-a-day Betsy transferred all the two thousand dollar clients' money into one bank account and the one thousand dollar clients' money into another, always leaving our PayPal account with two thousand dollars in it. "Just because," was Betsy's rationalization.

On the ninth day, from the yells of "What the hell?" and "Those bastards!" and other more profane curses, I guessed that something had changed on Betsy's side of the business. And probably not something that made her work easier.

I left the solitude of my room and the peaceful ocean waves soundtrack that was carrying Mother Teresa's clients' woes to higher places on this day and entered a space that had the energy of a high school gym locker-room after a critical game had been stolen by a bad call from the ref. I sat quietly until Betsy noticed me.

"Something wrong?"

Betsy glared at me.

"Like you always tell me, let the stress wash over and through you and out your crown chakra," I said, smiling, thrilled to be able to throw that one back at her.

"Screw my crown chakra," she growled.

"Who are you mad at?"

"PayPal. When I tried to move the money into our bank accounts today I was blocked. Our account has been red-flagged. So now, not only do we have to wait five days after the money goes into our normal bank account before we can use it, PayPal is holding the money too."

"Why?"

"We're making too much, too fast. They're worried we're not delivering the service."

"Well, have you contacted them?"

Betsy exhaled with the force of an angry bull staring down a Matador. She spoke in a tone reminiscent of a telephone operator—a mentally deranged telephone operator, "They provided a helpful link to their website which should answer any questions I have. If, after reading their policy, I want to challenge it, I can contact their friendly customer services reps at 1-800-screw-me."

"And?" I asked.

"And their policy of holding money for twenty-one days looks like it was written specifically for businesses like ours. Here's exactly what their email says," she started to read with an exaggerated tone of concern, "'We want to make sure that there are no problems with the orders, such as disputes, claims, returns, or chargebacks.' Blah blah blah, then 'Delaying the availability of payments for a specified amount of time is a common practice in the payments industry. Delaying access to payments helps make sure that sellers have enough money in their account to cover claims or refunds.' Blah blah blah and then this beautiful bit of information, 'If there are no problems with a transaction, the money will typically be released within 21 days after the buyer pays. If there are problems, such as a dispute, claim, chargeback, or return, we'll release the payment when the issue is resolved.' We're screwed," Betsy said, falling against the couch.

"I don't get it. What's the problem?"

"Really? You don't get it? Our own deal of you don't get your money back if you only pay a thousand dollars is over-ridden by PayPal's policy that customers get what they paid for. Anyone can get their money refunded."

"Well, only people who ask," I said.

"Yeah…and how long do you think it will take before clients start to realize that we have no proof that you provided a service? All they have to do is contact PayPal and say they didn't get what they were promised," Betsy said.

We sat in silence for several minutes before I suggested she go and sit in my cinnamon-scented sanctuary to try to find her calm place. I truly meant it as a helpful idea but it wasn't received that way.

After several minutes of swearing directed at God, the universe and her idiot business partner flowed over and through me and out my crown chakra, I asked Betsy what she thought our best move would be.

"Shut it all down," she said.

"But, why? So what if we have to wait twenty-one days to be paid. You managed to pull enough money out in the first week for us to live for six months.

"Maybe two months. Remember? My retirement money."

"So we have to wait three weeks before any more money flows to our bank account. Who cares?" I said.

"Tez, don't you get it? Once we get complaints PayPal will mark us as a bad-risk business. Mother Teresa's Advice will be dying a quick death once that happens."

"Well, maybe Mother Teresa's solutions can be sped up so they happen in a week? Or two weeks? That way nobody will complain."

"Tez, even if you do manage to make shit happen for these people, which, to be fair, we still don't know you can do on-demand, since we have no proof that you've actually done anything for anyone, they can all get their money back. You can't say, 'Well, PayPal people, I provided this service that ended her scoundrel husband's life in a way that matched his relationship crime.' It'll be their word against yours. And they'll win every time. Guaranteed."

It didn't seem like a smart move to correct Betsy, remind her that I wasn't trying to kill anyone, that I was focusing on providing loving solutions. Silence hugged us while I considered the potential impact of this new information and tried to think of something, anything, that would make Betsy feel positive about our business again.

"I know this will be more work, but maybe all we need to do is follow-up with every client, once-a-week or so, to find out whether or not anything has happened yet? And, once they're happy with the results, encourage them to post a positive review on PayPal and get that money released."

"You think I didn't already think of that, Tez? I'm not an idiot. But there are two problems. First, is that we have over one hundred paid clients as of today. I'm already overloaded doing what I'm doing. I can't add anything else to my plate."

"So, maybe we hire someone to do part of the work you're doing?"

Betsy moaned and shook her head.

"Why not?"

"Too risky. We don't even understand how this works. If we bring someone else in now, we could ruin everything. Or they could ruin it. We have to keep this between us. At least until we know if you even have any connection to some greater energy, or whatever."

"I thought you had confidence in my ability. You're the one who keeps telling me to have faith. Are you saying you're not sure this is working?" I suddenly felt the anxiety and fear of failure that had haunted me for the first weeks and months of our planning.

Betsy shrugged.

"No, seriously. Are you saying you're not sure I can pull this off?" I said, raising my voice for the first time.

She stared at the floor but didn't answer.

"So, you've been bullshitting me for the last, oh, four months? Telling me I could do this when you really aren't sure if I can?" I wasn't sure if I felt more anger or hurt. I know I felt betrayed.

"Well," she said, still looking at her slippers, "I believe that if this power is even possible, that you have it. What happened to all those guys and to d'Eddie and the Newfies, that's more than coincidence. It has to be something you're creating. But who knows if you can do it for just anyone. You don't even seem to understand how you do it. So, yeah, I have some concerns."

"Why didn't you tell me this before?

"Because one of us has to stay positive at all times."

"So why are you telling me now?" I asked, pushing a stack of magazines off the coffee table onto Betsy's slippers to get her to look up at me.

"Because I think we should shut it all down," she said, kicking the magazines off her feet. One of them flipped opened to our cleaner ad. We both stared at it for several seconds before I picked it up and placed it face-up on the table.

"Have you printed off all the new, paid-up client sheets?" I asked.

Betsy pointed to the kitchen table where a stack of papers sat.

"Have you read them?"

She nodded.

"Good. I'm not going to quit on the people who've already paid. Shut down the website if you want. But let's at least finish with this group before you quit entirely. I think with over a hundred clients we'll know pretty damn quick if Mother Teresa has something legitimate to offer or not. And I for one am feeling like things are happening."

I took the papers to my room and read each one

quickly but carefully, placing them into priority piles based on my best guess of how urgent the request and need for change was. I hoped that my analysis was close to my spirit guide's interpretation.

Since I didn't have the luxury of spending an hour in la-la land, visualizing each client's problem, waiting to see their solution, writing it down and having Betsy type it up and email it to them, I tried a new approach: I set my phone to beep every ten minutes and gave myself that long to address each client.

I read their story. I closed my eyes to visualize their situation. I opened my heart to feel their struggle. And I used my third eye to direct healing, white light to them so they could see their solutions themselves.

The third eye thing was a bit of stretch at first, but once that energy started flowing it seemed so obvious that if I could 'see' their situation when I meditated on their challenge, then they should be able to 'see' the solution. I mean, if I had some kind of psychic link to their brains or spirits or whatever the heck it was, and they were communicating with me by letting me see their situation, then why couldn't I answer the same way; tell them exactly what I saw with my mind? I figured they should see it pretty easily since the solution was their truth, not mine.

So that's what I did. For six hours straight. Beep. Read. Third eye, white light. Beep. Done. Read. Third eye, white light. Beep. And so on. All. Day. Long.

By the end of the next day, I'd sent white light to every one of the new clients. Even after Betsy shut down our website, twenty-one more sent money and emails.

And even though I still didn't understand how I was able to do what I was doing, I finally knew what to do. And for the first day it felt good. But by the end of the second day, all that sending healing white light to other people from my third eye seemed to be bringing my own life's challenges into clearer focus. And I wasn't sure I liked what I saw.

Chapter Twenty-Three

With the business shut down, Betsy and I faced two challenges. The first was that PayPal was holding almost one hundred thousand dollars that we might never see. I would have been fine with that had Betsy not jumped so quickly to invest all but the equivalent of two months' food and rent money that we did manage to have released into a one-year, locked-in investment.

And, because I'd felt rich for a couple of weeks and started spending money again, as though I already had it, I was deeper in debt now than I had been before the business took off. I'd bought myself a top-of-the-line, 15-inch MacBook and Sennheiser headphones so I could watch psychic development and education videos in my meditation room. Then I spent over fifteen hundred dollars on a cobalt blue KitchenAid just like Julia Child used. I also bought every single attachment available since I'd given up on getting these as wedding gifts. And, even though I was barely leaving the house, I bought an entirely new wardrobe and bedding made from sustainable fabrics that were sewn in fair-wage worker co-ops since I couldn't feel One with the Universe wearing petroleum-based yoga pants sewn by Bangladeshi children living slave-like existences.

Of course, I'd bought everything online and used my credit card, which I now had no way to pay back. I could hear my mother's disdain, "If you've got so much money you feel you need to give it away to the credit card companies then you should be tithing to the church." This was one area where I had to agree with dear, old mom.

But I was trying not to let my money troubles bring me down. I had to believe that PayPal would eventually release the payments. I had to keep faith that the work I'd done was having an impact and that our clients would all be happy with the results. Betsy, on the other hand, was not so positive. She was driving me nuts which was the second challenge we faced in the days after she shut down the business and furloughed us. With nothing to do, we were getting on each other's nerves so I was either staying in my room or going for solo walks.

Since Betsy didn't want to talk about Mother Teresa's business at all, I took it upon myself to send an email to each one of my clients, to ask them if they'd had a change in the area of their life they'd written to us about. From the first clients, I asked them to be specific so I could gauge whether I might have been responsible. I'd decided that if there were situations that I wasn't confident I'd helped with, I'd refund their money, without them asking and without getting Betsy's approval. I hadn't figured out how I'd do that since Betsy had the PayPal password, but I knew I'd figure it out when I needed to.

I snuck the orange pleather diary into my room while

Betsy slept. I didn't actually expect her to notice it missing from the pile of papers and books on the corner table in the living room, but I still wanted to be discreet so she wouldn't jump down my throat about interfering in her side of the business.

I started with Isabelle and her ass-slap-happy husband Ian. My file said I'd suggested she join him and his buddies in the celebratory spanking.

I wrote, "Dear Isabelle, I hope this message finds you and Ian happy and well. I'm writing to follow-up and see if the advice I provided for your challenge has resulted in any positive change. Please let me know if your problem persists and I will try another approach. In love and light, Mother Teresa."

Next was Louise, who's angry, mooch-of-a-boyfriend Luke was yelling at her kids and not helping pay bills. Of all our clients I most hoped my powers had worked to help her.

I wrote, "Dearest Louise, I hope you and your children are doing well and are excited about the winter holidays. I know it hasn't been a month yet since you wrote, but I was wondering if you'd seen a change in Luke. Please let me know. And, if there's been no improvement, I'd like to do two things for you: first, try another approach with your permission, and, refund your money. With warm wishes for a very happy new year, Mother Teresa."

I wrote close to fifty messages between midnight and 3:00 AM. And before I had to close my laptop and my eyes, I'd received one reply, from the Wrates in England.

"Dear Mother Teresa, You are a true Godsend. Your advice for our son, Isaac, to apply at the National Gallery didn't make a lick of sense when I saw it. Nonetheless, I encouraged him to check it out. It's only twenty minutes on the Tube. Well, wouldn't you know, their education outreach person left without notice and they were absolutely tickled with Isaac's experience having organized dozens of high school visits to his college when he was studying in the co-op program. He and Concepción moved out two days ago, into their own flat, and we couldn't be happier. Bless you, Mother Teresa."

"Yes!" I said out loud. I finally had proof, concrete evidence that I was actually connecting to these people. "Yes!" I said again. I was suddenly wide-awake. I wanted to celebrate. I wanted to wake Betsy. I jumped from bed and whooshed my door open, eager to burst into her room with the good news. But I stopped, hearing voices outside our apartment in the hallway. It was unusual to hear voices, even during the day, since there were only two suites on our side of the fire door.

I walked to the door and put my ear against it, to see if I could hear what was being said. It would have been unusual for old Mr. Grantham to have visitors coming or going at 3:00 in the morning. And then it occurred to me that perhaps he was sick and had called an ambulance. I wondered if there was anything I could do to help.

I put on my bathrobe and opened the door. The two people outside were not ambulance attendants—they were huge men dressed in black leather jackets and combat boots. Both had shaved heads and ugly faces. As quick as I could, I pushed the door closed again. But not fast enough. A boot blocked it. I yelled, "Get out!" and pushed as hard as I could but even with adrenalin pumping through my hundred-and-thirty pounds, I was no match and within seconds the two men were filling my small hallway.

"Is your name Mother Teresa?" the larger man asked with contempt. I'm not sure if it was my heightened intuitive sense or my spirit guide's guidance, but I knew better than to say yes.

The man pushed his way into the front room, giving me no choice but to step backward, bumping in to Betsy who had silently joined me. I looked at her and saw in her eyes the fear I felt in my own gut.

The smaller of the two men, who was at least six-foot-two and two-hundred pounds of muscle, spoke, "Which one of you is Mother Teresa?"

Betsy stepped forward. "I think you have the wrong apartment. In fact, check your GPS. This is Vancouver. Mother Teresa was living in Calcutta last time I checked," she said with a confidence that made me do a double-take.

"Don't be a smart-ass," the big guy said. "One of you two bitches is Mother Teresa. Which one?"

"Honestly, I have no idea what you're talking about," Betsy said. "And, if you don't leave immediately, I'm calling the police." She elbowed me hard enough to make me jump back and bump my bedroom door. I took the hint—intuition, guidance, fear?—and continued my backward movement into my room, locking the door behind me and calling 9-1-1.

The small guy spoke again, his voice carrying through the door, "One of you killed my brother. Where I come from that don't fly."

"Oh yeah? Where is it that you come from? Surrey?" I thought I heard Betsy say. I pictured her bloody body on the floor outside my door.

"Prince George," the second man said. I heard a grunt as though someone had been punched. It didn't sound like Betsy.

"Police, ambulance or—?" the dispatcher asked.

"Police. Two guys broke into our apartment," I said.

"Are you safe?"

"I'm locked in my room but my roommate is in the living room with them." My voice sounded like a child's.

"Police are on their way. Did you see them? Can you describe them?"

"Black clothes. Big guys. Huge," I said. I heard Betsy talking but couldn't make out what she was saying. And before the police arrived, the intruders were gone.

Betsy knocked on my door to tell me it was safe to come out. I told dispatch the thugs had left and that we were fine. She told me the police would be coming anyway to check around the building and to take a report. I thanked her and hung up, turning immediately to Betsy.

"What the hell was that about? What did they say to you? How did you get them to leave?" We moved to the living room where I cautiously opened the curtains, hoping to see nothing, but expecting to see the bogeyman waiting to break in again.

"Mistaken identity," Betsy said, as though two Girl Guides had accidentally knocked on our door.

"They asked which one of us was Mother Teresa! That's not mistaken identity. How did they find us? Why do they think I killed their cousin?"

It had been months since I'd had a nervous stomach. I hadn't experienced as much as a dry heave since Father Sparrow had passed. Body back to normal, I rushed to the kitchen sink and started retching. It wasn't terrible since all I'd swallowed was yerba mate in the last six hours, but it was no cup of tea either.

As I sat down with a glass of water there was a loud knock on the door. The noise startled me and I let out a small yelp. Betsy glared at me and shook her head

"What?" I wanted to cry.

She invited the two officers in. A man and a woman. They stood in the living room with Betsy while I stayed wrapped in my quilt on the couch. I explained that I'd heard voices and opened the door.

"You bloody idiot," Betsy said.

"What? I thought they were ambulance attendants."

"Probably looking for empty apartments to break in to. It's not unusual," the female officer said.

"Probably," Betsy agreed.

"No. They wanted me. They asked if Mother Teresa lived here."

"Sorry. Mother Teresa?" The male officer tilted his ear in my direction, as though he'd misheard.

Betsy jumped in before I could answer, "Obviously mistaken identity. I mean neither of us is Mother Teresa." She laughed facing the police officers and then turned her back on them and threw me a look that told me she'd kill me if I said another word.

The female officer pointed at me, "Why would you think they were looking for you?"

I looked at Betsy, desperate to understand her anger with me. Again, she answered for me.

"Tara's had a touch of anxiety. She always takes things personally. I don't know if you can still smell the vomit. We cleaned it up right before you got here. When she gets excited she...well, she kind of loses touch with reality, I guess."

"Is this true?" the female officer lifted her nose toward

the kitchen.

I nodded. "I guess."

Before the officers left they examined our front door and suggested we replace our old doorknob lock with a dead bolt and that we install a chain as well. We thanked them and Betsy apologized for inconveniencing them in the middle of the night.

It was after 4:00 AM by the time we were alone again. She waited until she heard the elevator door close before she tore into me.

"What the fuck were you thinking?"

"What did I say?"

"Telling them that you're Mother Teresa? Are you insane?"

"What's the big deal?" I asked

Betsy threw her hands in the air. "Never mind. I'm going to bed."

She turned off the light and left me sitting alone in the darkened living room. The uncomfortable feeling and image I'd experienced the day before returned, stronger, more clear. What had been a dark, faceless figure with a powerful, negative energy was now quite clearly Betsy in my mind's eye. I made it to the sink in time.

Before I let myself fall asleep, I focused a meditation on Betsy, filling her body with white light, visualizing her bones melting into white light, her organs becoming white light, her crown chakra funnelling healing and relaxing white light from the universe. As black Betsy became white light, I fell asleep.

Chapter Twenty-Four

I didn't wake up until almost noon and before I got out of bed I did another white light meditation focused on Betsy. It seemed to be working because the first words she said to me when I joined her in the kitchen were, "I'm sorry I freaked out at you last night. I was scared. You didn't do anything wrong."

"Thanks." I sat down and she made me a cup of coffee.

"I bought some bagels and cream cheese. Want one?"

I nodded. "Please."

We sat in silence. I watched her prepare my bagel and didn't see any of the dark energy I'd seen the night before. I decided it wasn't her energy that I'd picked up; that it was from the guys who broke in.

"How do you think they figured out where we live?" I asked.

"Probably our ISP number, you know, our internet connection code that's attached to our emails."

"So you think that I killed their cousin?" I suddenly

didn't think a bagel was a good idea. The coffee was threatening to make a return appearance.

"Tara, you did not hurt anyone so don't go getting all nervous stomach on me. I can even prove it," she said, walking toward the table where she kept my client notebook.

"It's not there."

She threw me a look.

"The notebook. It's on my bedside table," I admitted.

Betsy crossed her arms in front of her chest, "What were you doing with my book?"

I decided to try to avoid a fight so I didn't challenge whose book it was. A gift from her to me. Filled with my clients.

"I was sending follow-up emails to people. You know, to see if anything had happened for them yet."

Betsy didn't answer. She stood and stared. The toaster dinged and my bagels popped up.

"I thought if I could get some positive replies we could send them to PayPal as proof that the service is working so they'd release some of our money before three weeks is up."

"And?" she came back to the kitchen and started to spread cream cheese on the bagel.

"Only one reply so far. But it was positive. Remember the lady who wanted her daughter-in-law to move out?"

"No."

"Well, I told her where her son could find work and he got a job and an apartment. Or a flat, as she called it."

"But wait. You couldn't use the adviceforjiltedlovers email since you don't have the password."

"I created loversadvice at Gmail."

"Okay, good," she said looking relieved. Then she added, "Oh, Tara that is so unprofessional." Betsy banged her fist on the kitchen table.

As she placed my bagel in front of me I remembered the Prince George guys and got up to get the notebook myself.

"I guarantee you. Not a single client from PG," Betsy said, as I flipped from page to page. She was right.

"So what were they on about, then? And wait a minute—how did you get them to leave?"

"I told them…they were mistaken," she said with a shrug.

"And they believed you?" I had a hard time believing how easy that was.

"Oh come on, look at us. You're as much of a killer as piece of french toast, running and hiding in your room. And I look about as dangerous as…your breakfast."

"I guess. But I still don't get why they'd think it was me."

"For all we know, one of those guys could have been dumped by one of your real clients. And maybe she told the guy that she'd hired you and he was saying what he did to scare you. Or maybe his cousin did die and since you were able to get his girlfriend to leave him he thinks you're the all-powerful Oz and are able to cause a car accident. Or whatever."

"It wasn't me," I said, not to convince Betsy but to reassure myself.

After eating, Betsy left to spend the afternoon with one of her psychic friends whom she hadn't seen since the business started to boom. It was nice to have the place to myself. I took my laptop to the living room and opened my new Gmail account. I had thirty messages.

Some were short, "Job well-done. Thank you."

Some provided a little more detail, "He came home and apologized. He took the new car back and even though we lost a couple thousand dollars I don't mind because he's finally agreed to talk to a credit counsellor. I can see a better future already."

More than one note made me tear up.

"My daughter's sixteenth birthday would have been last week, and, thanks to you, my husband and I were able to talk about Marie without throwing blame at the other. For the first time in almost three years he stepped into my shoes and was able to feel the depth of my pain and I stepped into his and felt the hole he carries having lost his little angel. And then we both saw her. I was able to talk to her. Marie says she's happy now that her dad and I have stopped fighting about her. Marie asked me to thank you."

And then there were two that really confused me.

They both acknowledged that Mother Teresa's advice had helped them solve their problem, but each one also mentioned another person whom I supposedly helped. At first I thought one of the clients meant that the effect of the change had implications beyond her immediate family. But that's not how it read. And the other specifically mentioned someone else who had paid the fee and gotten the results they wanted. It was a first name that wasn't on my client list. She didn't describe the results except to say, "He got what he deserved. Nothing more. Nothing less."

I didn't like the sound of that and decided to follow-up. I had to tell a small white lie and said I'd lost all my emails from a certain day and that her friend must have been on that day since I no longer had her contact information. I asked if she'd mind giving it to me. The next day I had the name and email address of the mysterious client, Samantha.

I sent Samantha a message, like the others except I didn't mention the name of the man in her life. I asked her to share what happened so I would know if my powers had helped her.

"Dear Mother Teresa, The day Bobby died was the worst and the best day of my life. He was always jealous of time I spent with my mom, but he never hit me this bad before. I wrote to you just in time. He found the laptop I used to secretly Skype with my mom since he monitored all my phone calls. He got so mad he beat me pretty good. I said I was going to the hospital but he said no, he was leaving and he took the car. So I called a taxi and went to the hospital anyway to get stitches. He went to our friend's house and got drunk and they made him sleep on the fold-out couch and in the middle of night he got up and wanted to leave and they wouldn't give him his keys so he drank more and they think he leaned over the side of the couch and pulled the lever that folds it up and it folded up with him inside it and they didn't find him until the next day and it was too late. I promise I'll send the rest of the money after Bobby's death benefit is paid. And my mom says thank you from the bottom of her heart."

Her reply sent me to the bathroom to find Betsy's prescription for Ativan—no amount of Rescue Remedy was going to cut it this time.

I couldn't process this information. I wondered if Bobby was the mysterious cousin of the men in black but I couldn't bear to write to Louise again and ask where she lived.

I had to get out of the house, out of my head. Being the second week of December, I thought that walking around downtown, with all the lights and festive decorations would help distract me so I could get some distance from this feeling that I was involved in something much bigger than I understood.

Walking by the German Christmas Market I was drawn in by the smells of Bavarian sausages and fresh waffles, by the lights on the carousel with fantastical creatures to ride, and by the sound of a jazz band playing holiday classics. I paid the entry fee, got my free hot rum toddy, and sat down to listen to the high school musicians on stage. People sat beside me and struck up friendly conversations. It was so good to be around people, interacting with them face-to-face, not third eye-to-third eye.

The combination of Ativan, rum and the energy of so many happy people allowed me to totally forget why I'd left the apartment. I was feeling relaxed. And then, out of nowhere, my heart started to pound and my breath caught in my chest. I looked through the crowd of youth on the stage and saw Glen. He was with a woman our age, holding the hand of a child about five years old. They were waiting to buy giant pretzels. I dropped my head so he wouldn't see me and then immediately thought, *No, I want him to see me. I want to talk to him.*

I stood and starting walking, not sure what I was feeling other than increasingly light-headed since I couldn't seem to catch my breath. It was as if he sensed me approaching; as soon as I was speaking-distance behind him he turned and we made eye contact.

Even though my head wasn't sure what I was going to say, my heart knew what it was going to do—I grabbed him in a bear hug. It was a repeat of our first re-meeting four months earlier except this time I didn't let go in embarrassment. I didn't care who the woman and child were, I was happy to see him and everyone was going to know it.

When he hugged me back with as much force as I was holding on to him, I couldn't contain my joy. His hair smelled fresh and his jacket smelled of wood smoke. I wanted to crawl inside his coat with him. I pulled my head back to see him, to look into his eyes. But before I could bring him into focus he took his arms from around my back, placed his hands on my cheeks and kissed me. I was home. I would have stood, holding that kiss until all Kris Kringle's wrapping paper had been torn open. But the little girl was having none of it.

"Glen!" She pulled on his coat. "Glen, who is that lady?" She tried to push between us. "Glen! Uncle Glen stop ignoring me!"

He pulled away to answer her but first gave me a short kiss. Then another. And a third. I held my hands against his soft beard and pulled him back for one more.

"This is Tara," he said, looking at the little girl. "Tara, this is my niece, Amanda."

She looked at me and squinted her eyes. "If you want, you can call me Mandy."

Mandy's mom reached out and shook my hand, offering me a smile as warm and welcoming as the hot rum toddy I'd left on the table by the concert stage.

"It's nice to see that you actually do exist. I'm Beth. Glen's cousin. Mandy, let's let them catch up. Want to ride the carousel again?"

Neither of us spoke for a minute or longer after

they walked away. I didn't want my first words to be an accusation of betrayal. I didn't want to speak in a tone that showed anger. And I didn't want to cry. I waited for him.

"I didn't want to go. Can you, will you believe me?" he said.

"I want to. But I don't understand."

"Didn't you watch the film?"

I nodded. "Twice."

He sighed and pressed his eyes closed. He looked like he was in pain when he opened them.

"Is Betsy here?" He moved his head left to right, scanning the crowd.

"No."

He turned his head and we kissed again.

"Why did you leave like that? You thought I'd kill you? I promise, I won't," I said, desperate from him to believe me.

"I know you won't. But I…" He looked defeated, his shoulders slumped forward and his eyes were sad.

"What did I do?" Anxiety gnawed at my stomach.

"Nothing, Tara. You were perfect. You are perfect."

"Then tell me why you left. It doesn't make sense." Tears were overflowing.

He kissed my cheeks and my eyelids before he pressed his lips to mine again. Glen's tears mixed with mine during our long kiss. He looked confused when he finally pulled away to speak.

"I left because I was scared. Something happened that I didn't understand but it felt real. I made a promise I have to keep." Glen struggled, clearly wanting to tell me. "Watch *The Prestige* again. I love you, Tara. Please believe me. Maybe you can figure out how to fix this."

"Is Betsy part of this? Is that what the secret's about?"

Glen's energy became sharp, focused. "Tara, you *cannot* tell Betsy you saw me. Do—"

"Why? Why can't I tell her?"

"Tara, listen to me. Watch the film. Don't tell Betsy. Know that I think about you every day. Every single day. But we can't see each other until you fix this. Nobody else can fix it. Only you."

Glen took a step backwards.

"You're not going, are you? Please, can't we have dinner? I'll come to your house. I won't tell Betsy. I promise."

He stepped back to me and we kissed one last time before he walked away, leaving me standing alone by the pretzel hut, with twisting guts and a salt-stained face.

Five minutes later as I walked toward the bus, wishing for rain to hide my tears, my phone beeped. A new text message. From Glen.

The men who came to your apartment.

I'm sorry they scared you. I sent them.

It was to give you the message to watch the film.

You hid before they could tell you.

Delete this message immediately and please don't write back.

You can't let Betsy know we've been in touch.

I love you and I know you love me. XOX

I read the message twenty times, memorizing it before I hit delete.

I sat in the bus shelter on Granville Street for an hour, thinking. Now I understood how the two thugs— *Glen's friends?* — knew where I lived and why they'd left so quickly. And nobody in Prince George had died. I felt

198

much better knowing that.

Although Bobby's death had me baffled. There was no print-out of Samantha's request. And the payment spreadsheet Betsy shared at the end of each day didn't have an extra thousand dollars floating around in it. I figured there must be a logical explanation for the mix-up. I wondered if maybe, Samantha's friend might have taken the money and arranged to shut Bobby in the couch, making it look like an accident. I considered going to the police to report the possibility of foul play in Bobby's death. Sure, he was a bad man, but I was even more convinced now than I ever had been, that people could change. Even people who did terrible things. All they needed was to have their darkness diluted by healing, white light. And, it appeared, I was able to help them do that.

Chapter Twenty-Five

Exhausted from the emotional roller coaster I'd been on, I crawled into bed with my laptop and loaded *The Prestige* on Netflix. Before I hit play, I meditated, asking for help to see what I'd missed. I also brought amethyst Bob to bed with me, in case he had anything to add.

Well, between the meditation, Bob and knowing that the message I wasn't seeing was so important that Glen had sent 'thugs' to tell me to try, try again, I saw the film with entirely new eyes. And what I saw terrified me.

All I had to do was put Betsy in the role of the magician that I'd assumed Glen meant was me. Betsy as the duplicitous, murderous and powerful magician. In the film, one magician kills his friend's wife. I'd always thought that Glen meant for me to understand that he believed I'd killed James, Scott and Bob, my previous three lovers. But what I saw now was a more literal read of the film. It was *my* friend who was responsible: it was Betsy.

But I needed proof before I could confront her. Glen

had a hypothesis. And he wasn't afraid to hide his fear of Betsy. But I couldn't easily believe that the woman who'd been my best friend for twenty years would have hurt me so badly—three times. Four, counting Glen.

I knew I couldn't walk up and say, "Hey Betsy, are you the one who dropped the rocks on Bob's head and exploded a toaster in Scott's face and pushed James off the ladder?" For that matter, I wondered if she might also be responsible for Father Sparrow's death. I needed a plan. I needed proof. And, if she had used some psychic serial killer energy to off my lovers, I needed protection, at very least for Glen but maybe for myself, too.

A sea of Rescue Remedy would neither have rescued nor remedied me; a caravan of Ativan couldn't have calmed my nerves as I fell into a restless sleep that night.

I woke the next morning to find Betsy hadn't come home. She'd texted at midnight that she was sleeping at a friend's house. I was happy to have the morning to gather my thoughts and try to gain a new perspective on what I'd figured out the night before. Or thought I'd figured out. Of course, in the light of day, and with my third dose of anti-anxiety meds bringing balance to my nerves, the conclusions I'd drawn the night before seemed impossible and utterly outrageous.

To keep my mind busy and, to try to create some much-needed holiday spirit in our apartment, I pulled out The Way to Cook, a gift from my mother on my nineteenth birthday, the year she'd prayed I'd meet my future husband. She'd inscribed it with, "Every wise woman buildeth her house: but the foolish plucketh it down with her hands. Whether therefore ye eat, or drink, or whatsoever ye do, do all to the glory of God." Despite my lack of commitment to praising the God my mother had intended when I made Julia Child's plum pudding from this, my favourite cookbook, I did have to admit that my newfound spiritual connection left me thanking something, or someone. Using my new Julia-approved mixer to make my favourite holiday dessert was a glorious experience.

And by the time Betsy came home, I'd all but forgotten the crazy thoughts I'd had about her the night before. She arrived with a huge bottle of organic apple cider and a bag of cinnamon sticks, which we put on the stove to warm up. Between the pudding baking and the cider bubbling, our house smelled like family, holidays and love.

"Did you have a good time last night," I asked after she'd oohed and ahhed about the plum pudding.

Betsy nodded tentatively. "It was nice to get out and see Liz, yeah, but I don't know. She read my Tarot and it's left me feeling…" She sighed and slumped into a kitchen chair, "…out of sorts, I guess."

"What did she say?" I stopped stirring the cider and sat down beside her.

"It's not what Liz said, Tara, it's what the cards told me," Betsy said, rolling her eyes. No matter how connected to the universe I had become, it seems I'd never learn the lingo.

"Okay, then, Little Miss Literal. What cards did you draw?"

"Tower reversed," she said.

I hoped I remembered what this meant. I tried, "Big change coming? A warning of…death?"

"That's upright. I'd have preferred that. Reversed means, basically, I've pissed off the deities or broken some karmic law. Fuck."

"Did you pull other cards to try to figure it out?" I asked.

Betsy sighed. "No. I thought, what the hell. Let's leave it at that and let me wonder what I've done to piss off the universe." She rolled her eyes at me. "Of course I drew more cards."

Some of my negative feelings from the night before were starting to surface and no matter how nice the apartment smelled it couldn't mask the ugly energy that Betsy was oozing all over the kitchen table.

"Three of swords. The fucking three of swords. In the present position. Not the future or the past. The present." Betsy looked like she was going to shoot swords from her eyes. I was a little worried to ask what the three of swords meant. I could visualize the card: three swords stabbed straight through a red heart, like a valentine's heart, with clouds and rain in the background.

"Broken heart?" I tried.

"Seriously? No. In layman's terms, it means I've got some shit-bad karma and it's telling me to look deep inside at everything I do on a daily basis and figure out how I'm causing pain to others from my actions."

That's easy, I thought, *your crankiness causes me no end of stress*. But I didn't say that. "What else did you draw?"

"Magician reversed. Like I said, I'm fucked."

"Magician?" I mumbled. The front of my brain suddenly felt cold and I had a sharp pain behind my eyes. Rubbing my temples, I asked, "What does it mean?"

Betsy shrugged. "Doesn't make sense. Hey, have you had any more replies from clients?"

"Yeah," I said, distracted by a feeling that something should be making sense. Or maybe, that I didn't want to believe something that was making sense.

"Can you forward them to me? I'll send them to PayPal and see if that speeds up releasing our money."

"Sure," I said, standing up to get my laptop.

Back in the kitchen Betsy was opening her own laptop. I walked behind her and stood at the sink. I turned on the water as if to rinse some dirty dishes but watched as she typed her password into her user profile. Her fingers moved too fast for me to figure it out but what I could tell was that she started with letters, all from the QWERTY row, and ended with two numbers, the first she typed with her right hand, the second with her left. Her fingers never crossed the middle; she never touched the 5, 6, or 7 or the T, Y or U.

"Can you check PayPal to see if they've released any of our money yet?" I asked, hoping to get a glimpse of the total to see if there appeared to be an extra couple thousand dollars more than what Betsy had last reported to me.

"No need. Checked this morning. Send me the emails and I'll forward them. See if we can get some movement."

"Betsy," I said, hesitating, trying to find the right words, "One of the clients who was happy about my work made a reference to a friend of hers who also got the results she was looking for. The weird thing is, I didn't work with her friend. And, worse, her friend's husband died."

"Oh, great," Betsy said, sounding annoyed.

"Great?"

"I was worried this might happen."

"What? I didn't do it," I said, hoping she'd believe me.

"Of course you didn't. Someone's riding our success. Claiming to be you. Taking our clients." Betsy slammed her fist on the table and swore. "And it's my fault. Shutting us down opened the door for a fake Mother Teresa to come in and fill the gap. Shit. Sorry, Tez."

That wasn't what I was expecting to hear. Not that I knew what to expect, but a Mother Teresa impostor? How dare she? I sat with my thoughts for a few minutes while I forwarded the emails Betsy wanted. I felt such relief knowing that all my worry about Betsy having gone rogue was for naught. I gave myself a psychic boot to the head for mistrusting my best friend. But, as usual, I wasn't as quick with understanding what seemed to be so obvious to Betsy.

"Why are you so sure we have a copycat?" I asked.

"Welcome to success, baby. Imitation is the highest form of flattery. Blah, blah, blah," Betsy said. "I hope this phony has as good a track record as you do. She could totally mess up your reputation if she's not getting results."

"How can we find out who it is? Can we stop her? I hate the idea that someone else is using our name to do things I'd never do." My stomach lurched at the thought.

"Forward the email from the person who isn't your client. I'll see what I can figure out. And I guess I should open us up for business again. You good with that?"

"I never wanted us to shut it down in the first place, remember?"

"Hm. Listen, I gotta go. I only came home to grab clean clothes and my laptop. Liz and I are going to try to fix my bad mojo. Not sure if I'll be home tonight."

*   *   *

The next morning I awoke to Betsy's cheers. "We got it. They released the money. Most of it, at least."

I jumped out of bed and joined her in the kitchen. "How much?"

"One. Hundred. Fifty. Eight. *Thousand* dollars."

"For real? It's ours? Nobody can take it away?" I asked, disbelieving.

"I already moved it all to four separate accounts. PayPal can't touch it now. Taxman will take a chunk, but—"

"Who cares?" I yelled. "You put some of it into my credit union account? So I can pay my Visa bill?"

"You can pay it ten times over."

"Excellent. And have you done your magic to…" I was going to ask if she'd used her technical wizardry to unblock our website but saying the word *magic* filled my head with the feeling of a swarm of bees. I sat down on the floor.

"You okay? You look like you just saw the Grim Reaper," Betsy said.

"Dizzy."

"You need food. Let's go out. We haven't been to Sophie's on Fourth Avenue in yonks."

"I don't know."

"Come on, we'll take a cab. I'll buy." Betsy grabbed my arm to pull me out of my chair.

My mind was swirling. I saw Glen and the fear he showed when he'd asked if Betsy was with me at the Christmas Market. I replayed so many snippets of conversations with Betsy, times she'd told me how this man or that deserved his fate, deserved death. She hadn't spoken like that since Glen left, since we'd started our business. Respect for my feelings, I'd thought. And then my own aha about James: *I only ever see what I want to see with lovers.* And now the terrifying realization that this might also be true for my best friend. Could she be the other Mother Teresa? Could she have been the one who was responsible for my lovers' deaths? And Father Sparrow? And now the man who suffocated in the couch?

I couldn't ask her outright. First, I knew she'd never admit it. And, if I was wrong, she'd be incredibly hurt and I'd feel terrible. So I had to find proof, one way or the other. I needed her to leave me alone with her laptop for a few hours.

Chapter Twenty-Six

I had no credible way to get out of a celebratory breakfast with Betsy. And part of me really did feel like we deserved to celebrate. We'd done good in the world, helped a lot of people and we'd made good money doing it. I was living every sane person's dream. But the niggling feeling that I wasn't seeing the whole picture kept me subdued. Thoughts of Glen and what he was suggesting churned my gut.

"What's wrong?" Betsy asked, pointing at my fork which was pushing food around my plate, not into my mouth.

"I'm feeling a bit out of sorts."

"You look worried. What's bugging you?"

"Were you and Liz able to figure out why your card reading was so negative?" I asked, hoping to slide sideways into getting some information that might help me understand if Betsy was a threat to Glen or anyone else.

"You're worried about me?" She looked sincerely touched and put her hand on mine, gave it a little squeeze. I had to resist the urge to pull away. I smiled and nodded.

"Liz thinks that...how can I say this? She thinks I pulled the ominous cards because I'm not living with integrity. Basically."

Because you're using the same powers I have for evil, to kill people. Of course I couldn't say that. "What are you doing?" is what I asked.

"It's what I'm *not* doing," she said.

"Which is?"

Now Betsy was moving her hash browns around her plate, staring at them like she was trying to find the answer to my question in the pattern.

"You know I love you," she said, looking at her potatoes.

I laughed and stabbed at my eggs benny. "And you know I love you, too."

"Tara, I'm serious," she said, getting emotional.

"Sorry. But that's not news. You're my only family. Why in the world does Liz think that karma's going to get you because of me somehow?"

Betsy shook her head, "I haven't been honest with you."

The few bites of eggs I'd eaten started to hatch. I felt the baby chickens coming to life deep in my belly as I pictured Betsy as a murderous magician. All I could manage to say was, "Why?"

"Why? Because I was worried that if I told you, you'd be scared. That you'd push me away."

I couldn't breathe. I pushed myself back in my chair and faced the ceiling to create a straighter path for the air to push into my lungs. I saw the faces of my three dead lovers and then Glen. Beautiful, big-hearted Glen. I inhaled to speak but my body demanded more oxygen so I couldn't get the words out before Betsy.

"I love you, Tez. I'm *in love* with you. I don't just want to be your best friend and your roommate. I want…more."

Not what I expected to hear.

I felt relief for about a second and then my body filled with adrenalin. I was in full-on fight or flight mode. I did not want to hear what Betsy had said. She was right, I was scared. And yes, I was going to push her away. How could I not? She was my sister. And we'd talked about this. Maybe not in a couple of years, but we had the difficult discussion about her confused love for me and she convinced me she'd get over it. I honestly believed she had.

Those thoughts mixed with the ones I'd been having about her being responsible for all my lovers' deaths and I couldn't breathe.

"I…don't…" I stood up and grabbed my coat. I wasn't sure where I was going but I needed to think about this, not talk about it.

I stepped out onto the street and looked up and down Fourth Avenue. A bus was coming, heading in the opposite direction of home. I got on it and rode to the end of the line, UBC campus.

Autopilot navigated me to the library. I found a seat in a quiet corner and sent a text to Glen. I didn't set my hopes on expecting a reply but within minutes my phone pinged.

I called him immediately and whispered what had happened.

"I need some time to think. I still don't know if she's responsible for that guy's death. My gut says she is responsible for Bob and the others. She tried to kill you, didn't she? That's what you couldn't tell me. I can't go home. Can I please stay with you?"

Glen was silent for several seconds. Not a good sign. He didn't want me. I was trouble.

"I'm sorry," I said. "Of course you don't want me to stay with you. I'll find somewhere else. I'm—"

"No. It would be crazy to stay at my place. That'll be the first place she looks for you. And I don't trust her. Tara, I'm afraid of her."

"I'm sorry. I shouldn't have called."

"I'm glad you called. Tell me something—have you actually been able to help women the way your Mother Teresa website says you can?"

"Yes."

"You have confidence in yourself? In your...powers? Whatever it is that you and Betsy seem to have going on?"

"Yes."

"I want to help you. But we can't stay at my place. We'll have to go away..." His voice trailed off. The sound of waves crashing inside my head filled the silence.

"I have a job in Sacramento in four days. Come with me," he said.

I was overcome with relief and a sob escaped, too loud. Several people turned to 'shush' me.

I whispered, "Can we leave tonight? Can you change your flight?"

Again, silence. "I think we should drive. It'll be harder for her to find you, if she decides to come looking."

I slumped forward in my chair. "She doesn't have to know where I am to hurt me."

"She's not going to hurt you, Tara. At least, not

physically. Me, on the other hand…She was quite clear that if I stayed with you we'd be together until death did us part. And then it felt like she reached inside my chest. The pain was unbearable. She told me that I would die of a broken heart if I got in touch with you again. I don't understand it but, I have no doubt she's capable of fulfilling her threat."

Then why are you risking it now? She can still do it. I'm sure she's why Bob and the others died.

"No," I said, "I can't go with you. I shouldn't have even called you. It was selfish. I'm so sorry."

"I'll be fine. I have to admit I'm still having a hard time believing she has the power to hurt people, but if she does, I know you'll be able to protect me," he said.

The weight of his faith in me felt like being buried under the entire collection of spiritual books in the library.

"Go home. Pack light. We'll buy whatever you need. Don't forget your passport," he said.

"Where should I meet you?"

Glen was silent for several seconds then said, "If she's not home I'll pick you up at your place. Otherwise, text me where you are and I'll be there."

I felt like my bones were dissolving, and not into healing white light, but into overcooked spaghetti.

It was mid-afternoon when I got home to an empty apartment. Glen was going to pick me up at 5:00. I got packed in minutes and then paced. My energy was out-of-control. My mind screamed from image to assumption, idea to conclusion, around and around and around. I was dizzy just sitting. And then I remembered Betsy's laptop. I still wanted absolute proof that she'd been responsible. Or not. But at this point it was a conviction I was expecting—

and looking for.

With my mind racing I pulled out my own laptop and started to look at my keyboard, the letters on the top row, and started to write down all the words they could spell.

Tree, trotter, rotter, typewriter, prettier, report, pepper, tripper, pewter, typo, quiet. And then I remembered she hadn't touched the letters T or Y, that I only had the letters Q, W, E, R, U, I, O, and P to work with.

As soon as I rewrote the list, the first four letters helped me see the word, 'queer.' That looked promising. I put all letters into an online Scrabble app to see what words it would give me. I knew she'd typed more than four letters so I had eight words to choose from, assuming she hadn't doubled up any letters. Of all the words only one gave me hope: 'power.'

Queer and power. Two words I could see Betsy would relate to, possibly use as a password.

Then I looked at the numbers. Far right, 8, 9 or 0. Far left, 1, 2 or 3. That was an easy one, I guessed, '83,' the year Betsy and I were born.

I took Betsy's computer to my bedroom, heart pounding so hard I could feel the rapid beat in my triceps. When her home screen asked for the password I tried 'queer83.' The password box vibrated and said 'Try again.' I typed 'power83.' Not it. 'Queer83?' No. 'Power83.' The screen went blue and Mail launched. I was in!

It took me a minute to find a folder she'd labelled 'MTA4L.' There were over six hundred messages. I grabbed a USB stick and copied the entire folder. I didn't have the stomach to look at them now for fear of being caught. I closed Mail and launched Safari, hoping she'd used the same password for the PayPal account.

Even better, the PayPal home screen automatically populated with her email address and password. All I had to do was click 'Log In.'

When I saw the pending payment balance my vision blurred. My head felt like it had suddenly filled with helium. She'd lead me to believe, through her daily reports and how much she told me she'd already transferred out, that we had about fifty thousand dollars more being held. There was one-hundred-sixty-six thousand dollars still pending. That was way more than the money I'd brought in. And it felt like proof that she'd been taking clients as well. I wanted to see who these people were but I didn't have the clarity to figure out how to do that with my hands shaking and my head buzzing.

I closed the window and then typed PayPal into the navigation bar again. Betsy had used lovers@ adviceforjiltedovers.com as the log-in email. Easy to remember. I cleared the password field and typed 'Power83.' I was in. I logged out, shut off her computer and put it back where I'd found it. I could access the PayPal account from my own laptop anytime I wanted to now.

I lay down on my bed certain I was going to have a heart attack. After ten minutes I decided that I didn't want to face Betsy so I called Glen to ask him to meet me at the last station on the SkyTrain Expo Line, figuring it was as far south as the train goes and south was where we were heading. But when I spoke, I didn't say, "Meet me at the train station," I said, "Meet me at the church." I was as surprised as he was.

The walk took under ten minutes so I sat and waited. For two hours.

Although the sanctuary was dark and cold, it was oddly comforting, as unlike my last experience as possible. I knelt, for the first time in a decade, and said a small prayer of gratitude. In the time I sat I had an epiphany and made peace with both my mother and Father Sparrow. And they, I could feel, saw the truth in my unfortunate experience, forgiving both me and themselves for the hurtful words and thoughts that resulted.

When the warden came out to lock up the church I stood and gave her my condolences. She accepted with a warm smile.

"May I ask you about Father Sparrow's passing?"

"What about it?"

"The newspaper said he died of natural causes. Was he sick?" I asked.

She took a moment before she answered. "His passing was unexpected. But, I believe Father Sparrow experienced a natural passing, from this life to join our heavenly father. His body is no longer with us but his soul remains strong in our congregation."

"Do you think that we have the power to change lives with our thoughts?"

"Of course. Our thoughts create feelings within us. Our feelings become emotions. Our emotions dictate how we act, how we behave. And how we behave has a direct impact on everyone around us."

I felt like she was speaking to me the way she'd talk to a Sunday school class, not speaking down to the children but offering them a tool to better understand life.

"Can I ask you one more question?"

She smiled but started to walk toward the door, a sign that she was ready to lock-up and go home.

"Do you believe that people like you or I can have direct communication with God or some other power in the universe?"

"The power of God lives in every single one of us but it's easier to believe you're a victim than it is to look the God that lives within you in the eye and see how powerful you really are."

"Have you?" I asked as I stepped out on to the concrete landing outside the church.

She patted my arm and said, "Trust your heart. And keep faith." She closed the heavy oak door; the sound of the bolt lock was like an exclamation point to her final words. When I turned to face the street, Glen was waiting.

Chapter Twenty-Seven

After catching up with Glen for an hour or so, I decided it was important to create white light protection around us. Glen surprised me, not only with his acceptance of my suggestion, but with his knowledge of how to create a white light field.

"After the night that Betsy attacked me, I researched whether it was possible for her to do what she threatened. Obviously I'd felt it, but I wanted proof that I wasn't just imagining it. I find it truly hard to believe but…" Glen paused and shook his head.

After a long pause I said, "It is possible. I mean, if I have the ability to help create positive change in people's lives…" Now it was my turn to let the silence finish my sentence for me.

"I started to take chakra meditation classes," Glen said. "But I never felt like I was actually doing anything. It was relaxing, though." He turned and smiled. "The instructor talked about how to fill yourself with white light and then how to direct white light outward to others. I have no idea if I was doing anything, but twice a week I focused on hoping that it was true while I thought about you."

"You were doing the exact same thing I was?"

Glen shrugged.

A wave of guilt washed through me. I hadn't spent any time at all sending healing energy to Glen. I'd been so focused on helping women, our clients, I'd ignored the most important people in my life.

"Thank you," I choked out, trying to hold back tears. No use. They came anyway.

"What now?" he asked laughing.

"I don't think I could have done this without you. I thought Betsy and the amethyst Bob gave me were guiding me. But…it was you."

"Not at all. I think you were guiding yourself. But you didn't trust that you had it in you. All I was doing was thinking about you and sending you loving energy. Maybe it helped. I'd like to think it did, but whatever you were doing you were doing with your own power. Your own white light energy or whatever the hell it is! Your own love."

In that moment I had an epiphany. "We can change Betsy. We can do the same for her as you've been doing for me and I've been doing for the Mother Teresa clients."

Glen nodded. "I think we should try. And, I think we should also keep a lot of energy focused around us because if she gets mad…"

I undid my seatbelt, leaned across the stick shift, and kissed him. Although he accepted my kiss, he cut it short.

"I don't think white light will protect us from a seat belt infraction."

We drove as far as Olympia, a little south of Seattle, before deciding to stop for the night. It was almost 11:00

and I'd been in and out of sleep for the last two hours. Glen woke me as we pulled off the freeway to a Motel 8.

"It's not The Ritz, but I hope it'll do," he said.

"I'd be happy to sleep in the car, as long as it's with you."

Glen checked us in since we'd decided, at least until we were in Sacramento, that I wouldn't use either my credit card or bank card, to put some distance between us and Betsy. Of course, we knew she didn't need to know exactly where we were, but I feared as much that she'd show up in person as I did her energetic presence. More perhaps, since with Glen's and my combined white light energy I knew we could kick her dark power ass.

Although I'd expected Betsy's presence would be a constant travelling companion, as soon as Glen and I were in bed there was only one thing on my mind. With three more days before he had to be in Sacramento, he wasn't worried about waking up early so we stayed up until 2:00. I couldn't get enough skin contact. I wanted him wrapped around me, behind me, in front of me. Wherever he wasn't touching me, my body craved him. I couldn't lie still. I kissed every inch of him, spending extra time on his lips, his neck, the palms of his hands, and, his root chakra.

When his mouth was exploring me, melting into white light took on new meaning. My body and soul became one with Glen's. And the body and soul of the entire universe. With Glen, I knew that God existed and that heaven was a fifty-nine dollar hotel room with a scratchy polyester blanket and a dripping bathroom tap.

The next morning I awoke more relaxed than I'd felt in months. We made love, showered and left the hotel at check-out time.

"I don't ever want to lose this feeling," I said as we ate a decadent five dollar breakfast in a local greasy spoon.

"Is the toast giving you gas?"

"As much as I love her, or loved her, if I never see Betsy again I don't think I'd be sad." As soon as the words left my mouth I knew they were a lie.

"Can we make a deal?" Glen asked.

I nodded.

"Let's not talk about Betsy, say her name, refer to her, anything, until we get to Sacramento. Then we can try to figure out what we're going to do. But until then..."

"Okay. But it's going to be hard to push her out of my mind entirely."

"Impossible," Glen agreed. "So how about whenever you think of her you do whatever it is you do for your clients but, you do it for her?"

That felt like a good idea. "Deal."

*   *   *

We shared the driving for the next three days. We stopped for some great meals and ate some classic American, road trip fare: chicken fried steak with gravy and biscuits at Applebee's, seafood feast at Red Lobster, and buttermilk pancakes with blueberries at IHOP for Glen. I opted for a wheat-free omelette with bacon.

Arriving in Sacramento after dinner on the fifteenth, we got a small suite in a hotel a few miles from Glen's client's home. It had three rooms: a bedroom with a king-size bed, a bathroom with a shower and a separate soaker tub, and a combo living room-kitchen with the smallest fridge and stove I'd ever seen. Big windows overlooked a pool that had been shut down for the winter.

Glen expected his job would take a week, so we settled in with our sparse belongings.

Before he left the next morning to see his client, I turned on my cell phone so that we could stay in touch. I'd intentionally left it off until then, not wanting to deal with calls and texts from Betsy during Glen's and my 'no talk of Betsy' time-out. My phone pinged a couple dozen times, once for each phone message, text and email. Not all were from Betsy but many were. I braced myself but waited for Glen to leave before I dove headfirst into the tsunami.

Her first messages were apologetic. By the second day she was concerned about where I was. By day three she was angry.

Thanks for letting me know you were going away for a couple of days but I wish you'd stayed to talk to me. I'm so sorry. I never should have told you. I understand you're freaked out but you don't have to be. Nothing has to change between us.

Then,

Tez, please come home. I need to talk to you. I realized that what I did to you is what every one of my lovers has done to me. Don't run away. I know exactly what you're feeling.

And,

Tara, you have to call me. Let me know you're okay. I'm worried about you.

End of Day Two on the road,

Where are you? Call me. Let me know you're alive. Text me. We don't even need to talk.

The next morning,

Tara, you haven't used your cards in three days and you haven't answered your phone. If you're not dead, I'm going to kill you.

Her last text,

It's been four days and not a fucking word from you? I'm calling the police and reporting you as a missing person.

I was wrought with guilt. I should have stayed to talk to her. But I also wondered how she knew I hadn't used my cards and remembered I'd given her my online banking password when we were buying the magazine ads, so she could transfer money from my account to hers.

Until I knew exactly what she'd done with her Mother Teresa clients I didn't want to talk to her. I replied to her last text.

I'm fine. I'm sorry I bolted. I just need to think. I'll be home in a few days.

To help get my mind off of Betsy, I walked to the nearest mall, about twenty minutes away. Being ten days before Christmas, I splurged and bought some lights to string over the gas fireplace and a five-foot, pre-decorated, live tree. I hadn't celebrated Christmas since Scott died and was eager to create some new traditions with Glen. Waking up on Christmas morning in a hotel room in Cali definitely qualified as new for both of us.

Back at the hotel, I tossed a load of new clothes in the machine in the laundry room, put up the Christmas decorations and mixed up a batch of ginger cookie dough. I had to bake them six at a time in the miniature oven. The room filled with the smell of the holidays and I decided I was ready to face the reality of what Betsy had been up to during the hours I'd been soaking in my cinnamon-scented sanctuary.

Glen and I had talked the night before about whether or not I should jump down Betsy's rabbit hole to see what she had hidden. He was of the mind that since I had no involvement in her actions, that I shouldn't feel the need to take any responsibility, either. Although I finally agreed that I wasn't responsible for what she'd already done, he had to agree with me that if I, or we, had the opportunity to change her behaviour once we knew what she'd been doing, then it was our responsibility to do so.

I opened my laptop, plugged in the USB drive that held the Mother Teresa emails and transferred the folder to my own Mail program. I stared at the folder for several minutes; I was in no rush to open the first email. The oven timer dinged. I put the cookies on a cooling rack, dropped six more blobs of dough on the cookie sheet and set the timer for eight minutes.

Then I put the kettle on and stared at it until the timer dinged again, proving to myself that a watched pot does boil. Cookies out. Cookie dough in. Timer on. Tea in mug. I sat down at my laptop. Rather than reading the emails by date order I sorted them by name so all of Betsy's messages sat together. Scrolling through the first dozen, two things were clear: one, she had been providing a Mother Teresa service of her own and two, it was impossible to know if the service she'd provided intentionally brought harm to any person. A few of the clients did use language like, 'He got what was coming,' but that certainly wasn't proof that the man was dead. I didn't feel any closer to knowing the truth.

Ding. I took out the next batch of cookies and put the next half-dozen into the oven. I felt I had no choice but to call Betsy and ask her directly if the work she'd done had intentionally hurt anyone.

Chapter Twenty-Eight

I lay down on the bed and dialed Betsy. The phone only rang once before she picked up.

"You are such a bitch," she said with as much conviction as she'd have saying the Lord's prayer.

"Sorry." I replied instinctively.

"Do you know how worried I was? And what the fuck are you doing in Sacramento?"

"I'm here with Glen." I regretted the words as soon as they were out.

Silence.

"Are you still there?" I asked.

"Why are you calling? To rub it in my face?"

"No. I didn't mean…I'm sorry."

"How long have you been sneaking around with Glen?"

"I haven't been. I called him for the first time when I left Sophie's. I couldn't go home and didn't know who else to call," I said, telling a ninety percent truth.

"He dumped you. Why did you think he'd want to see you after so many months?"

"I was desperate. And hopeful. Turns out...he felt bad about leaving the way he did. And he was coming to California for work and I asked if I could go with him."

"So you jumped back in bed with Glen. You trust him more than you trust me?"

"I didn't realize it was a competition, Betsy. And actually, at this moment, I do trust him more."

"He walked out, no explanation and I've stuck by you for twenty years. And it is a competition because you picked Glen over me." I couldn't tell if her voice was shaking from anger or sadness.

"Betsy, don't. I'm sorry. I was wrong to run away. But like you said, you know how that fear feeling takes over and makes you bolt—"

"Yeah, but I always had the courtesy to at least say good-bye. And anyway, it is different. You and I are forever. Those guys...they never were."

A chill ran down my spine at the way Betsy said she and I were forever friends.

"So? You said you're sorry. Is that all?" she asked.

My turn to be silent. I'd lost the perfect words I'd prepared in my mind before I'd dialled.

"I need you to tell me the truth about something."

"Tried that. Didn't work out too well." Definitely more grief than anger now. The knots in my stomach pulled tighter.

"Why did you do your own Mother Teresa work on the side?"

Silence. Since it was taking her so long to answer, I figured she was trying to figure out how I knew.

225

She spoke slowly. "At first, I wasn't sure you could actually do what we said we were offering. And then when we got so busy, I was trying to keep the clients happy."

"But, how did you know you could do the work? Why didn't you tell me? And for that matter, why didn't you just give me more clients?"

"Tara, you were freaking out having to do six a day. We were getting twice that number. I had to step in and see if I had the same power. And, it turns out, I do."

"Same as me?" Disbelief filled my body, put my spidey-senses on high alert.

"Same," she said.

"You send white light and healing energy?" I was daring her to agree with me.

"In my own way, but yeah," Betsy said.

"Betsy, tell me, did you intentionally hurt any of your client's husbands or lovers or whatever?"

"No, of course not. We'd agreed, remember?"

"Yeah, I remember you fought against me," I challenged.

"But you convinced me and we agreed—nobody deserved to die."

"So, help me understand how Scott, Bob and James all died, Betsy. You were convinced I did it. But I know I didn't. How did they die?" I wanted her to admit that she'd been responsible and that she was wrong and that she was sorry.

"I don't know what to tell you. You'll never believe you had anything to do with those deaths but I know in my heart that you did. You just didn't understand your power."

Wrong answer. Very wrong answer.

Betsy continued, "Are you coming home soon? I started

226

the business again but I can't do it without you. There are certain clients that need your kind of attention, not mine. And I need you, Tara. I miss you."

Before I could answer, a piercing beeping filled the air. I jumped up from the bed and ran to the living room, realizing before I got there that I'd forgotten the cookies. Dark smoke filled the air. I opened the windows and the door to the suite, hoping to push the smoke outside but it got sucked into the hallway. Another smoke alarm started to sound and there was no way for me to turn them off. I hung up on Betsy without thinking and stood waving a tea towel to try to push the smoke outside.

Two men arrived with fire extinguishers, which they thankfully did not need to use. In the commotion I didn't hear my phone ring. After they'd made sure there was no fire, one radioed to have the alarms silenced. I had never been more embarrassed. The two men were gracious, assuring me I wasn't the first guest to burn a tray of cookies in the hotel.

My phone showed I'd missed a call from an unknown caller. I assumed it was Betsy and that the American phone provider couldn't identify her number. I ignored her message and dialled Glen. He didn't answer.

I spent the afternoon creating a spreadsheet of all of Betsy's clients—their names, their significant others' names, where they lived, how much they'd paid, if they'd paid the second thousand with a note saying the service had been received.

There were eighty-two clients. I decided to see if I could find out anything more specific about what had happened to any of these men. I couldn't email the clients and ask since it wouldn't make sense for me not to have understood our existing email communication so I started looking for news online. I figured that if I didn't find anything—an obituary, a news story about an accident—that would be good news. The media certainly wasn't covering any of my clients' stories.

Son finds job! Moves out at age thirty!

Husband stops drinking. Commits to counselling!

Surprised I hadn't heard from Glen by five, I called him again. The beeping dial tone reminded me I had a new message. I left a second message for Glen and then listened to the one that had been left for me hours earlier.

"Hello, Tara. My name is Constable Juan Leonardo, Canine Unit. Your husband has been in an accident. He'll be fine but he's at Mercy General Hospital. You can reach me before 4:00 PM at 916-264-5471."

I grabbed a cab to Mercy General. I tried to stay focused on sending healing white light to Glen but my mind kept taking me terrible places and it was hard to do deep, meditation breathing when I was holding my breath, trying not to burst into hysterics.

The cabbie was an angel. He spoke to me the whole ride over, saying exactly the right things. And, he didn't dump me off at the hospital, he came in to help me get to the right desk to find Glen.

The admissions lady wasn't so helpful.

"Are you family?" she asked.

"No. Yes, I mean, yes." I said.

"No? Yes? What's your relationship to Mr. Harris?"

"He's my husband."

Raised eyebrows from the clerk.

"We just got married. I keep forgetting."

She was skeptical but pointed down a hallway and told

me a room number. I ran.

Glen was sitting in a chair wearing a hospital gown. Three other people lay in beds in the same room. His arm was in a cast but he looked fine otherwise. When he saw me he stood up, and then immediately sat down.

"Dizzy," he said.

I dropped to a squat and hugged him.

"What happened? How are you?"

"I'm fine. Just a broken wrist. Nothing major. Oh, and seems I have a bit of a concussion, too, which is why they've kept me."

I held his face in my hands and kissed him gently. "What happened?"

"Damnedest thing. I was standing on the edge of a hole the guys had dug for a new waterfall feature and the ground gave out from under me. I fell a good ten feet onto my back. Hit my head and…" He held up his plastered arm.

"I tried calling," I said.

"Busted my phone. It was in my back pocket. Did you get a message from a cop?"

"I did. But not until just now. I didn't hear the phone ring. I am so, so sorry."

Glen smiled and tilted my face up to his. "It's all good. I didn't want you to worry. They should let me go home now that you're here. You're going to have to be a bit of nurse for the next few days, to make sure I don't have any concussion side effects like slurred speech."

"Oh, Glen."

He laughed. "I'm fine. It was a one-in-a-million freak accident."

Freak accident. His words hit me like a boulder. I fell

backwards from squatting onto my back and lay on the floor for a few seconds, reeling.

"Oh my, God. It was her." I pushed myself onto my knees and put my hands on Glen's legs to balance myself. "This happened after I talked to Betsy. She tried to kill you." Acid pushed up my throat. I gasped it back down as Glen rubbed my back.

I thought he'd be mad. He had every right to be. I'd almost had him killed. It was my fault. I sat back on the floor, pulling away from Glen's touch. Terrified that Betsy would know I was here now. That my coming here was putting Glen at risk again.

"I have to go. She'll kill you if I stay. I ruined everything. I'm so sorry."

A doctor walked in as I started to bawl. She put her hand on my shoulder.

"Your husband's going to be fine. He'll need a little TLC for a few days, but nothing to worry about."

I looked up at her, knowing she was dead wrong.

"He must love you very much. Heck of a survival instinct. I can't say I've ever seen anyone walk away from being buried under four feet of rock and earth. Quite a miracle."

I looked at Glen who was shaking his head and scowling at the doctor. I could tell he wanted her to shut-up. And I wished she had since I felt like I was the one who was going to be needing a nurse to watch over me for the next few days.

Seeing my distress, the doctor graciously added a short run of anti-anxiety medication to Glen's prescriptions: one for pain management, the other to ensure the abrasions on his back didn't get infected.

Back at the hotel I told Glen everything that I'd done that day. I tried to tell him exactly what I'd told Betsy. He didn't get mad. He didn't tell me to leave.

"We knew she was going to find out sooner or later. And guess what?" Glen asked, smoothing my hair.

I looked at him through puffy, red eyes.

"We're stronger than she is. White light beats black magic," he said, doing the rock, paper, scissors hand motion.

And God bless him, Glen's reaction was not to try to get revenge or hurt Betsy but to dilute her black with our white. "What shade of grey do you think we can move her to?" he asked me

"Betsy shades of grey," I snickered. "I love you so much."

"Three days of bed rest in a private room with you as my 24-hour nurse? I'm not the least bit upset about what happened," he said, coaxing me to lie down beside him. "And, I'm not the least bit worried."

"You're crazy," I said.

"Not at all. I have the authentic Mother Teresa to protect me."

I cringed, not wanting to be associated with the Mother Teresa brand ever again. "You know, Betsy is actually closer to the original Mother Teresa than I am. She, the real one, believed that we should all share in God's suffering to make up for the sins of the world."

"Well then, I think you need a new identity."

"And what would that be?" I asked, nibbling on his neck.

"Someone who's highly respected."

"The Queen of England," I said in a high English

accent. "Or, Hilary Clinton. Michele Obama. Although I don't think any of them will be willing to share their names." I laughed.

"How about, Tara 'Psychic-with-a-Heart' Holland?"

"That sure rolls off the tongue," I said, thick with sarcasm. "And you could be Glen, the White Light Knight." I was being sincere.

Chapter Twenty-Nine

The next three days were heaven on earth. I never dressed in more than the plush hotel bathrobe, which provided all the coverage I needed or wanted. Glen, with his casted arm, didn't have anything other than t-shirts that would fit without cutting them, and, since he had to keep the wounds on his back open to the air he, too, dressed only in a robe. It felt decadent. Glen hadn't shaved his head since we'd left Vancouver. It was growing in grey, which surprised me since his beard had only specks of white mixed in with the brown.

We ordered delicious and outrageously overpriced hotel meals and had them delivered at all hours of the day and night. I asked reception if there was a Scrabble board kicking around and before we could think of five, seven-letter words that start with the letter M, there was a knock on the door. A board and a velvety red bag were placed in my hand.

It was an old board. The kind that didn't fold in half

to fit inside a box. The same version both Glen's and my grandparents had had. It had wooden letter tiles and wooden tile holders. We played our first game imagining ourselves as an old farming couple from the 1940s. We tried to keep our words to the kind that our imaginary couple would have known and used—words about the weather, crops, animal husbandry and religion. It worked for a few rounds, but when we couldn't agree if *nor'easter* (without the apostrophe) was a legitimate Scrabble play word, we had to call on some twenty-first century technology and ask a search engine on Glen's iPad.

We listened to music, sat in silent meditation together, read to each other from online newspapers and e-books. We researched how to use the healing energy of the universe to make sure Glen didn't suffer any permanent damage to his broken right arm. And when Glen took his afternoon naps, rather than snuggle up with him, I logged in to Betsy's Mother Teresa accounts, copied files, took notes and did my best to interfere with the 'advice' she was providing new clients. I prayed that Glen's belief that white light beats black magic was true because I felt like I was putting energetic band-aids on the catastrophic injuries Betsy was trying to induce.

"How many new clients today?" Glen asked, grimacing as he arched his shoulders after napping, tearing the edges of new scabs.

"Drop your robe and I'll soften up that skin." I walked to the kitchen sink to wash my hands and when I turned around to put the special antibiotic cream on Glen's back, he was facing me.

"I'd rather you soften this first, please," he said, smirking at his erection.

An hour later we were back in our robes and working on a plan to expose all of 'Mother Teresa's' un-saintly activities.

"I think we should go to the police," Glen suggested.

"And say what? My best friend is a psychic serial killer?"

Glen nodded, "Why not?"

"Um, because it sounds insane?"

"You're right. But it's not unheard of for cops to use psychics to help solve murders. All we have to do is find one who would be open to the opposite idea—that a psychic could actually commit one."

"Or a hundred," I sighed.

"Or a hundred. We just have to give them the files you've collected from Betsy's emails and let them do their research."

Something about Glen's idea didn't feel right, but I couldn't put words to it.

"Can we act that out? You know, I'll be a cop and you be me."

"Weird, but okay," Glen said. "Uh, so I'm at the police station—"

"Which one? Are we going to do this here or back in Vancouver?"

"I was thinking here. Since we're here. And since the deaths are from all over. And I bet we'll be more likely to find a cop who believes in psychics in California than in BC."

I nodded.

Glen continued. "Hello Officer." He waited and jutted his chin toward me. "Hey, if I have to act, you have to play your part, Officer Holland."

"Sorry! Hello. May I help you?"

"I was wondering if you have any officers on staff who deal with psychics."

"Good one," I said. "I didn't think of asking that."

Glen smirked. "Well, why would you, *Officer Holland*?" he said with emphasis. "You're the person answering my question."

"Ah! I'm bad at this. Um, yes. Yes, we have an officer who works with psychics. Okay. Me as Tara, now. Are we going to do some research to make sure we go to a station where there actually is someone who won't throw us out as nut bars?"

"Good point." Glen nodded. "That way we know there's an officer who will have at least a little understanding about what we're talking about."

"Yeah, maybe we make an appointment so that you or I, whichever, just have to walk in and ask for that person."

"Better. So we get that officer into a room and hand over the file with all the clients and let them do their investigation of these people. Voila!" Glen said.

Unease grabbed my gut and I grimaced.

"What?" he asked.

"No. That won't work. Or it might not work," I said. "If we hand over the files with all the clients' names and they find a bunch of dead husbands and such, they'll blame the women before they peg it on a psychic serial killer. Don't you think?"

"Maybe."

"Well that would be terrible."

Glen gave me a confused look.

"You haven't read the files as carefully as I have. There were only a couple of women who actually said they wanted their guy dead. The rest just wanted to get out of bad situations. They weren't asking for murder as the solution. But since that's what Betsy gave them—"

"They might be charged with the crime or the situation that lead to the death. Right."

"And, worse," I added, "Some of those women have got kids. Imagine your dad has just died and now your mom is being charged with his murder. Those kids would end up in the system. Or at least some of them would if their moms were found guilty. We could end up creating more Betsies."

"Very good point. Okay, scratch that idea."

"Maybe. Or maybe all we have to do is adjust it a little. What if we found a cop who was sympathetic to the whole psychic thing and rather than giving the files to them, we only gave them a list of the men's names, nothing more, and asked them to look into them? I could say I'm a psychic who saw something and I believe there's foul play, and that my psychic friend, Betsy, might be responsible."

"Could work...what's the worst case scenario?" Glen asked.

"They don't believe me and we have to find another way to stop her."

Glen grimaced. "I think the worst case scenario is that they think you're responsible."

"Why would they think that? If it was me I wouldn't come forward to tell them about something so outrageous it's practically unbelievable."

"But if they talk to Betsy you know she'll point to you. She's already convinced herself that you were the one who..." Glen shook his head but didn't finish his sentence.

"They would be idiots to contact her. I mean, you don't call up a suspect and say, 'Hey, did you kill the guy at the end of your street? You do research, right? You gather evidence before you approach the suspect. I'm not worried about that," I said. And I wasn't worried.

"Okay, so the only other worst case is that even if Betsy is eventually arrested, she can still use her powers," Glen argued.

"But on who? If she's not getting input for where to send that black energy..." I looked at Glen hoping he could finish my sentence for me.

"She'll only have me to focus on." Glen fell backward on the couch and faked dying.

"Not even a little bit funny. But you're right. We'll have to double-up our own white light work."

He sat up. "So, we have a plan?"

"I'll ask Mr. Google what detective we should talk to."

Chapter Thirty

Aside from names of officers who'd worked with psychics on reality television shows, I came up empty-handed. The 'Contact' pages of the different police stations didn't help one bit. I tried another approach: media coverage of stories that involved police, using keyword searches.

"Why is it so easy to figure out all the officers who work in the canine units, but not in their psychic-friendly unit?" I complained to Glen.

"Maybe we should start by making some calls. Want me to help?"

"I'll start with Sacramento since we're here and it would be the easiest. I don't fancy driving all the way to San Diego."

"Christmas in Disneyland? Wouldn't be so bad."

"I love your positive attitude." I kissed him then stood to get my phone.

I felt nervous dialling, like I'd drunk a whole pot of espresso. "I hope this works," I said as the phone rang.

"Sacramento Police Department. Investigations Control Desk," a man with a Spanish accent answered.

"Oh, hi. My name is Tara Holland, and I'm calling with kind of a strange request," I raised my eyebrows and shoulders, looking at Glen.

He smiled and winked. I took a deep breath and continued.

"I think I have some information that you might be interested in. About some possible homicides."

"*Some* homicides?" he asked. "How many?"

"Um, like around a hundred?"

"One hundred homicides?" his voice went up a pitch. "All in Sacramento county?"

"Oh, no, not at all. They're from all over the world. Only a few are in California, actually."

"Sorry. You're telling me you have information on homicides from all over the world?"

"It's complicated. Do you have any officers who've ever worked with a psychic before?"

"Ah...you've had visions." I could hear him exhale loudly.

"No, not exactly. But I do have information that I think you should check out."

"How many of these alleged homicides are in Sacramento county?"

"I don't know, actually. I'm not from here. But I have a list of names I could give you. Of the men and the towns they lived in."

"Men?" he sounded surprised.

"Yes, they're all men."

"No women?"

"No. It's, like I said, complicated. Do you have anyone

I could talk to? Someone who believes in psychic abilities?"

"Can I get your number and call you back? Tara Holland, right?"

I suddenly had an ominous feeling that this had been a bad idea. I wanted to hang up but figured they probably already knew my number.

"Yeah. It's 604-555-8756."

"Give me an hour or so. I'll get back to you."

"One more thing. What's your name?"

"Sanchez."

"Thanks."

The hour dragged. Glen and I tried to play Scrabble but I was distracted and the letters in my rack simply wouldn't form words. When my phone finally rang I was as high-strung as a cello.

"Hello?"

"Ms. Holland?"

"Yes."

"This is Officer Sanchez, Sacramento County Police. Would you be willing to come in to talk to Officer Boyd?"

"Of course. When?"

"She's in this afternoon doing desk work. Could you come in today?"

"Absolutely."

Sanchez gave me directions for how to get to the station from our hotel and told me to bring all the evidence I had.

"Do you only want the California cases or do you want them all?"

"Bring everything. Boyd can sort out what she wants and needs."

"Okay." I hung up.

"I guess you're going to have change out of that robe,"

Glen said, tugging on the tie and opening it. He put his hands around my waist and locked me against him with his cast against my lower spine.

"Again? Are you crazy?"

"It's been hours. And we don't have to leave for…" He looked at the time on the stove, "…at least ninety minutes."

"I have to get ready though. I want to go through the files one more time. And I have to print out my spreadsheet at the front desk. And we should both shower…"

"Fine. But you owe me one," he said with a gentle pat on my backside, pushing me toward the bathroom.

"I'm glad you're feeling back to normal." I turned and kissed him.

"Good enough that I should probably go back to the worksite tomorrow. How many days until Christmas? Four?" He dropped his robe and turned on the water.

"Four 'til Christmas Eve. So…we'll just stay here, right?"

"I was hoping," he said as we stepped into the six jets of the spa-like shower.

My 'quick rinse' took twenty minutes with all of Glen's distractions. We got all we needed together in good time and made it to the police station ten minutes early. Glen let me do the talking to the man at the information desk.

"Hi. We have an appointment to see Constable Boyd at 3:30. I'm Tara Holland."

He smiled and nodded. "You Canadian?"

"Yeah. How'd you know?"

"In California we don't have constables anymore. It's usually Canadians who call officers that."

"Good detective work," I joked.

"Some cases are easier than others. I'll get Officer Boyd for you. If you want to wait over there." He pointed to a row of hard plastic chairs.

"Thanks," Glen and I said unison.

We sat, mostly in silence, until Officer Boyd arrived. I don't know what I expected her to look like, but it wasn't the woman who introduced herself to us. She stood inches taller than Glen and probably weighed fifty pounds more. She looked more like a linebacker than a cop who had a sensitivity toward psychics.

She walked us through a metal detector then down a long corridor to an office with nothing but a table and four chairs in it.

"Interrogation room?" I joked.

She smiled. "So, I understand from Officer Sanchez that you believe you have some information about some homicides. How many was it?"

"One hundred and twelve."

She raised her eyebrows.

"*Possible* homicides," I quickly added. "Some of the guys might be okay. I don't know. I just know that something happened to them all." I spoke too quickly, showing obvious nervousness. I leaned forward and rocked a little.

Glen rubbed my back.

"And where did you get this information?"

I told her all the details of Mother Teresa's Advice for Jilted Lovers, including the fact that I also had psychic abilities.

"So, if I understand this right, you're saying that both you and your friend have this power but you're using yours like Glinda the Good Witch, while Betsy is the Wicked

Witch of the West?"

Glen's jaw tensed. "Do you believe in psychic powers, Officer Boyd?"

She pressed her lips together and shook her head. "I don't know what kind of cop you were expecting to find—"

"Like on the reality TV crime shows," I said, feeling stupid as soon as the words left me.

She nodded. "Uh-huh." And then she shook her head. "Those cops are actors. Yeah, yeah, maybe they *were* police officers or detectives at one point, but they're always retired. Do it for the money. I would, too. Police pensions suck and those shows pay well. So, show me your file."

I pulled the sheets from the envelope the hotel had given me and handed them to her.

"This is all? What about the emails you talked about?"

"I didn't bring those."

"Don't you think they'd be helpful for me?"

"I guess, probably. But, I didn't want their wives to get in trouble."

"The wives?"

I realized my mistake too late. "Sometimes. But sometimes it was a mother or a mother-in-law or a neighbour or, you know, almost anyone. Not only wives." Even without the emails I'd probably just ensured that all the wives and girlfriends would be questioned. My brain pressed against my eyes.

"And I want to be one hundred percent clear—you don't actually know what happened to any of these men?" Boyd spoke slowly. "But you suspect they, or most of them, are dead. Killed by your friend's powers?"

I nodded.

"Okay. Leave it with me. I'll do a little digging and see what comes up."

"That's all?" I asked, surprised at how short the meeting had been.

"Unless you want to give me a sample of your power. You know, tell me what I had for lunch or something?" She was smiling and her tone was joking, but her eyes were not at all friendly. I regretted having told her as much as I had.

She escorted Glen and I back to the front waiting area and said she'd be in touch. "You're going to be at the same hotel? Not going home for Christmas?"

I looked to Glen and he answered, "Not going anywhere."

"Good. I'll be in touch."

Chapter Thirty-One

We stopped at the mall on the way home from the station so Glen could buy a jacket that fit over his cast. He'd had to go without one for our trip to see Officer Boyd. Of course, she'd asked how he'd broken it. He was vague, saying it was a workplace accident. We'd decided not to mention Betsy's hate-on for my boyfriends or Glen's own ability to channel white light, at least around himself and to me.

Glen left early the next morning to finish his work project. And even though we spent thirty minutes creating a protective energy field around him before he left, my stomach was in knots and I couldn't hide my fear.

"Please be careful. Don't stand near big equipment or on the edge of cliffs."

He held me tightly and promised that he'd be fine.

"Text or call me every hour," I ordered him.

"How about you text me when you need to know I'm fine. And I promise I'll reply within five minutes. Okay?"

"I'll text you a hundred times."

"Once an hour will do," he said smiling and kissing me. "Find something to do to keep your mind off of me. Keep focused on how we're going to stop Betsy from hurting others. I. Will. Be. Fine."

"I love you," I told him.

"I know. That's why I'm not worried. I love you, too. Now, go get dressed. I don't want to be imagining you laying about naked in your robe all day. I'll get distracted and might walk into a wall or something."

Glen left and I lay back down in bed with my phone set to the loudest ring option with vibrate on, in my hand. When it rang I almost had a heart attack. I'd fallen asleep.

"What?" I pressed the phone to my face without looking at it. "Are you okay?"

"No, I'm not fucking okay."

My whole body tensed.

"You told the cops I was killing people? Fuck you, Tara."

I dry heaved.

"Yeah, you want a reason for a nervous stomach? Oh, baby you have a good one now."

"Betsy, you…I…it's not…please don't hurt Glen."

"You think you're so clever, you and Glen? I've been doing this a lot longer than you have. You have no idea what you're up against."

"Betsy, I'm sorry, but—"

"Don't give me your bullshit 'I'm sorry.' You don't finger me then say you're sorry. Fuck. I'm sorry though. Sorry I didn't kill Glen that night. Or any night after for that matter. I didn't want to see your pain again. I was so fucking wrong."

"Please. Just let us be. I'll go back to the police. I'll say I was wrong. I'll find a way."

I wanted to scream. Why had Boyd gone to Betsy? She hadn't said anything about that. It never occurred to me that she'd get in touch with Betsy before talking to me again. I expected that the cops would work with me, not against me by telling Betsy they were on to her. Idiots. Them and me. I dry heaved again, straining my throat.

"You done?" Betsy asked, sounding irritated.

"Hm."

"You want to know the truth? Do you really want me to tell you?"

"Yes," I whispered.

"Okay. You figured it out. You were right. I killed your stupid boyfriends. But don't feel too bad. I killed a few of mine, too. That's actually how I figured out I had this power. I never told a soul. Not even you. I started to get suspicious after Dan, Paul, even Josh died."

"What? No, Josh went back to the UK," I said. "You told me that."

"He did. But a week after he left, his tour bus was in a crash. He died," she said with no emotion.

"But he loved you."

"He was smothering me. They all were."

I was speechless. I pressed my eyes closed to try to stop the room from spinning.

Betsy continued, "I actually didn't mean to. I didn't know that my thoughts created actions until the toaster exploded and killed Scott."

I was having trouble controlling my breathing.

"Remember," Betsy asked, "the night he died? We'd gone out for dinner. You invited me out to tell me that you and Scott were going to get married and he was looking for work in France. Remember?"

I didn't answer but I remembered.

"I didn't want you to leave. I thought about what would make you stay. And I saw Scott's head on fire."

"Betsy!"

"Whatever. You got over him fast enough, didn't you? God damn rockhead boyfriend."

"Bob was never a threat," I said more to myself than to her.

"*Au contraire*. I'd already lost you to Bob. In the month before he died how many times did I see you? Hm? How many? Do you remember?"

"I don't know," I whispered.

"Once. One time in the whole fucking month. The day you took me hiking at The Squamish Chief. And what did you talk about incessantly? The whole fucking time we were walking?"

I could barely hear her over the sound of waves crashing in my head.

"No? No memory? I'll tell you," Betsy said. "Rocks. Rocks and Bob. The one day I get to spend with my best friend and it was all about how wonderful Bob was. You said you weren't in love, but it was so obvious you were. I could see how scared you were to lose another man you loved. So…"

"You made me believe that I killed him by putting the rock on that shelf."

"Meh. Whatever. I did it for you. For us. And this is how you repay me? You tell the cops I'm a killer? Try to get me arrested?"

"But you are," I whispered.

"Everyone dies eventually. And guess what?"

I didn't answer. I didn't want to guess. I couldn't guess. My best friend of twenty years, my sister, my only family since Mom died was the Devil and I never saw it. Nothing made sense. My entire life seemed suddenly to be a joke. Everyone was laughing at me. I was a fool.

"Still there?" she asked.

I said nothing.

"No guess? Fine. I'll tell you then. You set yourself up and saved me. I'm walking. You're busted."

"What?" She wasn't making sense.

"They may not be able to pin a single one of Mother Teresa's jobs on you, but then, they can't pin any of those on either of us. Psychics don't get charged with murder. There's no evidence. No connection—"

"There's the emails. And the money." I said this but had a terrible feeling Betsy was right.

"Who do you think is going to be investigated?"

I didn't answer.

"It's not a rhetorical question, Tara. Work with me here. Who is going to be investigated?"

"The wives," I said, barely audible.

"That's right. And the girlfriends. And guess what?"

"What?"

"You're a girlfriend who's had three lovers die. And one almost die, but for the grace of God," she said with thick sarcasm.

"But you just admitted—"

"Your word against mine? Please. Nice of you not to mention your own lovers to the officer. Gave me a very easy shiny castle. Look, I said, she's the insane one. The real killer. She rigged a toaster to explode. She loosened a shelf. She pushed a ladder over. No witnesses. How convenient. And her current lover. Look what happened to him. What? The officer asked me. Oh, they didn't tell you?"

"Why?" I interrupted. I didn't want to hear what she'd said about Glen.

"Why what?"

"Why do you hate me?" I tried to think of something I'd done, some great wrong or hurt I'd put on her.

The silence was overwhelming. Somehow it was easier to listen to her rage than to not know what she was thinking. Just like always. The worst feeling was always when Betsy held hers back.

"Betsy? What happened to us? Why is this happening? You were my soul mate— "

"Don't talk to me about soul mates!" she yelled. "I was your convenience mate. Always there to pick you up when life shat on you. You are so fucking weak. You're nothing without me. Even this new power you have you only have because of me. Because I had faith in you when you didn't have it in yourself. And how do you say thanks? You try to have me arrested. Soul mate, my ass."

As I felt myself slip into my old role, the friend who was less, the friend who could be manipulated since it was easier than arguing, a powerful energy overtook me. Glen's voice. *You created yourself. All you needed was confidence to shine. And then my own voice. Don't listen to her. She needs you to be weak so she can be strong.*

"What do you want, Betsy? Why did you call?"

"To say goodbye. You won't get email or your cell phone in prison."

"I won't? But you're the guilty one."

"And the smarter one. Don't expect Glen to be waiting for you when you get out."

The phone clicked. She hung up. I ended the call and dialed Glen.

"I'm fine," he said with a laugh.

"I'm not. Can you come back? Please. Betsy's framed me for your accident and Scott and Bob and James. I don't know what to do."

"Make yourself some tea. Stay calm. I'm coming. Be there in twenty minutes."

Chapter Thirty-Two

Sometimes I amaze myself. After I hung up with Glen I took three deep, chakra-cleansing breaths. I was actually able to calm down and focus.

Lawyer. I'll need one.

Money. To pay the lawyer. No problem. Except…what was the problem?

Dammit. Betsy had access to my account number. She could transfer out every dollar if she wanted to. I had to beat her. Move it to my credit card? But what if she had that information, too? I couldn't trust that anything of mine was secret or private.

I logged in to my online account. The money was still there. I was so focused on how I'd protect it I didn't worry that Glen might be hurt on his way home. I didn't think of Glen at all. He startled me when he rushed into the hotel room.

"Are you okay?"

"That's it! I need your credit card."

He looked at me sideways.

"Hurry. Please."

Glen pulled his wallet from his work pants and handed me his Visa card.

"No you hold it. I'm going to set your card up in my account so I can make a payment to it. I need you to read the number to me—"

"What's going on?"

"I'll tell you in a minute, just read me the number, please."

Glen stood on the other side of the coffee table as I set up his credit card account as a payee and moved all but one thousand dollars to his Visa.

"Can I talk now?" he asked, sitting down beside me.

"I had to protect the money before Betsy took it."

"Why would Betsy take it? She has way more—"

"She knows we went to the police. Boyd called her! Can you believe it? I can't believe it."

"But why give me all your money?"

"Betsy has the online log-in information to my bank account," I said, as though Glen had asked the dumbest question ever.

"So," he hesitated, "why didn't you just change your password?"

"Uh...uh? Oh, uh, because...I'm...an idiot?" I started to laugh. "I was so focused on how to get the money *out* of the account it never occurred to me to block her from getting *in*."

Glen shook his head and laughed with me. "So what's going on with Betsy? How did she frame you?" He sounded calm. His energy was calm. The effect was, calming.

I told him about our conversation. He didn't think

that her accusation would be taken seriously.

"But, on the off chance that the police are morons…" his voice trailed off.

"Lawyer?"

His eyes darted around the room but his head didn't move. It was as if he was reading words on the walls.

"What?" I asked, squeezing his triceps.

"Yeah, lawyer. But I was also thinking that you're going to have to give up all the information and emails. And not only the ones Betsy was sending, but the ones you sent to your clients as well."

"They'll see the difference right away." I was encouraged by this idea, even though it meant throwing Betsy's clients under the bus to save myself. Now I was the one reading invisible words around the room.

"You said that the emails from clients Betsy 'advised,'" Glen made air quotes, "never asked for their husbands to be hurt, right?"

I nodded.

"They'll be fine," he assured me.

"Okay. Let's print them all out then. Will you come down to the business centre with me, keep me company? It's going to take awhile."

The front desk was busy with people checking out. All the computers in the business centre were taken but that didn't interfere with our work. I plugged my laptop in to the printer with a cable I borrowed at the front desk. I was on the honour system and told to tell them how many pages I'd used once I was done.

After an hour or so, the noise in the lobby quieted and only one person remained in the room with us. Glen and I chatted quietly about the situation, using vague words in case our office mate was a nosey parker.

"That's Betsy's done. Now mine."

"Do you want a cup of tea?" Glen asked.

"Love. And a biscotti as well?"

"I think I can manage that." He kissed me and said he'd be right back.

And he did come right back. About thirty seconds later without tea or a cookie.

"What's up?" I was sitting, facing the door to the business room.

"Turn around. Back to the door," he whispered in my ear with an urgency that I knew I shouldn't question.

I sat still and silent until Glen spoke again. "Unplug your laptop— "

"But I'm not—"

"Tara, trust me. We have to finish this somewhere else. We have to go right now. Like, now!"

He grabbed the stack of papers I'd printed. I grabbed my laptop. He took my hand and walked us out the side door of the hotel, not past the front desk. My insides turned and my face got hot.

Glen looked at me and took a deep breath in and exhaled loudly. I copied him.

"Let's get a cab," he said.

"We don't have our jackets. I don't have my wallet."

"We're good. I have mine."

We walked two blocks in silence before we found a cab. I got in silently and waited for Glen to give the driver an instruction.

"Can you take us to the public library?" he asked.

"Which one?"

"The big one."

"That's a good thirty minute ride," the driver warned.

"Fine," Glenn said, handing four twenty dollar bills to the driver.

"Oh, it'll be more than that."

"That's fine. Just so you know we're not going to rip you off."

Glen squeezed my leg.

"What?" I mouthed, without saying anything.

He grimaced.

"Betsy?" I asked.

"No." He leaned over and kissed my cheek and whispered "police," into my ear.

Glen and the driver made small talk for the duration of the drive, talking about landscape architecture and water shortages. It took every ounce of energy not to hyperventilate. Even though I tried to focus on my breath, it seemed I was regularly forgetting to exhale, which was making me light-headed and tired.

When we arrived at the library, Glen paid the rest of the fare. We walked up the steps but once we reached the top Glen stopped me from opening the door. He turned back and saw that the cab had left.

"We're going to that mall," he said, pointing down the block.

I shivered. He put his arm around me.

"We'll get jackets. I've been thinking I'd like a new one, cause you know, the one I bought yesterday is so... yesterday's fashion." He smiled and squeezed my hand.

"Do you think they were there to arrest me?" I'd asked the question in my head so many times in the last half-hour I wondered if Glen had already answered.

"They have nothing to arrest you for," he said.

"Then why did you want to get out of there so fast?"

"Just being cautious. Even if they only want to ask you questions, you should be prepared. Right?"

Inside the mall, we found a store that had a copy machine with a USB port. We bought a stick drive and transferred the rest of my files then printed them out, paying a dime for each page. Glen did most of the work. I was too wobbly to stand so I sat on the floor beside him. Once we had one copy of every email, we used a normal copier and made two more copies of the full set of documents. One for the police, one for Glen and I, and the third set for the lawyer we were going to find, which was our next job.

"Can I even be arrested in California for a crime I *allegedly* committed in BC?"

"I have no idea."

"The Consulate should be able to help, right? Isn't that what they're there for?"

He nodded. "They'll have a list of lawyers, too, I suspect."

"This is all going to be much ado about nothing, right?" I asked him, expecting a smile and laugh. But Glen looked more worried than I felt, which made me feel more worried than he looked.

I spoke to the Consulate and had them email me a list of lawyers, which I forwarded to Glen. We bought new jackets and then Glen bought himself some breakfast in the food court. I opted for a light meal of chewable, natural ginger, anti-nausea pills.

Once our stomachs were sated, we walked back to the library, which is where we spent the rest of the day, reading the emails and highlighting the passages that we thought were relevant. We worked as one, with the three piles of documents in front of us on a large table, reading the same pages and watching what the other was marking so we could follow suit on the other two files. We spoke little. Stopped to pee twice. Kissed a few times. And, for the most part, I was so engaged in the task that the reason for its undertaking stayed far enough from the front of my mind that I didn't suffer from anxiety. Much.

We never spoke about what would happen if I was actually arrested. It was both obvious that we were preparing for that possible outcome and something that I wasn't going to say aloud for fear I'd make it real.

Thirty minutes after we arrived back at the hotel, when there was a knock on our door, my day of keeping it together fell entirely apart. I was taken away, sobbing uncontrollably. No handcuffs, but a firm grip on my arm.

Glen was told he could follow in his own car. I don't know if he did or not, since I didn't see him again.

Chapter Thirty-Three

I was taken to the Pre-trial Services Center in Sacramento, which was a co-ed facility with a separate sleeping building for women. The evening I arrived, the space was about two-thirds full; forty women, like me, awaiting trial dates. That seemed to be where the likeness stopped between myself and the majority of the other women. For the first time in my life, I was a minority; the rare white woman in a rock garden featuring varying shades of brown. Prison, it seemed, was prejudiced against women of privilege, which, I most obviously was. And, although my first reaction was to fear my new cell mates, I made a conscious effort to extend compassion to each and every face that scowled at me or called me Martha.

Having spent most of my waking hours over the last six months in my cozy and warm, cinnamon-scented meditation room, and the last week wrapped up in Glen's arms, the harshness of my new, temporary home was a terrible shock to the system. The first assault was textural.

Where my meditation room had been soft, with my fabric chairs and bright wool rug, my rich-coloured walls and mahogany wood door, and my hotel room had been warm with the bed and Glen in it beside me, the Pretrial Center was ice cold. Most of the walls were brick and all were painted white. There were some walls that sang; walls with a big red arrow and heavy blue words in all capital letters, like "WEIGHTS," "WORKSHOP," and "SOUTH YARD." I thought of the words I'd hung on my wall, perhaps as large as these, but painted on three canvases in calligraphy-like font, and all small letters, *sat*, *chit*, *ananda*—being, consciousness, bliss in Sanskrit.

Walking along the corridors in the main building I had a strong déjà vu. Everything felt so familiar. Turning a corner I almost stepped on a man in an orange jumpsuit. The strong smell of paint, perspiration and Pinesol grabbed hold of my nose hairs and dragged me back to 1999 and the penitentiary-like high school I'd attended.

Every door in this facility was metal and painted a dull baby blue, adorned with a metal handle, a lock, and tiny window that looked out at other blue doors. All the railings—which seemed to be everywhere—were metal as well, but painted a dirty salmon colour. The floors were polished grey concrete that attacked my spine with every step, a high contrast to the gentle give and take of my meditation rug sitting atop a sixty-year-old oak floor.

And the light. It was all fluorescent. Daylight was only to be found outside. That was probably the hardest adjustment to make, especially while walking down a thirty-foot long corridor, six feet across with nothing but white bricks to each side, grey concrete underfoot, and row upon row of glaring tube lights above. It was impossible to feel joy in this place.

Although my sleeping quarters were small, I appreciated having a bunk-mate. Belinda was thirty-two years old. This was her third time in remand; the other two visits ended in short stays at the Folsom Women's Facility. She liked it there and wasn't upset that she'd be going back.

In addition to the necessities I was allowed to bring with me, I had Bob. My lawyer successfully argued that my amethyst constituted a religious symbol, like a crucifix for a Catholic, or a crescent and star for an Islamic believer. I rarely let him out of my hand. Having Bob helped me settle into my new situation much more easily than I thought possible when I first walked the halls.

The first few days of jail life didn't look like anything I'd seen on television and for that I was grateful. I was grateful to be locked up with women. I was grateful for Bob, although I would have preferred to have Glen with me. Glen promised to visit once a week, which was all he was allowed. And, once she stopped looking at me with suspicion, after three days, I was grateful for Belinda, too.

"Can I hold your egg?" she asked one night after dinner, during our quiet time.

I hesitated. I didn't want to share Bob. I felt he was mine, nobody else's. The thought made me sit up straight on my bunk. "Huh," I said.

"Can I?" she asked again.

"Sure." I handed her the amethyst like I was giving her one of my great-grandmother's ancient glass Christmas ornaments.

"It's warm," she said smiling. "You talk to him," she said as a statement, not a question.

"I do."

"I know. Sometimes you talk out loud. It looks like you're asleep but you start talking."

"Really? Sorry. I didn't mean to disturb you. I guess I don't notice when I'm meditating. I don't know. I don't actually understand how any of this works. I kind of…" I didn't know how to finish my sentence.

"I know exactly what you mean. You start doing something and even if it doesn't make sense, at a certain point you do it because it feels like you've always done it."

"Yeah," I said smiling, "just like that."

She sat back on her bunk, staring at Bob, rolling him in her hands. "You haven't asked why I'm in here. You're the first who didn't come in and ask in the first ten minutes," she said.

"You didn't ask why I'm in," I said.

"No need. We all know what the new girls are in for."

"I guess I knew that by the way everyone looked at me funny."

"No, I think it's cool. I think what you're doing is great. I don't care if you kill men or not. As far as I'm concerned we'd all be better off without them."

"Is that what people think? That I'm in here for killing men?"

She shrugged, "Maybe."

"I didn't. I swear. And, if I did, then I deserve to be in here. But I honestly didn't. It was my best—" I stopped myself, not able to call Betsy my best friend anymore. Not even able to think of her as a friend. My mind wandered to Glen and tears rolled down my cheeks. I curled up on my bunk and closed my eyes, wishing Glen was curled in behind me.

Belinda gave me about a minute before she asked,

263

"So, do you want to know why I'm in here?"

I nodded.

"Kind of the reason I was hoping you'd use your power on my ex-boyfriend. You know, all the women in here want you to use your power to get back at their men. None of us would be here if we didn't have an asshole man pushing us."

"I...honestly...that's not what I did."

"Yeah. Whatever."

"What happened? What did he do to you?" I asked. Hoping that she'd give me something to work with that wouldn't involve axing her ex.

"You want this back?" she asked, pushing Bob forward toward me. "I was a drug mule. I got hooked up with this guy, Jack. I knew he was a dealer, but he was good to me. Never hit me or hurt me. Bought me nice things. Never talked smack about me the way some dealers talk about their girls. So, he had a mule and she got caught so he asked if I'd do it once for him. Just once."

"And you got caught for helping him once?"

"No. I carried kilos of blow across the border for two years before I got caught."

"How? Sorry. Am I being too nosy?" I asked.

"Whatever. I don't care. He'd fill two condoms and I'd shove one up my ass and the other in my twat. I carried two condoms into the states every day for almost two years."

She saw my shock.

"I was working in Blaine. I have dual citizenship. There are lots of us who live in Canada and work in Washington. We cross in the Nexus lane. I got my pass years before I met Jack so..."

"So you did it for two years? How'd they catch you?"

"I gave myself in. I got sick of it, you know? I told Jack I wanted to stop, but once he had me, he had me. You know? He'd use threats. Say if I stopped he'd turn me in on an anonymous tip. Said he'd tell my family or worse, get my little sister to work for him. Shit like that. And it worked for a long time."

"What happened to change it?"

"I don't know. I didn't plan to turn myself in that day, but when I got to customs, instead of taking the Nexus lane, I went to the normal lane. And when the Customs Officer asked if I had anything to declare, I said, "Yeah, three-hundred-and-fifty grams of cocaine. He looked at me all serious and said I shouldn't joke like that. I told him I was serious and asked if I should pull over and come in. He waved me to the parking area."

I was speechless. Heartbroken. Then outraged. "How long did your boyfriend get?"

"No time. I never turned him in. Told the cops I was doing it on my own."

"*Why?*"

"I don't want him to have any reason to bother finding me when I get out. I'd have to do the time anyway, so why make it harder on myself later? You know?"

I shook my head.

"See why I was hoping you'd use your powers to help me? I *hope* he won't try to get back at me when I get out, but, you never know, right? These guys aren't normal."

Chapter Thirty-Four

My fourth day in jail coincided with both Sunday, the day Glen could visit, and Christmas Day. Although I'd not been able to talk to him directly, my lawyer, who I did see daily, kept me up-to-date. Basically, assured me he hadn't become Betsy's next victim.

Since I'd not been in long enough for Glen to pre-register his visit, he had to take a chance with the group of first-come, first-in families who'd decided at the last-minute to visit their moms, sisters, daughters, wives, best friends. Visiting hours started at 9:00 AM and only went until 3:00 PM and since there was no way to know where he was in the line, I had no idea if I'd get to see him or not. The morning dragged. While Belinda celebrated in the dining hall with other inmates, decorating a tree and making gifts, I sat on my bunk stressing. I tried to remember the exact words I'd said to Glen about wanting this Christmas to be unlike any other and beat myself up for that request. The universe gave me exactly what I'd asked for.

At 1:12 my name was called. I ran to the visitor's area and was met by a growly guard.

"First visit?" she asked, sounding bored.

"Yes."

"There is no touching. You are allowed one kiss hello and one goodbye but no physical contact other than that."

"I can't hug him?" I asked, my chest heaving at the thought of having Glen within touching distance but out of reach.

"Well, there won't be a wall between you, so technically, you can hug him if you want to. But most women resist the urge," she said, looking at me with eyes that told me she could tell I was going to break the rule.

My breathing was fast, panicked. I knew I wouldn't be able to resist. My arms felt disembodied. They were going to reach out to him no matter what my brain told them. My whole body longed to be in Glen's arms.

"And, if I don't resist, what will happen?"

"Full body search after the visit. Including cavities."

I could tell this guard had no desire to be looking inside my cavities. Merry Christmas, have you got a gift in there? I weighed my own desire against hers and knew what I was going to do.

After the longest ten minute wait of my life, I was lead into a room with several card tables, most with two chairs, some with four. Glen was already seated. My heart exploded and I ran to him. He stood up and as I pushed around the table to throw myself into his arms I knocked over two chairs. The guard on the inside of the room appeared to be in better spirits than her colleague. She walked over to us without any rush and waited until we'd finished kissing before she placed a large orange sticker on my back.

"Once your visit is over, please report back to me. Don't leave through the regular door," she said with a sympathetic smile. "And keep your hands on top of the table for your visit, please."

"Can we hold hands?" I asked.

"Well, you're already getting the full post visitor exam so…sure. Why not. Merry Christmas."

Glen picked up my hands and placed them against his face. "Merry Christmas," he said between kisses. "How are you?"

I nodded and tears rolled down my cheeks. "I'm okay. I miss you. How are you?"

"Hanging in there. This isn't quite how I'd imagined we'd spend out first Christmas together." He smiled.

"Going to be hard to beat this one for originality, next year." I managed my first smile in five days.

Glen pushed a book and an iPod across the table. "Sorry they aren't wrapped."

"You shouldn't have. I didn't get you anything."

We sat in silence holding hands and looking into each other's eyes for minutes. It was heaven to have Glen's energy so close. I wanted to breathe him in so I could feel him deep inside me.

"So what have you been doing? Have you gone back to the job site?" I asked.

He shook his head. "I can't focus on work. They understand. I'll get back to it once you're out of here. And," he paused and pressed my hands tighter, "I'm heading back to Vancouver tomorrow—"

"You're leaving? What about…" I stopped before I finished the sentence. How could I expect Glen to give up his life while I sat in here? Of course he had to go home. His life could carry on as usual. My being in here wasn't reason enough for him to stop working.

"I'll be back next Sunday, don't worry. And I have a guaranteed visit since I'm travelling more than two-hundred-fifty miles to see you. A double-long visit, even."

"You're coming back?" The love I felt for Glen flowed down my face and dripped on the card table with a melamine top.

"I'll be back every Sunday that you're in here. That's a promise."

"The lawyer said this could take a month. Worst case scenario."

"I know. But it won't get to that. That's worst case, Tara. She hopes we'll have you before a judge in the first week of January. This holiday is pushing things back since the courts are basically closed for the next ten days. They're only seeing emergency cases." Glen picked up the iPod and put it in my hand. "You won't even miss me—"

I wiped away tears to tell him he was wrong.

"There are a few songs on here, the ones from our road trip down, but most of the tracks are yours truly, reading from this book." He pointed to the one on the table. "Just me talking to you. There are lots of guided meditations in the book and I thought it would be nice to be able to lie back and close your eyes and feel like we were doing them together."

"Do you know how much I love you right now?"

"If it's half as much as I love you, then I'm a lucky man," he said. "Oh, they wouldn't let me bring in headphones. Something about you being able to buy them from the store? So there's a hundred dollars in the book, in case there's anything else you need. I was told shower slippers are a hot commodity."

"Absolute fashion necessity to get in good with the local power brokers," I said.

More silence, soaking in the feeling of Glen's skin on mine.

"Have you gotten in touch with Betsy? Does she know I'm in here?"

Glen's chest rose and he looked down at the table.

"You haven't?" I asked.

"Oh, I have. She's absolutely unapologetic. Says this is where you're meant to be."

"You know, she may be right."

"Tara." Glen's tone had anger in it. "Don't start to believe that. You know it's not true."

"No. No, I don't mean it like that. I know I'm not guilty. But I'm meeting so many women in here who need the kind of help I can give them. It's almost like I had to come here to see what I'm actually meant to be doing with this gift."

"You are…an exceptional human."

"Let's hope so, because I really need to help Betsy more than anyone else." I felt a tinge of guilt since helping her was less about Betsy and more about keeping Glen safe and getting myself out of jail. "You're okay, right? No 'acts of God' or anything?"

He flexed his arms and hunched his shoulders like an overbuilt body-builder. "Hulk is not afraid. Hulk is strongest one there is."

"My green, white light knight." I placed my lips on the palm of his hand and breathed him in.

"Ten minutes," the guard said.

"This wasn't long enough."

"I'll be back next week. Do you want anything special to celebrate New Year's Eve? A fancy hat, maybe?"

"A fancy hat with you hidden inside so you can magically appear in my room at midnight. Hey, do you think you can get hold of a Tesla machine to transport yourself inside?"

"As appealing as it sounds to be locked up with you, I think my time would be better used trying to get you out."

"Since I'm getting the glove anyway can we please spend our last few minutes hugging?"

Glen stood up and walked over to the guard. He had a quiet conversation with her and she laughed. When he came back, he grabbed me and held me like he'd never let me go. I pressed my cheek against his chest to feel his heartbeat.

"Will you bring me a new iPod next week with the sound of your heart so I can sleep with it beating beside me?"

"I'll bring you a new iPod with something different from what you have on this one. And more of me talking to myself, pretending you're with me."

"No heartbeat?"

"I think I'll record a night of me snoring, so you don't miss me so much."

"I will never complain about your snoring ever again," I said.

"Time's up ladies and gentlemen. Merry Christmas to all and to all a good night," the guard said.

Chairs scraped. Families following the rules touched hands, but stayed on their sides of the tables. Glen and I kissed until the guard tapped me on my shoulder.

"Time for him to go, honey."

I looked into Glen's wet eyes but only saw a blur through my own. "I love you so much."

"I love you, too. I promise we'll get you out of here as fast as we can."

Chapter Thirty-Five

The post-visit, full-body cavity search wasn't nearly as bad as I'd imagined it would be. The guard was respectful and clearly didn't approach the job with the mindset that she was going to look until she found something. Thank goodness.

Aside from giving me clear directions about how to stand, bend and breathe, she didn't say much but a few times it sounded like she was going to laugh. After I'd redressed, she wished me a Merry Christmas and opened the exam room door to let me leave.

I paused and turned back. "Can I ask you something?"

She raised her eyes and nodded.

"What did Glen say that made you laugh?"

She smiled.

"He seems like a very nice man."

"The best." I agreed.

"He asked me if I'd ever done a cavity search on a Canadian inmate before and when I said I hadn't, he told me to be prepared for a lot of apologizing." The guard smirked.

"How many times did I—"

"Eleven!"

I laughed, bowed my head and said, "Sorry."

She handed me my iPod and the book Glen had given me.

"Is the shop open?" I asked.

"Not today. Ask around. Someone will lend you headphones, a nice, polite lady like you."

Before I went back to my cell I found Belinda and asked if I could borrow her headphones. No problem.

I spent the rest of the afternoon and night listening to Glen's voice, reading from the book, interjecting funny commentary. Telling me he loved me. And when I was too tired to focus on his words anymore, I played the track he'd labelled 'My heart is yours." Ninety minutes of the sound of his heartbeat. I loved him even more knowing he could read my mind. I slept better that night than I had since I'd arrived.

On Monday, Belinda dragged me away from iPod Glen to attend the career skills training class she was in. I thought it was going to be a waste of time—I knew what my career was. I was a technical writer—but I had an epiphany when the facilitator asked us each to write down one word to describe what we're good at. I didn't write, *research* or *writing*. I wrote *magic*.

When it came time to share and explain our one word, I knew exactly what I did well, "I help people find their power."

"How do you do that?" she asked.

"As a writer I explain difficult ideas in ways that

regular people can use the information to do things like…
understand how contracts work, or make sure they get the
credit card that best serves them. And then, most recently,
I was helping people see that they had answers to some
pretty hard personal challenges."

"And how did you do that?"

"I…just…meditated for them," I said, afraid that the
answer would draw a negative reaction from the facilitator
and the group.

"Will you meditate for me?" asked a young woman
with cornrows and big brown eyes.

I nodded.

"And me?" a thirty-something Hispanic woman asked.

"Sure," I said.

"Is it like praying? I can pray with you. Look. That's
what I wrote on my paper. It's what I'm good at," the
oldest woman in the class said, holding up her paper,
smiling broadly.

"I'd be honoured," I said.

"What's your name?" Brown Eyes asked.

"Tara."

"She's *my* bunkmate," Belinda said, putting her arm
around me.

For the next three days I couldn't leave my cell. There
was a line-up of women wanting to meet and meditate
with me. Belinda found a small speaker that allowed
Glen's spoken word meditation to be played for three of
us to listen to together.

Word travelled quickly and quietly about my meditation
classes, as they were being called. Everyone wanted a
chance to try it out before my trial date. Nobody believed
I was guilty anymore and they all 'knew' that once I left I

wouldn't be coming back.

Belinda took on the work of scheduling times for women to sit with me, starting with the ones who'd been in custody the longest since they had the greatest chance of leaving soonest. My lawyer said I wouldn't be out before New Year's Day but was hopeful I'd have my case seen before a judge in the first week of January.

I did the math to figure out how many women I could see a day without interfering with my own meditation. It was a rigorous schedule.

Wake up at 6:00 AM and meditate on Betsy and then Glen.

Breakfast and shower from 7:00 to 8:00.

Meditation with an inmate from 8:00 to 9:00.

Betsy and Glen time, 9:00 to 10:00.

Inmate from 10:00 to 11:00.

Mandatory group therapy time, 11:00 to noon.

Lunch and socializing, noon to 1:00.

1:00 to 2:00, Betsy and Glen time.

2:00 to 3:00, inmate meditation.

And so my day went, until lights out at 10:00 PM. And even then I didn't completely shut myself down. I slept with Glen's heartbeat, focusing on sending him protective white light until I fell asleep.

The inmates I saw on the first day—seven of them—all shared their stories of how they came to be in jail before we turned on Glen's guided meditation. As these women opened up to me, I found myself raging inside, feeling the kind of hatred I imagined Betsy must have channeled to do her style of Mother Teresa advising and it scared me. I worried that I might not be strong enough to keep myself from sending dark energy toward some of these men. It was another epiphany for me and, I hoped, helped me become more attuned to the kind of energy Betsy needed to heal her own wounds.

I found it almost impossible to sleep that night having heard so many terrible stories, felt the constricting energy of so much pain, seen the terror on the women's faces. My body was alive with frenetic, angry energy. Even Glen's voice couldn't calm me down enough to sleep well. When I awoke I knew I couldn't spend another day like that.

Chapter Thirty-Six

The women who came to see me on the second day had an entirely different kind of experience. They had a Tara 'Psychic-with-a-Heart' Holland experience. And on Day Three, with help from the guard who'd allowed Glen and I to hug, I was given a room where six of us could sit together. Since nobody was sharing stories, having us all meditate together made a lot of sense.

I brought amethyst Bob with me and encouraged everyone to spend some time holding him.

"It feels like it's vibrating," one woman said.

"And sometimes he…I mean, it, talks to me. I know it sounds weird, but I can hear the voice of the man who gave it to me."

"Is he dead?"

"He is. But he feels very alive in the amethyst. That's how I started to believe in this power. Before then…I didn't believe in anything," I admitted.

"So what do we do?" A woman in her thirties bounced

anxiously in her chair. "How do you meditate?"

I realized at that moment that my plan to ask them to sit and think about nothing was off-base. I'd forgotten how long it had taken me to be able to do more than berate myself for not emptying my mind when I first started to try meditating.

"That is a very good question. What's your name?"

"Amy."

"Excellent question, Amy."

She smiled large and grew a little in her chair.

I took in a deep breath to get centred.

"Okay, so you know I've never led a class before. You're my experimental group, so at the end of the hour you have to give me honest feedback. Deal?"

They all nodded.

"Meditating is hard. Not impossible. And probably not the hardest thing you've ever done in your life, but you may not get it right way. Be patient with yourself. Okay?"

Nods.

"First thing is to sit in the right posture. What I'd like you to do, is put your first finger against your thumb, like this." I held my hands up and showed them. "It's like making the okay hand sign. Okay?"

Many women laughed and waved their hands at me.

"Now, place your hands lightly on your knees, like this." I put my hands, palm down on my knees. I noticed two women having trouble reaching their knees. "If you're more comfortable with your hands higher up on your legs, let them fall where they feel right."

The two women nodded and relaxed their arms with their hands mid-thigh.

"Close your eyes if you're comfortable doing so. If not,

find a spot on a far wall and focus on that spot until all you see is a blur. Let your eyes relax as if you were doing a 3-D puzzle."

"I can never do those," a voice on my left said.

"Shh," from all around me.

I kept my eyes open while I spoke.

"You all know, I have a crystal, my amethyst that I use to meditate. Some of you know I call my crystal 'Bob,' after the man who gave it me. Bob was one of my lovers who died. Before I got here I never let anyone touch Bob. I was possessive of him the way many of our men have been possessive of us. Not wanting to share us with our families, or our children, our best friends, and absolutely never with male friends, no matter how innocent the friendship. But Belinda taught me to trust others with Bob."

I saw that the amethyst had moved to Amy.

"Amy, you keep Bob as long as feels right for you." She nodded and smiled at me. "And when you're done, it could be after five more seconds or five minutes, tap your neighbour to the right—sorry I don't know your name—"

"Sandra."

"Amy, you tap Sandra on her leg and pass the amethyst along. Let it go around until everyone's held it. When Bob gets back to me, I'll put him in the middle so anyone who's drawn to him can hold him again."

Belinda gave me a thumbs-up of encouragement. I mouthed, 'thank you,' to her. I closed my eyes.

"I'm going to share with you all the things I do when I'm focused on helping someone find a better place to be. It's what landed me in here with you all. This helps keep me grounded and able to both pull white light into my body and push it out to others in need of it."

I took a deep breath. I could tell many, but not all the women repeated my action.

"I want you try to empty your mind, which is not easy. It took me months before I could do it without falling asleep. But if I say these words in my mind, it keeps me focused and awake. Ready?"

Nods and few 'yeahs'."

"Breathe in clarity, breathe out peace. Say it with me if you'd like."

I repeated the phrase a dozen or more times. Small voices whispered around me.

"Okay, as best as you can, continue to follow my breathing. Slow, deep breaths. Really inhale into every part of your body. I know it sounds strange, but imagine the nice, clean air going into more than your lungs. Picture it going deep into your belly all the way down into your uterus. Imagine it as pure healing oxygen. As you breathe out, picture anything dark that lives inside you or your organs leaving with the air you exhale. Inhale pure air. It's called white light. Exhale what no longer serves you. Breathe in clarity, two. Three. Four. Five. Hold the white light inside as long as you can. Then breathe out peace, two. Three. Four. Five. Let go of anything that no longer serves you."

I breathed and counted for ten inhalations and ten exhalations, to get everyone relaxed. Hopefully receptive to the next step.

"Now I want you to repeat, either in your mind or quietly out loud, 'I love myself. I deserve unconditional love."

One snort but other voices whispering, mumbling the words.

"Don't forget to keep breathing as you repeat the words, 'I love myself. I deserve unconditional love. I love myself. I deserve unconditional love.' If you're having trouble saying these words, picture an event or an act you did that you're proud of. Something—it may have been years ago when you were a child or it may have been yesterday—anything that makes you smile on the inside. Picture yourself smiling at yourself, feeling joyous and see if that helps you say the words, 'I love myself. I deserve unconditional love.'"

I opened my eyes again. Amy was still holding Bob, rolling the amethyst back and forth between her palms, her lips moving with the mantra, tears rolling down her cheeks and neck. At that moment, for the first time, I understood the power of the universe. I knew that my gift had nothing to do with asking some spirit guide to help women-in-need, and everything with creating the space for people to connect to the loving power of the universe themselves. I also knew that I would never again ask for money to share my gift. I hoped that Glen wouldn't mind sharing his life with an income-free, ex-convict.

After twenty minutes of quiet chanting, I interrupted one last time.

"When you're ready, bring your awareness back to the room, back to my voice."

Everyone opened their eyes slowly, cautiously, looking around the room.

"How is everyone feeling? Doing okay? Anybody fall asleep?"

All heads turned back to Belinda who was breathing lightly, head tilted forward, clearly dozing. A few chuckles.

"Leave her. She'll probably wake up for this next part,"

I said. "Now, I'd love for anyone who feels comfortable doing so, to join me in a mantra, a chant. This is the mantra I repeat in my mind almost constantly. I say it to myself when I'm frustrated or scared. I said it to myself a lot the day I got here and was getting stink eye from some inmates. The mantra is easy, but it's in Sanskrit, which is this old language. It has enormous potential and power; it has the ability to expand your awareness and raise your level of consciousness, and to benefit all mankind."

"Was that in Sanskrit, too cause I didn't understand a word of it," one of the younger women said. A few others smiled and nodded.

"Basically, the words mean wisdom, consciousness and bliss. You can use the mantra like a prayer or a wish even. As I understand it, it doesn't actually even matter if you understand what the mantra means, simply saying it will help you connect with universal love. And I know that sounds flaky! Sometimes I marvel at the things I think, but...it works. I promise.

"Start by breathing in clarity, two. Three. Four. Five. And then breathe out peace, two. Three. Four. Five. I love myself. I deserve unconditional love. Say that a few times."

I hadn't asked them to close their eyes but they all had. I could see by the softened look in their jaws and foreheads that the meditation had at least worked to relax everyone.

"Now repeat after me, Sat."

"Sat," a couple of women whispered.

"Chit."

"Chit," one more woman added her quiet voice.

"Ananda."

"Ananda," I heard another voice in the mix.

"Sat. Chit. Ananda. Sat. Chit. Ananda. Sat. Chit. Ananda."

I repeated the three words over and over until everyone in the room was chanting with me. I spoke a little louder. The others increased their volume. I softened my voice and the room quieted. And then, I changed the chant, quietly speaking, "I love myself. I deserve unconditional love." The new chant spread quickly and, without my prompting, became louder and louder. One woman stood up and tapped her fingers on her collar bone in a slow rhythm as she chanted. Another woman stood and joined her. Two more women. Then all six of us were standing, tapping and chanting, "I love myself. I deserve unconditional love."

Amy took my right hand in hers and reached for Sandra's hand. Before long, we were all holding hands, arms raised high above our heads. A victory stance. Every face wet with emotion. Joy? Grief? Relief? It didn't matter. It was movement. And connection. And it was good.

I did this four times a day. Belinda became the door monitor to make sure nobody came more than once a day, since many women wanted to. By the third day of the group sessions we had a rhythm. The same five women came at their same time until one was released and her seat would be filled by a new face. Belinda gave up her chair on the second day, choosing instead to meditate in our room with iPod Glen reading meditations.

When Belinda offered to focus her meditations on helping Betsy feel love, I wept.

Chapter Thirty-Seven

I was much less angsty on my second visit with Glen. I still broke the no touching rule and had to apologize to a different guard for requiring her to explore my orifices. But she was kind and even thanked me for the work I'd been doing to help inmates relax. She said it made her job easier.

When I was called to the visitor's room the following day I was surprised since Glen was heading back to Vancouver and my lawyer had told me on her previous visit that it would be a week before she'd be back; it had only been four days.

"Look at you, little miss popular," Belinda teased. "You're not going to force another guard to ruin another pair of perfectly good gloves, are you?"

I smiled. "I don't think it's Glen. And no, I won't be wasting gloves for anyone else."

I walked casually to the visiting room and asked the guard who was there to see me. She looked at her paper and said, "Betsy O'Connor."

"Betsy?" I waited for the floor to give out from underneath me. For my knees to melt and leave me collapsed in a pile of confusion. For my stomach to rebel. But none of that happened. In fact, I felt myself stand a little taller, my inhalation become a little deeper.

Okay. I can do this. I'm ready to face her.

The door opened and I saw her profile at a table near the far corner of the room. She looked toward me when the heavy door clanged closed. Neither of us smiled. She didn't stand up. There was no rush of emotion like my two greetings with Glen.

"I assume you want me to sit down," I said when I reached her table.

She nodded.

We sat in silence for several minutes, making eye contact, looking away. Several times she sounded like she was going to talk but then she stopped. For a change, it was me who took the lead.

"I'm not sorry I told the police about you," I said.

Betsy scratched her nose then bit her finger.

"And I'm not sorry that you spun it around and landed me in here, either. In fact, thank you," I said.

"Thank you?"

"Yeah. I am sorry that I ran out on you like I did. That wasn't fair. But…in my defence, it wasn't just you telling me you loved me that freaked me out. It was all the other stuff that I'd figured out. I was scared."

She nodded. "Why 'thank you'?"

"I've heard so many stories about dysfunctional relationships since I got here. And it made me realize that for our entire friendship, since I was ten years old, I've let

286

you be in charge. I gave you all the power. I liked taking the backseat. I didn't have to make the hard decisions, I just had to go along. And then when I'd try to, you know, get into my own driver's seat and you'd get pissed off, I didn't understand. But now I do."

"You have no idea how hurt I was when you walked out of that restaurant. I felt like I was a little kid again, being ditched by yet another family."

"Betsy—"

"Let me finish. Please. But then I realized that I was manipulating you." Betsy smiled. "Just like I used to manipulate those foster families. I lied to you. I mean, I told you the truth, I do love you, but that wasn't the whole story."

She stopped talking and stared at the table. I reached across and touched her hand. She pulled away.

"Don't," she said.

"Sorry."

Betsy looked up and shook her head. "You don't have to be so goddamn apologetic about everything, Tara. I knew you'd react badly if I told you I was in love with you and in one way that's what I wanted. I wanted you to reject me to prove that I'm unlovable because, well, look at me."

"Betsy—"

"I fucked up. I know that. I did some terrible things. Unforgivable. And I'm not going to ask you to forgive me because I don't deserve it. I intentionally took away people you loved because I was afraid I'd lose you. And then James, well...he was different. He hurt you and I wanted to hurt him back."

I wanted to be angry but couldn't find the emotion. My heart knew that Betsy had always acted from a place of love with me. She always had my back but I'd been a fickle friend whenever a man came into my life. It was never intentional but the result was consistent: my attention would drift and I'd leave Betsy in the lurch. An image of Glen and our first coffee date popped into my head.

"I couldn't ask for a better friend," I said.

"But I wanted—I *needed*—you to be more than you could ever be."

I looked into her eyes and waited for an explanation.

"In my whole life you're the only person who's ever loved me for who I am, even when I fuck up, which I know is a lot. Even though your mom was judgmental, you know she loved you. I never had that. But I had you. Until you started dating and falling in love with guys. Something in me would go off like it did every time I was kicked out of one foster family and into another."

"You never told me," I said.

"What was I supposed to say?"

"So, why are you telling me now?" I asked.

"Because I need you to help me change. When we started the business and you stood up to me and said you wouldn't kill anyone, that nobody deserved to die no matter how awful they were, I knew I couldn't tell you what I'd done. But I wanted to keep doing it."

I wanted to stay open-hearted but that didn't ring true and I had to call her on it. I shook my head and pointed a finger toward her. I spoke calmly, like a teacher reciting facts. "No, you kept the secret long before then, when you killed Scott with the toaster, then Bob with the rocks."

Betsy moved in her chair but didn't speak.

"You said you want to change. I don't know what that means," I said. "Ten days ago you lied to the police and here I am. Two weeks ago you almost killed Glen. You said you've started the business again. How many men have died in the last week because of you?"

"None," she said.

"None?" I raised my eyebrows in disbelief.

"I actually haven't done any work. I read the letters but can't do anything. I can't do what you do because I feel hatred toward these guys, but I know that what I was doing is wrong. I don't want to do that anymore."

"Why the sudden about-face?"

"You tell me," she said with a small smile.

"You think I'm responsible?"

Betsy nodded.

"So if I stop—"

"Please don't," she interrupted.

We sat without speaking for a minute or more.

"Betsy, why are you here?"

"To make things right," she said.

"And what does that look like to you?"

"You come home. We start the business again, on your terms. No secrets. Nobody dies."

"I'm not giving up my relationship with Glen," I said.

She nodded. "I know. And I don't want you to."

"Really? Kind of hard to believe, don't you think?"

"Everything that's happened, that we've both done over the last six months, is kind of hard to believe, don't *you* think?"

I smiled and agreed. "How do you see this working so that nobody gets hurt? I mean *nobody*."

Betsy's energy changed. She leaned forward and started to talk with her hands. "We move out of your apartment. We can both afford to get nice places now.

I think we should each get our own places in the same building. Near Glen's house is fine. I'm happy to live over by the Drive. And we should rent an office space that has a room where you can meditate on your own and another room for small groups to meet together to meditate, and another office for a bookkeeper or business manager—"

"You've put a lot of thought into this. And it sounds… interesting. Great ideas to consider. But what I meant was, how can I be sure you won't freak out one day and try to hurt Glen again, or worse?" I leaned back in my chair and stared into Betsy's eyes.

She followed my posture and said, "I'm not that person anymore."

"And what do you need me to do?"

"Exactly what you're doing right now."

"Which is?" I asked.

"Sending me loving white light. That's all I ever really wanted was to know you love me."

I felt relief and then concern. "You know I will never love you as a lover, right?"

She laughed. "The idea is actually kind of gross, isn't it? Like being intimate with your sister."

I nodded and smiled.

"Why did you say what you did at the restaurant then?" I asked.

"I was afraid. I knew I was losing you and I hoped that, I don't know, that if I said I was in love with you that you'd see me differently…I don't know. It was stupid."

I nodded and laughed. "Well, you were right, sort of."

"Glen really does love you," she said.

"I know. But that doesn't mean I can't have you both in my life."

"I know," she said nodding, "and if you and I keep working together then…"

"You won't feel left out?"

"Yeah."

"I'm sorry I ran off like I did. That was a horrible thing to do," I said.

"I'm sorry I drove you away. And… did all those other things. Forgive me?"

I stood up and Betsy followed. We stepped around the table and hugged. Five seconds later a tap on my shoulder and two on my back told me I'd be getting the personal post-visit exam again. I laughed and called "sorry" to the guard who shook her head and said, "We've got to get you out of here."

Chapter Thirty-Eight

On the morning of the day I was to leave for my trial, all the women gathered outside of our shower room. The shower room was much like a public pool, with six shower heads along one wall, no privacy curtains. Showering was always a group experience. Typically, I'd be waiting my turn mid-way down the line, but on my last morning, all the women ahead of me moved me forward until I was first in line. Nobody else had started their shower, which was strange since, at this rate, the women at the back would be late for breakfast.

Also unusual, nobody was speaking. I wouldn't characterize a normal morning as rowdy, but this was quite out of the norm. Without speaking I undressed and turned on my water while five other women did the same. Over the sounds of water hitting the tile and gurgling down the drain holes, a quiet chant started, "Sat. Chit. Ananda." It grew louder. I joined in, almost singing the words. I turned off my water to let the next woman have her turn but was told to stay, that each woman wanted to say good-bye and good luck and thank me personally. Tears of joy joined the water in the drain. *Om sat chit ananda.*

I dressed and had a tear-filled breakfast with my new sisters before I was put in handcuffs and moved to the court room. My lawyer met me and explained the process, reminding me to answer questions with as few words as possible.

"Is Glen here?" I asked.

"Of course," she said, squinting as though to say, *What a dumb question.* "And Betsy's here, too."

A knock on our door and a Sheriff poked his head in. "Time to go."

My hands suddenly became cold. I rubbed them together to create heat. I blew into my palms. And, as I pulled my hands away from my face I saw a ball of blue-white light cradled in them. It was as real as my flesh. I stared at it and it seemed to pulse. I pressed my palms together and opened them. It was still there. Blue-white light.

"Tara." My lawyer brought me back to the moment. "Let's go. And say as little as possible. Please."

In the end, the only words I said in court were, "Thank you."

Betsy had recanted, told the police that she'd lied about my being involved in my lovers' deaths. And since the investigations of their deaths showed nothing that would directly or indirectly link me, I was told my record would not reflect the time I'd spent awaiting trial. Betsy, however, was charged with making false accusations and sentenced with a fine and one hundred hours of community service, to be served in Vancouver.

My mysterious knowledge of so many unusual deaths was something the Sacramento court did not want to deal with.

"Of the three men in Sacramento county who were on your list, all were investigated. Our officers find no reason to suspect wrong-doing and I for one, have no interest in starting a witch hunt. I would encourage you, Ms. Holland, to return to Canada, and, if you would like to pursue your own allegations of wrong-doing against Betsy O'Connor, to do so in your home jurisdiction." He banged his gavel once and said, "You're free to go."

I pressed my hands together in prayer position, placed my thumbs against my collarbone and tilted my head to the judge. "Thank you."

Betsy and Glen walked toward me but stayed on their side of the wooden gates, separating the audience from the counsel table. I looked at them then to my lawyer.

She nodded. "But don't leave. There's still paperwork to do."

I threw myself into Glen's arms and buried my face in the nape of his neck. We didn't speak. When I finally looked up, I saw Betsy standing a few feet away. Her eyes were closed and her palms faced us. The white light that she was directing to and around Glen and I was the brightest, most beautiful I'd ever seen.

Chapter Thirty-Nine

And, we all lived happily ever after.

For about ten days.

Because even though Betsy had *seen* the light, she wasn't able to embody it.

I still can't believe I was so naïve to think she'd actually changed...

Acknowledgements

Virtually every author says it, and now I know it's true: this book would still be under my bed were it not for the support of a pant-load of people.

Cathleen With, my mentor in the Vancouver Manuscript Intensive. Cathleen did not help me with this specific novel but her support with my first manuscript (never to be pulled from under the bed!) gave me both the confidence to move forward and the reality check that I needed to read and write 100,000 more words before considering sharing my work with the world.

Elizabeth Dawson, the Thelma to my Louise, who has read every word of fiction I've ever written and who provides harsh and loving feedback.

Eileen Cook who development edited the first draft of this novel and showed me which darlings I needed to kill.

My Mountain Mavens critique group, Michele Fogal, Joanna Drake and Mary Ann Clarke Scott. There are no words, only deep love.

Jennifer Duhamel Conover; I used that wrong for you!

All of the members of the Greater Vancouver Chapter of the RWA who come out to monthly meetings and share their experience and support. In particular my Atta Girl partner, Angie Gregson, who cheered me on through over fifty agent rejections.

To all of my ARC readers and reviewers. The fact that you raised your hand to read my novel gave me confidence to keep pushing this book along the bumpy and complicated publication path.

An extra special thanks to Kerryn Reid who caught twenty-five typos in my ARC. I shake my head at my sloppiness. And to Terry Mitchell who summarized the story so nicely in her review that I used it as my back cover copy.

Finally, thanks to Liam, Dave and Marcus. You are the reason my inner-Tara beats out my shadow-Betsy.

Thank you all!

Reading Group Guide

1. At what point in the story were you hooked? Was there a question you wanted to have answered that kept you reading?

2. Readers experience Tara and Betsy very differently. Some become frustrated that Tara is weak at the start of the book, others feel she is not a good friend to Betsy, while others like Tara but despise Betsy. Did you have any strong feelings about either of these two characters? Did your feelings for Tara or Betsy add or detract from your enjoyment of the story?

3. If you had to assign this novel to one single genre, what would it be and why?

4. What are the main ideas or themes that the author explores in this novel?

5. Did you find Tara's character arc (her emotional growth) plausible?

6. If you found yourself in Tara's situation how would you have reacted to events like learning your best friend had killed your lovers or was responsible for your ending up in jail? Would you have any "white light" for Betsy?

7. If you had Betsy's powers, are there situations where you might feel justified in using them as she did? In what situations would it be okay to be a psychic serial killer?

8. Were you surprised at any point in the story? Did the plot leave you guessing? If so, at what points?

9. Were there any passages that struck you as insightful or have stayed with you? What are they?

10. Did the novel make you think about you own values and attitudes towards women who are different from you, such as female prisoners, rape survivors, or serial killers?

11. Is the ending satisfying?

FIND OUT WHAT HAPPENS TO GLEN!

www.AdviceForJiltedLovers.com

Go to Tara and Betsy's website to sign-up for updates. You'll be the first to know when the next book is available.

Tentatively called *Mother Teresa's Karma for Lying Lovers*, it focuses on Betsy as the main character.

Sign-up and I'll send you Chapter 1 once it's been edited.

www.AdviceForJiltedLovers.com

CPSIA information can be obtained
at www.ICGtesting.com
Printed in the USA
FSOW04n0537210416
19439FS